OUT OF THE OVEN AND INTO THE FIRE

Dwain Gordon Fuller

ALSO BY DWAIN FULLER

Gardenia Transplanted
with Faye Christopher Fuller

The Adventures and Misadventures of Payston Peters

The Oven

ISBN 979-8-89238-472-8 Hardback
ISBN 979-8-89269-746-0 Paperback

DEDICATION

To Dr. James P. McCulley, longtime Chairman of Ophthalmology at the University of Texas Southwestern Medical School in Dallas. A man with a tough exterior hiding a very kind heart buried somewhere deep within. Jim, our family remains eternally indebted to you.

"The greatest secrets are always hidden in the most unlikely places."

—Roald Dahl

"Life is like a maze in which you try to avoid the exit."

—Roger von Oech

ACKNOWLEDGMENTS

It is said that to live a long time one must pick his or her parents carefully. Equally important is to choose the right life partner. I am not a believer in the theory of romantic elective affinity as espoused by the poet Robert Browning, but after running hard to escape the commitment of marriage for seven years, I succumbed and have been blessed ever since. Continued thanks to my wife, Patsy, for reading all of the chapters of my novels as they come off of the printer and making certain that I have not wandered too far off into the weeds or made egregious typos. My second son, Matthew Fuller, who is an English teacher, read the entire manuscript and pointed out errors in syntax and grammar and made helpful suggestions. My first son, Christopher, also read the chapters of this novel and gave needed encouragement.

Once again, I must express my appreciation to Professor Susan Ford Wiltshire, former Chair of Classics at Vanderbilt University and an old friend from high school, who convinced me in my retirement that writing fiction could be as gratifying as operating on retinas.

Lastly, I am extremely fortunate to have a remarkable editor like Cynthia Orticio who has eagle eyes and manages all of the many things necessary to prepare a manuscript for publication. My novels would never have been birthed without her. Thank you, Cindy.

—Dwain Fuller

TABLE OF CONTENTS

INTRODUCTION

This novel is a sequel to The Oven, *which is a high-action CIA thriller set in a medical school class in 1963.* Out of the Oven and Into the Fire *can be enjoyed without first reading its precursor. However, the following brief synopsis may be helpful to a new reader.*

Atwood "Woody" Stressel is a newly trained CIA clandestine operator who has been embedded in the first-year class of Grantland Medical School in an attempt to solve the mystery of disappearing undercover CIA personnel. Woody is only told of a strong suspicion that there is a mole in the CIA who has been turned by Russian agents and who is fingering operators who are kidnapped and tortured for classified information, then murdered. However, no bodies are ever found. The CIA has information that suggests that someone at the medical school is involved.

Woody meets the mysterious and alluring student Alina Karnitsky (Ava Volkov) across the cadaver table in gross anatomy. Alina speaks fluent Russian, and Woody soon learns that Alina is an expert at weapons and street fighting. He is concerned that the woman is a Russian agent as well as a medical student, but has trouble convincing his CIA case manager to conduct a thorough background check. Woody cannot afford to flunk out of medical school, but his only hope of passing biochemistry is with tutoring from Alina.

During a nighttime excursion, Woody discovers the mutilated body of a pregnant woman in a vat of formalin in a heavily secured backroom of the gross anatomy lab. As Woody starts to uncover pieces of the missing operator puzzle, he becomes the target of assassination attempts. Alina tells Woody that his only chance of survival is to trust her to protect him. There are many twists and turns in the plot of this story that will keep the reader guessing until the very end.

CHAPTER 1

WALKING CORPSE

Ava Volkov (formerly known as Alina Karnitsky) and Woody Stressel had been moved from Langley to Camp Peary near Williamsburg for continued security. They had been there for six months and were growing restless. The constant adrenaline rush that they both had experienced while playing a high-stakes cat and mouse game as pseudo first-year medical school students was gone. Ava, who formerly was an undercover agent for the KGB, had been granted permanent U.S. residency for the role she had played in saving the lives of Woody and also his CIA manager. Both she and Woody had been offered protection while they decided whether to accept the CIA's offer to provide new identities for each of them.

Ava was teaching combat and surveillance skills to the new recruits of the clandestine CIA service at The Farm, which was part of the 9,000 acres occupied by Camp Peary. All of the carefully-screened candidates had assumed names, and Ava had no access to intelligence information. The gunshot wound to Woody's shoulder had slowly healed. He had a desk job helping classify and channel low-level incoming intelligence information—a job that he hated. But Woody and Ava both knew that they were high-value targets for the KGB as well as the Chicago crime syndicate, who had been partners in making CIA agents and other murder victims' bodies disappear in the crema-tion oven at the Grantland Medical School.

Woody and Ava were sitting at a back table in one of the dormitory cafeterias during lunch and commiserating about how boring their lives had become after the end of their medical school intrigue.

Ava said somewhat wistfully to Woody, "If a genie appeared and offered me one wish, I know just what I would ask for."

Woody smiled. "But what if I refused to become your permanent boy toy?"

Ava shook her head and replied with a frown, "You egotistical men think women spend every waking hour fantasizing about luring them into bed. My one wish would not even involve you. As I told you once before, I would wish that I had never been ensnared by the KGB and could just be a normal woman in medical school working to become a pediatric oncologist."

Woody shook his head and said, "There's just one flaw in your wish. If the kind genie did grant your request, you would never have met me."

Ava's eyes flashed angrily, "Don't flatter yourself, Mr. Stressel. Good-looking men are a dime a dozen."

"That may be true, but how many of them, in addition to being incredibly handsome, are experts at street fighting, weapons, and high-level espionage and can take care of a woman?"

Ava said sharply, "You are so annoying! We both know that if you and I went into a dark alley, only I would walk out. The last thing I need is a man to protect me!"

Woody smiled and reached across the table and took Ava's hand. "I'm just pulling your chain, my beautiful Miss Volkov. I find you very attractive when you are angry. Now, let's think what I would wish for from your mythical genie."

Ava jerked her hand back from Woody and snapped, "Being a typical man, you probably would ask for a Brobdinagian anatomical male enhancement miracle."

"Slandering me by using a big word that I don't even know is very condescending and unkind, Ava."

Ava let a flicker of a smile cross her face and replied, "In Russia even the slow children read *Gulliver's Travels*. You must have had a very impoverished elementary school reading list."

"Well, after that demeaning remark, I'm not going to share my secret genie wish with you. So there."

There was a pause in the conversation, then Ava got a very serious look on her face.

"Woody, I need to tell you something important. This morning I found this envelope that had been pushed under my door. The sheet inside makes me wonder just how safe we are here at The Farm."

Ava took the sheet of paper out and gave it to Woody. He looked and slowly shook his head. On the paper was a short EKG strip that ended in a flat line. There was a crudely lettered Russian phrase in red ink that Woody could not translate.

He hesitated, then said to Ava, "That Russian phrase is not familiar to me. What does it mean?"

Ava replied slowly, "The best English translation is 'walking corpse.' I don't know about you, but I now feel incredibly vulnerable."

"Surely you don't think the KGB or the criminal cartel has penetrated this super secure CIA training base," Woody said with concern.

Ava replied, "The CIA Assistant Deputy Director who sold out to the Russians shared a great deal of very sensitive information with the KGB. And there is no telling how much information was extracted from the kidnapped CIA operatives who were tortured before being killed and incinerated in the medical school cremation oven."

There was silence, then Woody said, "We both need to be very careful. Let's meet for lunch tomorrow and discuss what our options are. Maybe we should agree to let the CIA change our identities and take our chances in the world outside."

* * * *

Woody and Ava met in the cafeteria for an early lunch the next day. They went through the line and found a table in a corner.

Woody asked, "How's your day going so far? Any new death threats?"

Ava replied, "I spent the morning teaching the eager new trainees how to garrote someone with a piano wire. There is a know-it-all from the Bronx in the group whose father is a police chief. The man is just as annoying as Justin Noble was in our medical school class. The fellow volunteered to play the victim in my demonstration, and it was all I could do not to cinch up the piano wire and say, 'Oops!' How was your day?"

"I think I got my death warning this morning. When I returned to my room after breakfast, I found a small bowl of oranges on my night stand. I thought that was rather strange. When I studied the oranges with a good light and a magnifier, they all had what looked like a very subtle needle penetration through the skin.

"I took a slice out to the patio and let one of the squirrels eat it. The squirrels are very tame and are used to being fed. I watched the one that ate the orange slice carefully. After about fifteen minutes, it started having seizures and keeled over dead."

"Strychnine," Ava said quickly.

"Bingo," Woody replied. "I have requested a meeting for both of us with our operations officer Robertson for tomorrow afternoon. I think that our days at this uber secure training facility are numbered. The envelope and poisoned oranges have to be the work of your KGB. There is no way regular criminals could penetrate this CIA facility. But I may be able to conjure up a possible option for us to stay alive, at least for a while. I need to work out some troublesome details before we discuss it. But it's back to work for both of us now."

CHAPTER 2

FARM QUESTIONS

The following day Ava and Woody were ushered into the office of their case manager whom they knew only as Robertson. He was a lean and muscular man with a hint of early male pattern baldness and a prominent chin. The officer had penetrating green eyes that stood out on his angular face. It was hard to judge Robertson's age, but Woody and Ava had agreed on the early forties. Robertson was known for being all business with no interest in becoming a personal friend of anyone who entered his office. It was rumored that he had made a name for himself by being a CIA assassin early in his career. Incongruously, there was a small picture on the credenza behind his desk of a very pretty woman and two young children.

Robertson indicated for Ava and Woody to sit down in the two chairs in front of his desk. The officer was writing on a yellow legal pad and continued to do so for a minute or so before he looked up and asked with no inflection, "What can I do for you two people?"

Woody replied, "Both of us have received recent death threats while here at Camp Peary and do not feel safe with our current government protection."

Robertson's face remained impassive as he replied, "I find that very hard to believe. There are few places on earth as secure as The Farm. Please explain."

Ava produced the piece of paper that had been pushed under her door and reached across the desk and gave it to Robertson. He studied the paper, then said, "This EKG tracing shows ventricular tachycardia ending in a flat line that suggests that the patient died. The Russian phrase for 'walking corpse' makes the message rather plain. The first thing I need to do is to see if the hall surveillance camera shows someone delivering this message. The idea that Langley has been penetrated by the KGB or any criminal element is almost impossible to contemplate. Is this the only threat that either of you has received?"

Woody answered, "When I returned to my room after breakfast yesterday, I was surprised to see a small bowl of oranges on my night stand. Under magnification, each of the oranges showed a small penetration site that suggested a needle stick. I took an orange segment and fed it to one of the friendly squirrels out on the patio. Within fifteen minutes the squirrel had seizures and died. There has to have been strychnine injected into the oranges. I brought all of the oranges in this double plastic bag."

Robertson closed his eyes for a minute as if in deep thought, then abruptly slammed his fist down on the desk. "The damage that bastard John Claiborne did to this agency by selling out to the Russians is proving hard to repair. The thought that there may be a mole at Langley or Peary makes me sick to my stomach."

Ava said, "Woody and I think we may be safer if we accept the CIA's offer to give us new identities and let us take our chances out in the real world."

"That can be done," Robertson said, "but it will take some time. You will need new names as well as a host of manufactured documents such as driver's licenses, bank accounts, passports, credit cards, and social security numbers just for starters. And you have to understand that to be safe you must be cut completely off from your families for at least several years."

Ava said with anger in her voice, "The KGB had my parents in Russia killed when I started cooperating with the CIA. My brother was shot while he and I were working undercover for the KGB at Grantland Medical School. I have no close family remaining."

Woody added, "My only close relatives are my mother who is a language professor at Yale and my younger sister. They started living together in New Haven after my father died from a heart attack last year. My mother knows that I am in some sort of secret government service. She will understand my dropping off of the radar for a long period. I really don't want to spend my life being baby sat by the CIA here."

"There is a great deal to consider before one or both of you commit to becoming a totally different person for your personal protection," Robertson said. "And understand that it would be advisable for the two of you to separate permanently. It is much easier for us to hide a single person than a couple."

Woody shook his head. "Ava and I have been through way too much together to split up now. I don't think either one of us will agree to that stipulation."

Robertson frowned, then gave an almost faint smile. "I am aware of your heroism in service to our country. The two of you make a very lethal team together. Perhaps watching each other's back will be safer than being solo. But it will be up to the director to decide if the agency will agree to that. My suggestion for now is that the two of you take several days to carefully consider your options. I will provide security for your rooms. And I will have our lab assay the oranges for any type of poison, as well as having the surveillance film from Ms. Volkov's hall evaluated. Let's plan to meet again in one week."

* * * *

Woody and Ava left Robertson's office. Once they were in the hall, Ava started to speak. Woody gave a quick shake of his head and said, "Let's grab a cup of coffee and go out to the patio."

The two sat down with their coffee on a bench. Ava said, "Good call, Woody. I don't think that it's safe to talk anywhere there might be a listening device."

"Agreed," Woody responded. "I'm betting that Assistant Deputy Director Claiborne was not the only CIA mole that the KGB cultivated. If we went through the CIA process to be given new identities, there is a real chance that whoever the remaining mole is would immediately finger us and send executioners to our new location. There is clearly someone at Peary who would be happy to have us killed."

Ava was silent for a moment then said, "I think that our best chance is to disappear without consulting the CIA and depend on each other to stay alive. But that option brings up the problem of money and being able to eat. If we let the CIA help us disappear, they would almost certainly provide income for at least a while."

Woody smiled and said, "And how could we maintain your lavish lifestyle of living in a luxurious penthouse like you did during our brief med school journey? Surely you had a sugar daddy of some kind. Hmm. Were you ever a casual playmate for Premier Khrushchev?"

Ava gave a small shriek and dashed her hot coffee on Woody's lap. "You are such an impossible horse's ass!"

Woody winced and said, "Ow! That coffee's hot. I think I may have third-degree burns of my male parts."

Ava laughed and replied, "Maybe you will turn out to be a late-in-life castrati and can get a job singing soprano in one of the cathedrals of Europe."

There was a moment of silence. Then Woody asked quietly, "Ava, do you trust me completely? This is a very important question. Think carefully before you answer."

Ava hesitated, then replied, "In a fire fight or a street brawl, there is no one I would trust more than you. But if you are asking if I would trust you to be a forever soulmate, that's a much tougher question."

Woody said seriously, "Ava, I'm not proposing to you. But there is a great deal that you do not know about me that will be critical if we decide to try to stay alive as a team. We both need to get back to work now, but let's meet for lunch tomorrow—that is, if we survive the night. Too bad that Langley made us surrender our weapons."

Ava stood up and replied, "Works for me. I may be worn out by then since tomorrow morning we are doing mock hand-to-hand combat. The students are always hoping to land a good hit on me. There is one man that troubles me. He is very strong and appears to have had previous training in Russian Systema and Brazilian jiu-jitsu. Of course, they are all here under assumed names, and I am not permitted to know anything at all about their backgrounds. This fellow would probably be a great fit for the CIA as an assassin."

Ava smiled and said, "And, one other thing. The coffee stains on the front of your pants make it look like you wet yourself. I think that I'll just walk inside by myself if you don't mind."

CHAPTER 3

TESTICULAR IMPLANTS

The next day Woody was seated at a table in the cafeteria waiting for Ava to join him for lunch. He looked up and saw her approaching somewhat slowly. He looked up and immediately saw bruises on her neck. Woody stood up quickly and took her hand and asked with great concern, "What in the world happened to you? You look like someone tried to choke you to death."

Ava sat down and replied hoarsely, "Exactly. I think that I am fortunate to be here and not on a slab in the morgue. That strong fellow I mentioned yesterday wanted to take me on in a demonstration of hand-to-hand-combat with all punches pulled of course. He headed straight for me, and I gently tried to block him with my forearm, but he body slammed me and put me in a front chokehold and started squeezing very hard. I tried to shout 'enough!'—but I could barely speak. It immediately became apparent that he planned to choke me to death. I began getting dizzy."

"Oh, my gosh!" Woody interjected. "How did you escape?"

"The man was so sure of himself that he had not bothered to wear any groin protection. I kneed him so hard in the crotch that I heard his testicles explode.

"He gave a loud scream and released me as he fell to the floor. There is no question that he intended to kill me. Surely, he will be dropped from the program after he gets out of the hospital sporting his spiffy new testicular implants. All of our mock combats are filmed, so there can be no question what happened here."

"Ava, do you think this man is a KGB mole or was just paid a fortune to try to eliminate you?"

"I don't know the answer to that, but the man that fought me has a distinct Slavic accent. Staying at The Farm seems to be a death wish."

Woody replied, "I'm beginning to think that we would be safer walking through Central Park in New York City at 2 AM wearing fancy jewelry and rolling a wheelbarrow full of thousand-dollar bills. I see two options for us: One, stick around here for a while and see if we can lure the KGB mole or moles out into the open so we can eliminate them, or, two, escape from The Farm and hide out in a place so remote that even Sherlock Holmes and a pack of bloodhounds could never find us."

Ava asked, "Would this mythical safe place have nice restaurants and a place for me to get my nails and hair done each week?"

Woody smiled, "How do squat toilets and miles of desert sound to you?"

Ava frowned and said, "Please. I am a refined lady and need certain niceties to survive."

"Well, then, my lovely princess, the question you need to answer is whether you would prefer to have the latest French salon hair style and perfect nails lying in a morgue with a bullet hole in your chest or to be alive and well with frizzy hair and chipped nail polish. Unfortunately, you seem to have only a Hobson's choice."

Ava slowly nodded her head. "We both know the answer to that question. But there are some difficulties with reaching the secret Nirvana to which you allude. The CIA will never agree to let us go out on our own without at least some type of surveillance, as well as new identities. And I just know that they are going to strongly suggest cosmetic surgery for both of us to change our appearances."

Woody shook his head and said, "Never turn a crazy plastic surgeon loose on the Mona Lisa or her handsome companion. Neither of us is ever going to agree to surrender to facial revamping. Remember what a close call you had at the funeral home when Randy and his son Tiny tried to turn loose a maniac with a scalpel to remake your face before incinerating both of us in the cremation oven."

Ava teared up slightly and said, "Just thinking about it makes me shudder. I can't tell you how much I enjoyed plunging the large needle into that goon's eye."

Woody said, "The other life-threatening problem is that if we let the CIA change our identity and relocate us, the KGB mole at Langley or Peary would certainly share this information with the KGB, who would waste no time sending out a hit team. Of course, leaving this compound without CIA approval will be very difficult. And if we do that, we will have not only the KGB and the crime syndicate looking for us, but also CIA trackers."

Ava shook her head slightly and said with a hoarse voice, "We just don't have a really appealing option. The way things are going, it will be just a matter of time until we both end up very dead if we stay here. Yesterday you asked me if I trusted you completely and said that there were things about you that I would need to know if we decide to stay together as a team trying to survive. Would now be a good time to elaborate on that?"

Woody said, "Let me just say that I have some resources that you do not know about, including access to land in a very remote place. This property is owned by a crazy maternal uncle, so our family name Stressel does not exist in any record base. If we could get there undetected, I think that we would disappear off of the radar for a least a while. The closest town is 20 miles away and has a dwindling population of less than a thousand people."

"Is this the charming place you mentioned with squat toilets and a fascinating desert view? And, most importantly, does the distant small town have a Parisian hairdresser as well as an upscale nail salon?"

"Out of luck on both counts, my lovely patrician, but there is a general merchandise store that sells guns and camouflage gear. But before I go into more detail, my vote is to stay alive at The Farm until we meet with Robertson again and see what he has learned from the hall surveillance cameras and the testing of the poisoned oranges."

Just at that moment, a woman came up to their table and said, "I'm Mr. Robertson's secretary. He asked me to find you two and request that you come to his office immediately."

Ava and Woody stood up and followed the woman out of the cafeteria. "Kiss up and kick down—the mantra of the CIA," Woody whispered to Ava. The woman ushered them into the reception area of Robertson's office and asked them to sit down.

"Mr. Robertson is on a very important phone call and may be tied up for several more minutes. He really needs to speak with both of you, so don't wander off."

After 20 minutes, Woody approached the woman's desk and said, "We both really need to get back to work. Perhaps you could give us a convenient time to return to see Mr. Robertson."

The secretary gave Woody a cold stare and said, "Mr. Robertson asked to see you now. It would not be wise to make him unhappy."

Suddenly the inner office door opened and Robertson beckoned Woody and Ava to enter.

"Have a seat. I have some disturbing information to share with you."

Once they were seated, Robertson said, "Two things. First, the captured hall camera images showed no one near Miss Volkov's door during the night or early morning when she allegedly found the note on her door. Second, our very excellent lab found absolutely no evidence of strychnine or any other toxin in the oranges Mr. Stressel presented to me. I am beginning to wonder if Miss Volkov may have prepared the death note herself for some unknown reason. And the alleged squirrel death is difficult to believe."

Woody said, "Sir, if I may ask, was the assay for strychnine done with the old Prussian blue test or something more accurate like chromatography? Do you have a copy of the laboratory report that I could see?"

Robertson frowned and tersely replied, "The lab report was read directly to me by the head chemist. I am not at liberty to show you a written report. And, unfortunately, there is a third thing to discuss that I view as very serious. Miss Volkov, I have been told that you caused serious injuries to one of our trainees this morning in what was supposed to be mock hand-to-hand combat. He is threatening to sue the U.S. government and you personally."

Ava stood up and said sharply, "No disrespect, Sir, but look at my neck. These bruise marks occurred when the trainee attempted to choke me to death. Fortunately, all encounters are filmed and will verify what I said. If I had not responded forcefully, there is no doubt that I would now be laid out in the morgue."

Robertson had an angry look on his face and retorted, "I asked to have the film from this combat to be processed immediately. Unfortunately, there is a new technician in the film department who stupidly exposed the film and ruined it."

Ava said, "There were at least ten trainees who witnessed this combat, and they can certainly tell exactly what happened. Have you spoken to any of them?"

"Miss Volkov, since there is a potential suit pending against the government and you, the trainees have been given explicit instructions not to discuss this matter with anyone except legal counsel for the CIA. I am going to have to relieve you of your teaching duties until this matter is resolved."

Robertson stood up and said curtly, "You both are now dismissed. And in view of the fact that there is no substantiation that either of you is actually at risk in your present situation, I am going to discontinue the previously instituted protection for you. There is no safer place for you in the world now than where you are. At a later date we can revisit a possible change of identity."

CHAPTER 4

BEAUTY AND THE BEAST

Woody and Ava were ushered briskly out of the office by the secretary. As they walked down the hall, Woody motioned in the direction of the patio. Once they found a bench away from the building and sat down, Woody said, "Robertson may be a legendary CIA super stud, but I have never trusted him ever since he was assigned to us as our operations officer. Did you see anything in his office that struck you as unusual?"

Ava thought carefully, then said, "The picture on his desk really seems out of place. Robertson is certainly not handsome, and he strikes me as a really mean SOB. However, the woman in the photograph was very beautiful, as were the two small children. It would be hard for me to believe that a woman like that would be attracted to Robertson."

"You are very observant, my brilliant companion," Woody said. "Anything else about the photograph that caught your eye?"

"Well, there was a blurred image of some type of car behind the woman and children," Ava responded.

Woody said, "Bingo. I am certain that the car was a Cadillac Eldorado Brougham, the most expensive car in the world, even more pricey than a Rolls Royce. If the people in the picture were his wife and children, and the car belongs to the family, that would be very interesting. It is hard to believe that a career government employee could afford such an expensive set of wheels."

Ava thought for a moment, then said, "Perhaps his wife has all the money."

"Possibly. But it is clear that Robertson does not have our best interests at heart. He has to know that you were the victim of an unprovoked attack today. And there is no way the man whose testicles you crunched two hours ago has already threatened to sue. He's probably still in surgery."

Ava responded, "It seems very convenient that the film from this morning's combat matches was allegedly exposed and lost in processing. And there has to have been someone who posted the note on my door that the hall surveillance monitor would have shown. I found Robertson's suggestion that I possibly wrote the note myself infuriating. I would love to take him on one on one. He would be needing testicular prostheses himself, as well as other emergency services."

Woody said, "Robertson is clearly lying, but what would his motive be? He is a prototypical CIA lifer. It is hard to believe that he could be paid enough to become a KGB mole."

Ava gave a faint smile and said, "Maybe his wife is a princess like me and is expensive and high maintenance."

Woody squinted his eyes as if deep in thought, then said, "I don't trust the report that he gave us on the oranges. There had to have been some type of toxin to kill the squirrel so quickly, and strychnine would be the most logical choice. We need to get out of here ASAP before we both become statistics. Any bright ideas?"

Ava answered, "What we need is official permission to exit Camp Peary very quietly and without CIA surveillance or a change in our identities. Then we can head for your Shangri-La, replete with squat toilets and miles of barren desert."

Woody replied, "Beats the heck out of being dead. Being sweaty and hot with frizzled hair and no makeup may make you utterly irresistible."

Ava smiled and said, "We both know that I am already utterly irresistible. And besides, I thought that you were considering a vow of permanent chastity? That's definitely something that I can help you out with. But back to the question at hand. I have a longshot idea that I need to think about before we discuss it. And since I no longer have a job, I will have plenty of time to work on this idea."

Woody said, "I am more than open to any ideas that you have. What say we meet for dinner in the cafeteria? And, my fair princess, watch out for poisoned apples.

"And whatever you do, don't kiss any toads."

After Ava left, Woody stayed seated on the bench on the patio searching his brain for a plausible way to exit the Camp Peary compound safely. He heard footsteps and looked up to see a person about his age wearing a lab coat and carrying a cup of coffee approaching him. The man smiled and said, "You have to be Woody Stressel, the tremendous linebacker from Grandview High School. Do you mind if I sit down?"

Woody nodded and replied, "Sure, go ahead. You look familiar. Should I know you?"

"I'm Tre Neuman—Neuman, just like Alfred E. in the Mad comic books. When you were a senior at Grandview, I was a sophomore. Since I played in the band, I got to see all of your ball games that year. We all wondered why you didn't take a Division One scholarship and play college ball, as good as you were. It was quite a shock to see you sitting on the bench on the patio of The Farm. We all understand anonymity here, so I won't ask what your job is."

Woody said, "I won't ask either, but I would guess by your lab coat that you may be a laboratory technologist."

"You are certainly correct. Nothing I do is really classified, so I am free to talk."

Woody's mind was spinning. "May I ask what part of the lab you work in?"

"I have an MS in biochemistry and work in the toxicology section."

Woody said, "I bet you see all sorts of weird things. Do you ever deal with anything as dangerous as strychnine? That would really be scary."

"Funny that you mention that. We actually assayed some oranges yesterday as a lab unknown and found strychnine in them. Apparently, this was just to test the sensitivity of our new gas chromatography system. There was no report to file. But there was enough strychnine in each orange to do a person in quickly. However, nothing exciting and sinister here. The oranges were just a check on how good we can be with unusual toxicology samples."

Woody said, "It sounds like your lab does some really important work. To answer your question about football, I had decided to become a lawyer and didn't think that I could play ball and make good enough grades to get into law school. But as you can surmise, I ended up working for the government."

Tre gave a thumbs up sign and said, "Working for Uncle Sam is not all that bad. Hard to turn down free healthcare and a good retirement. And the government is financing my PhD studies at Georgetown. No complaints from me."

Woody extended his hand to Tre and said with a smile, "It has been a real pleasure meeting you today. Best of luck working on your doctorate. I need to head back to work now. Hopefully, we can talk again soon. Take care."

CHAPTER 5

OMPHALOSKEPSIS

Woody was seated at the back of the cafeteria when Ava arrived wearing a high-collared sweater to hide the bruise marks on her neck. She sat down and Woody asked, "How was your afternoon of indolence, my fair damsel?"

Ava frowned and replied sharply with a raspy voice, "Try not to be the south end of a horse heading north, Mr. Stressel. Actually, I had a very productive afternoon practicing omphaloskepsis."

Woody shook his head and said, "There you go again using big words just to make me feel inferior. Please remember that I am an illiterate football jock who had one too many concussions."

Ava replied, "I hope that your britches are fireproof since all of your lies are about to ignite them and char your hiney. As I recall, you graduated from high school as valedictorian and actually made Phi Beta Kappa in college, despite a C in organic chemistry. I am shocked that you do not know that omphaloskepsis means meditation while gazing at one's navel."

Woody smiled and said, "Please get your facts straight, fair princess, before you indulge in inaccurate verbal abuse. I'll have you know that my organic grade was not a C, it was a magnificent C+. But we have much bigger fish to fry than working on my vocabulary and your veracity. I unearthed a bit of fascinating information on the patio after you left today."

Ava said, "I am all ears. Talk on."

"Just after you departed with your snide remark about my pants, a fellow with a cup of coffee came up and introduced himself. It turns out that he was two years behind me at Grandview High School and remembered me as a football player. I learned that he works in the toxicology section of the lab here. With a few discrete questions, I extracted the information that the lab had tested their new gas chromatography system yesterday by analyzing some oranges—all of which were loaded with strychnine. Since the assay was allegedly a test, no official report was generated."

Ava's eyes narrowed. "Yikes! So, Robertson was flat out lying to us about the oranges as well as the possible lawsuit from the fellow who tried to kill me this morning. What do you think his motive is? According to what we hear, Robertson has been a legendary CIA star for years. It is hard to believe that the KGB or any other group could turn him."

Woody paused, then said, "All true. But if Robertson is working both sides of the street, the cleanest way to get us killed is to make things so dangerous here that we leave Camp Peary and become easy targets on the outside. Explaining how both of us got erased at this uber secure facility would be hard to explain to the CIA director."

Ava shook her head in agreement and said, "So, even if we acquired completely new identities, including cosmetic surgery, all Robertson would have to do is finger us once we left to assure our prompt elimination."

Woody nodded and said, "I think I have a brilliant hypothesis. Neither the oranges nor your choking was intended to kill us. Both happenings were meant to make us so nervous that we would get out of Dodge as fast as possible."

Ava shook her head, "Get out of Dodge? What is that supposed to mean?"

Woody replied, "You must have never watched Gunsmoke on TV. I can explain the phrase later. As I think back, the needle tracks on the oranges were not too subtle. The plan was for me to see the penetrations and become suspicious. Of course, there never could have been an official report of poison in the oranges since that would raise all sorts of hell here."

Ava said, "One little problem, boy genius. How do you explain the fact that I was almost choked to death?"

"Ava, the man wanted to scare the pee out of you, but his intent was not to kill you. I would bet a large amount of money that he was on the verge of letting you go when you smashed his testicles. Remember, whoever desperately wants their hands on us will plan to torture us and extract as much information as possible. That would be nearly impossible here at Camp Peary."

Ava asked, "Does that mean staying here for the long haul is our best survival option?"

Woody shook his head. "This place is no longer secure, so at some point the KGB, or whoever else is after us, will compromise and settle for just getting us eliminated here at The Farm. Of course, they would miss out on all of the fun of torturing us by whacking off random body parts to extract classified information."

Ava said, "Since I don't have any body parts that I really want to sacrifice, let me tell you about my survival idea. We both agree leaving here is our best chance to celebrate another birthday. The problem is that with all the security of Camp Peary, escaping would be near impossible. We need an official pass to leave. And I think I know a way that could make that happen."

"I have my bunny ears up tall. Let's hear your idea."

Ava continued, "I know that you recall that we were extensively debriefed by the director himself when we were still at Langley. He was so grateful for our work in saving Sanderson that he bypassed protocol to obtain permanent residency for me. You may have forgotten that he gave me his personal card as we left. I didn't show you, but there was a handwritten note on the card that said, 'Here is a number that you can always reach me on if either of you need anything.'"

"And?" Woody asked.

"And, I called him during my afternoon of so-called indolence, and the director was very gracious. He is taking a chopper from D.C. to Camp Peary tomorrow morning on business. The director asked us to meet him in his private office here at 10 AM. He is the one person who has the power to grant us a 'Get out of Camp Peary free' card. So, remember when you get up tomorrow morning to take a long shower, brush your teeth, and put on deodorant. I myself plan to be even more fetching than usual."

Woody replied, "As you know, my body hygiene is always impeccable—fear not. And for added good measure, I will drench my sculptured body in Old Spice cologne tomorrow."

Ava sniffed, "Old Spice has always been better at attracting flies than hot women."

CHAPTER 6

LOOSE LIPS SINK SHIPS

Ava and Woody met for breakfast early the next morning. As they sat down to eat, they saw Robertson enter the cafeteria. He paused long enough to give them a penetrating stare, then grabbed a tray and joined the serving line.

"If looks could kill, we'd both be flatliners like the message pinned on my door," Ava observed. "Why would a person who is allegedly a CIA hero even consider turning dirty?"

Woody mused a moment, then asked, "Don't you believe everybody has a price? That bombshell wife of Robertson has to be very high maintenance. If he wants to continue a connubial open-door policy each night in bed, I bet that he has to keep the shekels coming in."

Ava shook her head. "You men are so disgusting. In your testosterone-inflamed world, every human action always comes down to sex."

"Yep," Woody said with a sly smile. "Why do you think I hang out with you?"

Ava gave him a quick kick beneath the table that made him wince. "Woody, I don't think you learned a great deal during your few months in medical school, but I hope that you remember what dyspareunia means. Well, you are about to enter into a long period of apareunia in your life."

"Surely a fate worse than death," Woody said. "I offer humble apologies on bended knee."

Ava said, "I will consider your apology—contingent on continued better behavior from you. But let's concentrate on staying alive. Sex is likely not a high priority of dead people."

Conversation stopped as Robertson approached their table and loomed over them. He transfixed them with a steely stare, then said ominously, "I have no idea how you got an appointment with the director. We have been very good friends for a long time. My wife is his daughter. So, keep in mind the old adage, 'Loose lips sink ships.' I would hate to see something really bad happen to the two of you—particularly the woman."

Robertson continued his cold stare at Ava and Woody for several more uncomfortable seconds, then turned on his heel and dumped his tray on an empty table as he left the cafeteria.

"Mr. Personality," Ava said. "How in the world did he ever talk the director's daughter into marrying him? And why is he trying to terrorize us?"

Woody answered, "My hypothesis remains the same. Robertson wants to scare us into going AWOL from Camp Peary and then set us up for the kill in the outside world with no protection. Perhaps there's big money in it for him from the KGB or maybe from the crime syndicate, which also has a score to settle with us. I don't think Robertson is clean despite his alleged hero service for the CIA."

Ava asked, "How are we going to play it now that we have been threatened by the director's son-in-law? Do we tell the director that we think his son-in-law may be compromised?"

"We'll tell him everything straight, and let the director draw his own conclusions about Robertson," Woody answered. "Somehow we have to convince him to help us get out of Camp Peary."

* * * *

At 10 AM sharp, Ava and Woody arrived at the director's Camp Peary office and were ushered into the inner sanctum by his male secretary. The director rose from behind his desk and extended his hand. He was a handsome man with striking blue eyes, perfectly groomed steel-gray hair, and wire-frame glasses. After shaking hands with Ava and then Woody, he said, "Please, take a seat. It is so nice to see you two again. Our government will never forget your service to the country."

Ava said courteously, "We know how frightfully busy you are, Sir, and are honored that you made time to see us."

The director smiled and said, "How can I help you? When Ava and I spoke, she conveyed a sense of urgency."

Woody said, "We will be brief and to the point." He paused, then continued. "Ava and I are not safe here. Our lives have been threatened. There is little doubt that the secrecy of Camp Peary and The Farm has been penetrated. John Claiborne was not the only traitor in the CIA."

The director's face took a look of great concern. "Those are very serious charges. I hope that you can substantiate them. Camp Peary is one of the most secure compounds in the world."

Woody replied, "Sir, we would not be here taking your valuable time with pure conjecture and a wild conspiracy tale. Here are the straight facts with no punches pulled and no intent to incriminate any specific person or persons."

Woody then proceeded in a calm, concise way to detail the threatening note on Ava's door, the oranges with strychnine in them, and the choking episode with Ava. When Woody related Robertson's denial of the positive lab test, the director's face hardened.

Ava interjected. "Sir, you can still see the bruises on my neck from the choking.

"The man who attempted to strangle me clearly had previous training in martial arts, perhaps the Russian Systema or Brazilian jiu-jitsu. He was a professional. We think that it's just a matter of time until whoever is behind this finds a way to eliminate Woody and me right in the middle of Camp Peary."

The director sat silently for a minute, then said, "What would you have me do?"

Woody said, "We want to be allowed to leave Camp Peary without CIA protection and fend for ourselves. Neither one of us wants a new identity or a surgical change of our appearance."

The director replied, "There is no doubt that you two are a formidable pair, but I think that the KGB or whoever else is looking for you will track you down and torture you for information. It won't be pleasant for either one of you. I don't think that I can agree for you to be out on your own. You both have valuable information that foreign governments would kill to obtain. But I understand your concern in the present situation. Perhaps we can arrange to isolate you in a small area of Camp Peary with guards around the clock."

Ava shook her head and said, "You are describing a prison. We both had rather be dead than spend our lives like that."

Woody said, "I completely agree, Sir. But I think that I can present a plan for how Ava and I can disappear safely for a long period of time."

The director bowed his head for a minute, then looked up. "Here is my suggestion. You are both to stay in your present situation for now, but I will arrange for unobtrusive security, both day and night. We will meet again in a week. If at that time you can present an utterly convincing and detailed plan to me for how you can stay safe outside of here and without government security, I will consider it."

The director stood, and Ava and Woody knew that the meeting was over. As the two left the office, the director added, "Based on the bad experience that you had teaching hand-to-hand combat, Ava, I think that it is unwise for you to continue your role as an instructor at this time."

As Woody and Ava walked down the hall, Ava said softly, "Squat toilets and endless desert, here we come. Upchuck."

CHAPTER 7

CRAZY UNCLE WILBUR

Woody and Ava left the director's office and headed for Ava's Camp Peary efficiency apartment. After they entered and sat down on the small couch, Woody put a finger to his lips. Ava nodded in agreement. They both were suspicious that their apartments might have listening devices.

Woody nodded at Ava and said, "The director is really a nice man. He's probably right that we are perfectly safe here and are just being overly suspicious. It is hard to believe that there is any place more secure than Camp Peary under CIA protection. Looks like we are going to be here for the long haul."

"Woody, I have to agree with you. I'm going to ask our case manager if I can attend the Mandarin school in the compound. Might as well do something productive if we are going to be here for a long time. What say we go grab a cup of coffee?"

Once the two of them were safely on the patio and away from other people, Woody said, "I hope that we didn't lay the manure on too thick in your room. But we have to be really careful where we talk. We have to communicate on the principle that even the walls have ears."

Ava shook her head in agreement. "Let's just make the magical assumption that the director is willing to let us vanish from Camp Peary. I would love more details about where we go, how we get there, and how we keep from being a death statistic once there."

Woody said, "My idea is rather complicated. But here goes. I have a crazy step-uncle named Wilbur Wilbanks who for years has lived on a small ranch way out in the boonies of the Trans-Pecos desert in far west Texas. He was in the Army Special Forces in World

War II and received the Medal of Honor for bravery in the assault on Normandy Beach. But he was never the same after the war. He began hearing voices and acting irrationally. The Army gave him a medical discharge with a diagnosis of paranoid schizophrenia. He also received a nice pension.

"With that money and some other funds that he had inherited from his father, who was a very successful attorney, Uncle Wilbur bought one hundred acres of land in the desert and built a very secure compound. I took a road trip at the end of my senior year in high school and drove a 1955 vomit-green Pontiac station wagon from Dallas to a small town called Barlow way out in the desert. There was a gas station, a small general store, a bar, and a seedy-looking hotel. A man at the gas station told me how to find Uncle Willie's place, which was twenty more miles farther into the desert on a nonexistent road. He also told me that no one ever went near the compound since Crazy Wilbur was prone to shoot at people who trespassed on his land.

"It was a tough trip out to the compound since that part of the desert was an anomaly with very fine sand that made tire traction almost impossible. The fellow at the gas station said that my uncle had a beat-up pickup truck with large sand tires and would drive into town once a month to buy supplies and food at the general store. People avoided him since he was usually talking to himself and had a wild look in his eyes."

Ava shook her head and said, "If that is where you are planning for us to go, I may just stay here and ask Robertson to give me a slice of orange to eat. It sounds ghastly. I note that you have not mentioned any civilized amenities at Wilbur's place. What about water?"

Woody replied, "You will be thrilled to learn that there is a nice desert aquifer that provides water. My uncle was something of a genius and rigged up a pump system that supplies running water to the house and barn."

Ava gave a faint smile and said, "The lodging has just gone from a no-star to a tentative half-star. Is this the place with squat toilets?"

"Actually, you just have to go out of the back door and walk fifty yards to what Uncle Willie calls a 'squat cactus,'" Woody said with a grin. "You have to be very careful not to back your bare bottom into one of the large cactus spines."

Ava shook her head with a frown and said, "You are about to get another hot cup of coffee thrown on your private parts for lying. Better tell me the real potty accommodations before it's too late."

"Just funning you, Ava. Don't be so sensitive. There are actually two bathrooms with flush toilets and perfumed toilet paper flown in from Paris each week."

Ava lifted her hand with the coffee cup and drew back as if to throw.

Woody said quickly, "Cross my heart about the flush toilets. The fancy toilet paper was just a little poetic license. My uncle put in a huge septic tank that he said would last 30 years without needing pumping. He also has a giant buried propane tank and a generator."

Ava put the coffee cup down and said, "OK. I believe you. The accommodations have just been upgraded to a weak one-star. Since there is no safe way to communicate with your uncle, how do you know that he will not shoot us on sight? And why would he agree to let us stay there?"

"Ah, highly intelligent questions. Wilbur might indeed shoot at us. When I drove up to his gate in my station wagon and started honking the horn, he came hot footing to the gate toting a Russian AK47 and with a snarling Rottweiler at his side. It took me several minutes to convince him who I was. The dog never liked me, but Uncle Willie and I got along fine for the week I was there. He has a huge cache of weapons and let me fire several of his exotic guns. The most unnerving thing was Willie's screams at night when he dreamed about storming the Normandy Beach and seeing so many of his comrades blown to bits by German machine gun fire."

Ava frowned and said, "This place sounds worse by the minute."

"Beats being dead," Woody said succinctly.

Ava gave a small sigh, then asked. "How, pray tell, do we get to Uncle Wilbur's paradise without being tracked?"

Woody smiled and answered, "I thought you would never ask. Simple. We parachute in."

Ava had a look of disbelief on her face. She shook her head and asked, "Woody, have you completely lost your mind? Do you seriously believe that the director is going to arrange a private jump for us into some God-forsaken desert hell hole?"

"Yep," Woody said with a nod of his head. "What's the matter, my fair princess? Are you afraid of heights?"

Ava frowned and answered, "KGB training makes The Farm look like day care. I have over 20 jumps under my belt."

"That's good," Woody replied, because this jump will have to be at fairly high altitude and done at night if we want to avoid any curious eyes. The good news is that there is an old Army training air field dating back to World War II in the area, so it won't be totally strange for an aircraft to be heard up high in the night sky."

Ava rolled her eyes and said dubiously, "If you can sell this cockamamie scheme to the director, you could do a land-office business selling glow-in-the-dark condoms at a nun's convention."

Woody replied, "Genius idea, Ava. But let me sell the director on our relocation plan first, and then we can look at business opportunities."

CHAPTER 8

SECURITY BREACH

The next morning Woody and Ava were back on the patio with coffee and sweet rolls they had taken from the cafeteria. Summer was fast approaching, and the Virginia day was muggy with low clouds.

Ava took a sip of her coffee, wrinkled her nose, and said, "This coffee tastes like it could be used to strip the rust off of an old iron fence. Nasty."

Woody got a sly smile and said innocently, "Mine tastes great. Wonder if yours got the dose of strychnine?"

"Not funny, Woody. Not funny at all."

Woody said, "Just offering a bit of early morning humor. The last thing our enemies want is for us to die here. They are not going to miss the chance to whack off body parts and extract as much information out of us as they can. And for that to happen, we have to be out in the real world."

Ava said with a small shudder, "I have absolutely no interest in being a whackee."

"Agreed," Woody replied.

After a pause, Ava asked, "Did a night of sleep clear your mind of your wacko plan about hiding out at your crazy step-uncle's desert spa and retreat?"

"Au contraire. I stayed up late working on a proposal that the director will not be able to turn down."

Ava said, "If you are going to insist on pursuing this hare-brained scheme, I have a few pertinent questions for the relocation genius."

"Fire away," Woody replied.

"Number one, what are we going to do for food?"

"Fret not. Uncle Wilbur was totally into independence and isolationism. When I was there, he had a huge storeroom full of all sorts of survival food. No reason to think that he hasn't kept it fully stocked. And if push comes to shove, one of us could always figure a way to get into Barlow for some supplies."

Ava sniffed and said, "Adding K rations to a veritable desert paradise makes a couple of tasty orange slices from Robertson sound better all the time. Moving on to number two—what about weapons?"

"Uncle Wilbur is certain to have enough weapons and ammo to outfit a platoon of soldiers. Firepower won't be a problem. But, remember, our goal is to disappear for a while and not have the need for guns—except to shoot desert critters."

"Got it," Ava said. "Now for a really critical third question. What happens if your crazy uncle won't let us stay with him?"

"Don't think that is a worry. I am certain that I can sell us as delightful companions for him ... particularly when I tell him that you are eager to take over all of the cooking and cleaning chores."

Ava pointed a finger at Woody and said, "Careful, Big Boy. Remember my organ clamp from gross anatomy. I travel with it at all times. If you try to volunteer me for menial chores not befitting a princess, I might have to break it out."

Woody smiled and said, "I have been warned."

"Moving on," Ava continued, "Question four is what we will do for money. We certainly can't use a credit card. And will we assume different names?"

"Pertinent questions," Woody answered. "I have enough cash to last for several months, courtesy of a real uncle who left me some funds when he died a few years ago. We will need to assume new identities without CIA help. My idea is to grow a beard and let my hair grow out to change my appearance. No doubt you can do some similar things to make yourself less recognizable."

Ava pursed her lips and said, "I think there is almost zero chance that the director will agree to this insane plan, but if he has gone totally daft and does agree, I guess I'm game."

* * * *

A week later Ava and Woody found themselves once again in the director's office at Camp Peary. The secretary told them that he would be there shortly. After a few minutes the director arrived and asked them into his inner office. He seemed a bit harried and concerned.

Once the two were seated, the director asked, "Any more threats?"

"No, Sir," Woody answered.

The director had a grave look on his face and said, "I cannot go into detail, but there does appear to be a security breach here at Peary. We are working hard to remedy the problem. I have to agree that at the present time you two are not safe here. Our intelligence tells us that each of you is a high priority target for the KGB. There are also some crime figures who would like to get their hands on you.

"The CIA and the FBI have not forgotten your bravery and service to the country and want you to be safe."

Woody said, "Sir, we really want to leave and take care of ourselves. Being essentially incarcerated here or elsewhere with constant surveillance is no better than a prison sentence. I would like to present my plan to you which I think offers safety as well as some degree of normal living."

The director listened without interruption while Woody outlined his plan for disappearing into the western desert of Texas. In closing, Woody added, "We think this plan will only work if no one at Camp Peary knows anything about it. And not to be rude, but that would include our manager Robertson."

The director put his hand on his chin while he digested Woody's remarks. Then he slowly said, "That has to be the most bizarre plan I have ever heard. I see lots of potential problems and risks. Right off the bat, I see no way I could arrange for a plane to take you near your uncle's hideaway to jump without arousing all sorts of suspicion."

Woody quickly responded, "I have a lifelong friend in Odessa who runs a skydiving school. He has a Cessna, and I know that he would fly us out to Uncle Wilbur's place. I trust him implicitly. The only tricky part would be getting to Odessa without alerting the KGB or the crime people."

The director did not speak for a minute as he seemed to be deep in thought. He finally spoke and said, "The CIA and your country are deeply indebted to both of you for service that risked your lives on a number of occasions. I do want to help the two of you find some type of near-normal life. My primary concern would be the fear that you could be captured and tortured. I have been advised that neither of you is in possession of any highly classified CIA information compared to the previous leaks. Your possible painful execution would be my first worry."

Ava spoke for the first time. "Neither one of us would expect or want any CIA protection once we leave here. Our goal is to disappear for several years in hopes that at a later date it might be safe to take our heads out of the desert sand without getting them whacked off."

The director put his hand to his forehead. "This is so highly irregular. I have to give this some more thought. You two were responsible for identifying Assistant Deputy Claiborne as a traitor to the CIA and his country. And now you seemed to have unearthed another CIA traitor here at Peary who may have already compromised more clandestine operatives and shared highly classified information. These are very dangerous times for our country."

Woody said, "If you can just help us get to Odessa under the radar, we will handle things from that point on and will not expect anything from any branch of the government."

The director said, as he arose, "Let me have a day or two and I will get back to you. Thank you for coming today."

CHAPTER 9

DESERT BOUND

The next morning Woody received a message from the director that he and Ava would be picked up at 11 AM by a government helicopter and taken to Langley to prepare to testify with the director before a Congressional Committee concerned about leaks in the CIA. The message also said to be prepared to stay three or four days.

Woody met Ava for breakfast. They both took their trays out to the patio. Once they felt safe to talk, Woody relayed the message and said, "We are out of here! The part of the message about being prepared to stay several days is code for 'you are not going back to Camp Peary.' That means that the director has figured out a way to get us safely to Odessa."

Ava said, "I sure hope that you are right. The thought of the desert and meeting your crazy uncle has given me anticipation tachycardia. Let's hurry through breakfast, then go to our rooms and select a few essentials for the trip. We need to pack light so it won't look like we're leaving for good."

Just as they were finishing their breakfast, Robertson strolled up. "I understand that you heroes are going to D.C. to testify before Congress. Leaving the safety of Camp Peary is a huge gamble. I'd guess the odds of you two coming back alive is a lot lower than you might think. D.C. is a very dangerous town. All sorts of accidents could happen," he said ominously before he turned and strode back into the building.

Ava said, "Well, that's a nice ray of sunshine to start the day. Robertson seems super pissed that we are getting a two- or three-day pass outside the hallowed walls of Camp Peary. Your theory that Robertson is being paid big money to get us to leave here and become easy targets for the bad buys does not comport with his warnings."

Woody said, "He's grumpy because we are leaving under the director's protection which will make it hard for anyone to drag us off and begin removing various body parts while listening to us scream out classified information. His goal is to terrorize us into making an ill-advised dash from Camp Peary, right into the arms of the people who are making him rich and funding his nights of connubial bliss with his hot wife."

Ava asked, "Do you think the director has suspicions about his son-in-law possibly being on the take? That would really be a sticky wicket investigating his daughter's revered CIA husband for possible treason."

Woody replied, "If Robertson has been made party to our talks with the director, our days are numbered. We have no choice now but to trust the director."

* * * *

The government Bell Huey skimmed over the green Virginia countryside and reached Langley in less than 30 minutes. A car met Woody and Ava and took them to CIA headquarters. They passed through screening and were ushered into the director's main office. He joined them promptly.

The director had a very serious look on his face as he spoke to Woody and Ava. "Please sit down. Thank you for coming on such short notice. There is much that must be done in a short period of time. I want to update you on recent developments and your request to leave Camp Peary permanently and fend for yourselves without CIA protection. Initially, I was not enthusiastic about Officer Stressel's plan. But things have changed.

"Intelligence tells us that there are at least two people based at Camp Peary who are KGB informers. They apparently have been offered a large sum of money to eliminate both of you. Unfortunately, we have as of yet not identified these people with certainty. We cannot guarantee your safety at Peary short of locking you both up in a cell with round-the-clock guards. I think that you should reconsider assuming new identities and letting us quietly relocate you somewhere in South America."

Woody replied, "Sir, we would much prefer your helping us get to Odessa and letting us assume all responsibility for our own safety."

The director said quietly, "I was afraid that you would not agree to a complete identity change and relocation. Trying to isolate in the western Texas desert would not be my choice, but I will help you do that with some nonnegotiable stipulations. First, Officer Stressel has to resign from the CIA with no prospect of ever returning. Both of you will need to sign a statement that leaving CIA protection is one made of your own free will, and that you will have no expectation of any government help in the future.

"Lastly, you must agree in writing that if either of you is ever captured by a foreign government or a criminal entity, the U.S. government will have no obligation to attempt to secure your release."

Ava and Woody looked at each other, then said in unison, "That is what we want."

The director said, "I feel like I am releasing my teenage son who has just received his driver's license out on the streets with a hot new Corvette and no automobile insurance. One other thing that you need to know, the KGB desperately wants to capture Miss Volkov to make an example of what happens to KGB agents who are turned by a foreign entity. If they get their hands on her, it will not be pretty."

Ava looked directly at the director and said firmly, "I understand, Sir, and I am not afraid."

A brief smile played across the director's face. "You two are a remarkable team. I have been fully versed about your lives as undercover agents in a freshman medical school class. Your lives to date would make a compelling movie. There is one other thing that I need to bring up. It is none of my business what relationship you two have, but I would suggest that you pose as brother and sister, not husband and wife, until you study the common law statutes in Texas."

Ava and Woody exchanged glances and nodded in agreement.

The director stood and said, "Now I need to go testify before a Congressional Intelligence Committee in a private session. Very few people will ever know that you two were never invited."

The director pushed a button on the intercom module on his desk. A woman who appeared to be in her late 30s entered the office quickly.

"This is Officer Reagor, who is an expert at her craft. She will show you to another secure room where you can sign papers and learn more about traveling to Odessa. You will need to come up with preferred names so Reagor can arrange for your new ID cards. We will shred your old ones. What the officer has to tell you may make the difference between living and dying. So, pay very close attention."

Ava and Woody stood as the director walked over to them. He shook their hands firmly and said, "I admire both of you greatly and wish you well." He paused a moment as if there were more he wished to say, then abruptly turned and left.

CHAPTER 10

DESERT PREP

Officer Reagor was all business. She led Ava and Woody briskly down the hall to a small office and pointed at chairs for them to sit. She sat down at her desk and looked intently at the two people in front of her as if trying to reconcile their choice to leave CIA protection with their past history of bravery and service to the agency.

Ava judged Officer Reagor to be in her late 30s. She had the body of a runner with muscular calves. Her white forelock and dark green eyes combined to give her an exotic look. Ava thought to herself, "If I had 20 minutes and a makeup kit, I could make this woman almost attractive."

The officer said firmly, "We have a great deal to do in a hurry so you can be ready for your trip to Odessa—Texas, not Russia. I must say that I, like the director, have grave reservations about you two deciding to leave CIA protection and heading out into a very dangerous world. But we all make choices in life—some are wise, and some are foolish.

"I am an expert at placing people in our witness protection plan. Even though you have chosen not to take advantage of this, I can tell you things that will increase your chances of surviving. So, listen up.

"First, it is critical that you do not contact any old friends or family members. Period. Second, absolutely do not return to any place where you have previously lived. Your job is to blend into the background wherever you end up. Avoid standing out by dress or by actions. Be very careful meeting new people. You both will have new names and must practice them until they are second nature. A slip in using a real name can be deadly. I understand that both of you are fluent in Russian. Never, ever speak any Russian in public. Now, Ava and Woody, take turns and please repeat the sentence, 'It is time for all good men to come to the aid of their country.'"

Ava repeated the sentence with precise articulation. Woody followed.

Officer Reagor listened intently, then said, "Ava, you have a very slight Russian accent. Woody speaks pure lingua Americana. This means that posing as a brother and sister will be treacherous and would necessitate explaining different backgrounds. The safest thing will be to present yourselves as companions, perhaps boyfriend and girlfriend. The director has some concern about the Texas statutes of common law marriage, but it seems to me that you have much bigger things to worry about than that.

"It is critical that I help you develop a new past history that is convincing. You also need to be flawless in explaining what has brought you to your new location. I will work with you for the next few days on this and other things. The fact that you plan to isolate in what sounds like a desolate part of Texas will be to your advantage. Your trip to Odessa is scheduled in five days. I will tell you more about it when all details are final. Use this afternoon to work on your past history stories as well as new names. Pick very common names that will not stand out.

"Once you both sign release papers, I will show each of you to your secure quarters which have a connecting inside door. You will only be able to leave when I come to take you to a safe place to work on names and a believable past history.

"Meals will be brought to your rooms. Any questions?"

Woody asked, "We had to have our weapons stored when we arrived at Langley. Any chance of getting them back before we travel?"

Officer Reagor shook her head. "Retrieving your weapons would be like flashing a neon sign that the two of you are not coming back to Peary. I have been told that Ava has a Russian pistol which could be a deadly identifier. We will provide each of you with a new weapon before you leave here. No doubt both of you are hungry. I will walk you to your quarters where food is waiting. Expect to see me at your doors tomorrow at 7 AM sharp."

* * * *

Once Officer Reagor had shown Ava and Woody to their rooms, she closed each heavy metal door, which was followed by a clicking of the lock tumblers. Woody waited a minute and tried to open his door to the hall. It was securely locked. He next tried the deadbolt on his side of the connecting door and was able to open it. But the door on Ava's side was locked. He tapped 'SOS' in Morse code. After a few seconds Ava tapped back, "I'm in the middle of a bubble bath, then I need to do my nails." After a brief delay, she opened her door. "Welcome to my palatial quarters."

Woody came in and sat on the small, hard bed. He looked around and said, "These rooms are tiny with no windows. It's just like being confined to a cell on death row."

"Don't try to spook me, Woody. I have complete trust in the director."

Woody answered, "Did you check out the biceps on Officer Reagor? I bet that she and Robertson were colleagues in the CIA death squad. Do you trust her?"

Ava said, "We are as safe as a baby in a womb."

Woody said wryly, "Better watch out for a knitting needle coming through your door."

Ava replied, "Enough graveside humor for now. We need to start thinking seriously about new names. They need to be common names that don't stand out and won't be remembered for being odd. I was thinking about 'Mary Patricia White.' That's about as generic as you can get."

Woody said, "I was considering 'Hercules Samson Studly' for myself. What do you think?"

Ava shook her head and replied, "I think 'A. H. Studly' would be better."

Woody replied, "Do the initials stand for anything? I hesitate to ask."

Ava smiled wickedly and replied, "I'll give you a clue. The 'A' stands for another name for a donkey."

Woody laughed and grabbed a pillow and threw it at her.

"Actually, I can match your bland 'Mary Patricia White' with 'Michael Robert Smith.'"

"Tell you what," Ava said. "Let's hold off on first-naming each other until we run our potential new names by our CIA trainer in the morning. Go get the bag lunch in your room, and the soon-to-be Mary and Michael can have a romantic dinner together. Then we can work on coming up with believable past histories to present to our former CIA female assassin in the morning."

CHAPTER 11

A NONDESCRIPT VW CAMPER

As promised, Officer Reagor came for Woody and Ava at 7 AM. As she tapped on each door, there was the subtle sound of the dead bolt retracting. With a curt nod, she led the two of them to a new room that had a projector and screen. There was coffee, orange juice, and sweet rolls waiting.

After Ava and Woody sat down, Reagor said, "You have ten minutes for breakfast. I'll be back then to start my instruction." She then took a key out of her pocket and walked to the door. "I will be locking you in for your safety. Don't dawdle over your food."

After the door closed behind Reagor, Ava looked at Woody and said, "Just like I insisted, Mr. Stressel, we are in fact as safe as babies in a womb. The director is clearly determined that we leave his headquarters alive."

Woody replied, "Mr. Smith to you, please. Mr. Stressel no longer exists."

Ava shook her head. "Hold your horses, Mr. Stressel. Officer Reagor has not yet sanctioned our new names."

Woody replied, "I am confident that she will love our name choices. In fact, she might conjure up a slight smile. Did you notice that Reagor is just bubbling over with cheer this morning? She's even grimmer than yesterday. I would bet my last penny that Reagor has lots of CIA travel miles in her file with a host of CIA-approved kills."

Ava nodded. "I don't know if you noticed, but Reagor quickly surveyed my room to make certain that my bed had been slept in. She obviously is not aware of your recent vow of lifelong chastity."

Woody gave a sly smile and answered, "Vows taken by the head are often trumped by other body parts. Besides, I never really took a vow. But I also noticed that Reagor gave my room a rapid visual once over."

Ava said, "She'll be back any minute, Woody. You better wolf down that sweet roll if you want it. I have a feeling that eating will not be permitted once our session starts."

The door opened and Office Reagor walked in briskly.

"Breakfast is over. No more food or drink while we work. Before I start, let me clarify a few things. First, you both should have been smart enough to know that you should never assume a safe speech area unless you are certain. I would have thought that you would have noticed that small microphone hidden in the overhead light fixtures of your rooms. So, to clarify things, I have zero interest in whether you two are having a sexual relationship or not. Second, it is a total waste of your time to speculate about my CIA career. All three of us have served this country well. That's all that I am going to say about that. Now down to the business of keeping you alive, if possible.

"First, I want to discuss your trip to Odessa, which is challenging to arrange. As you know, it seems certain that there is a security leak at Camp Peary. Your chopper trip to see the director under the pretense of testifying to Congress was not a secret event there. Whoever would like to capture you will be monitoring the exit gates at Langley hoping to establish a tail. So, our first problem is to get the two of you out of here without detection. In four days, Saturday the 25th of July, we plan to smuggle you both out at night in the back of a plumbing truck that will take you to Staunton, Virginia.

"There the truck will enter a warehouse at the edge of town. Inside is a beige 1960 Volkswagen camper with curtains. It is totally nondescript. The two of you will drive this vehicle to Odessa, Texas, which is about a 26-hour trip. When one of you is driving, the other should always be in the back with the curtains drawn. People interested in harming you will likely be looking for a couple.

"There is a partition that obscures the area behind the driver. Inside the partitioned area is a small bed, a chemical potty, water, and food items. When you stop for gas, only the driver should be seen. The person in the back may have to rely on the potty, depending on urgency. There is no air-conditioner, so expect to be hot. Hydrate frequently. There is a small fan for the driver and one for the person in the back. Changing drivers should only be done on a stretch of road when there are no other vehicles and no houses or businesses are in sight. You are both high-value targets. Expect the KGB to use a full-court press to find you.

"I would suggest that you drive straight through, alternating driving with sleeping. When you stop for gas, spend as little time as possible at the station and try to find small stations that have few, if any, customers. Avoid unnecessary conversation with other people and don't try to win any friends along the way."

Officer Reagor paused and asked, "Everything good so far? Any questions? No? Then I am going to dim the lights and project a proposed route for you. We have decided that the fastest possible route will be safer than a slow route on backroads. Memorize this route and the cities and towns along the way. Part of your trip will be at night, so stay on the route and don't miss a turn and wander out into no-man's land. And—very important—don't speed. A stop by the highway patrol might blow your cover. We will prepare each of you a North Dakota driver's license once we have agreed on your new names. However, these licenses won't be searchable in the national database since they are bogus. Any questions thus far?"

Woody asked, "What happens when we get to Odessa?"

Officer Reagor replied, "We quickly vetted your friend Clarke Driver who runs the skydiving business. You likely know that he was an Army Ranger with a number of jumps himself. Once we were as certain as we can be on short notice that Clarke is trustworthy, we discretely contacted him, giving as few details as possible. He is more than willing to fly you over predetermined coordinates at night. His suggestion was that you jump from 2500 feet when there is high cloud cover. Landing at night is always tricky, so be careful. A broken ankle in the middle of nowhere would be a problem."

Ava said, "It is going to be difficult timing the meeting since our ETA may vary depending on weather and possible car trouble."

Reagor responded, "We have planned your drive closely so that if you leave at 10 PM, you should arrive at around midnight. The camper has been thoroughly inspected and should make the trip with no problems. Clarke plans to be in the back lot of John's Truck Stop on Highway 20 outside of Odessa at your projected arrival time. He will be driving a black panel truck with no signage. The driver should join Clarke first, then the second person can follow when he or she is convinced that there are no prying eyes."

"There are more important details to follow, but for now I will accompany you back to your quarters and give you more time to work on your new histories and names. At noon lunch will be delivered to you. Then at 1 PM I will escort you back to the training room to consider your new names and to see how good you two are at rewriting your personal histories. We still have a great deal to do before Saturday."

CHAPTER 12

NAME CHANGE

Woody and Ava were sitting on the bed in her room discussing how to contrive believable new personal histories to conceal their true identities. They had already agreed to present 'Mary Patricia White' and 'Michael Robert Smith' to Officer Reagor as potential mundane names that would not call any attention to themselves. Once the names were settled, they moved on to trying to devise a history for Ava to explain her slight foreign accent. The discussion was interrupted by a firm knock on the door.

"Come in," Woody said. There was the quiet sound of the tumblers in the door lock moving, and then the door swung open to admit Officer Reagor with a brown bag in each hand.

"Lunch time," she announced as she sat the bags down on the bed. "Government gourmet as per usual. I'll be back to get you in thirty minutes to take you to the same teaching room."

Reagor left, shutting the door behind her, and waited for the door lock to reset.

Ava said, "Did you detect just the slightest touch of humanness there?"

Woody shook his head and pointed to the light fixture.

Ava mouthed "My bad," and pointed to herself.

Woody articulated "dummy" silently in response.

Ava gave him a death stare and pointed to his crotch and made a scissor-cutting sign with two fingers.

The two then opened their brown bags and found Spam sandwiches, potato chips, and a rock-hard brownie. Ava wrote "Yuk!" on a piece of paper and passed it to Woody. He shook his head in agreement, then wrote back, "I can hardly wait to see what culinary treats have been stashed away for us in the camper!"

At 12:30 PM sharp there was a rap on the door and Reagor entered. "Meal time is over. Time to get back to work. Follow me."

Ava and Woody trouped down the hall dutifully and were led back to the same room they had been in that morning. Once they were seated, Officer Reagor locked the door and walked over to stand in front of them.

"Before we get into names and new past histories for each of you, there are a couple of important points to cover. For you to survive your high-risk choice to leave CIA protection, it is critical that you both blend in with the background wherever you are. Never, ever stand out. Avoid confrontations. Also, I need to talk about your appearances, which absolutely must be changed.

"First, Mr. Stressel is very muscular, which is obvious in regular clothes. His physique could serve as a memory guide for people. Woody, for the trip we are going to have you dress in a tan, baggy leisure suit with pants and a long-sleeve top that will conceal your muscles. The pants have some subtle padding up front that will give you a small pot belly. And, Woody, I would strongly advise you to grow a beard that is not outrageous and also to let your hair grow longer and stay unkempt. Looking a bit like a hayseed will be in your best interest.

"Ava, you will need modification even more than Woody. It is obvious that you are an attractive and shapely woman. You will need to dress in nonrevealing clothes that de-emphasize your bust and hips. And as much as you will hate it, clipping your hair short will add to your chances of survival. I assume that you are a natural light brunette. Using a color rinse to darken your hair would be prudent. I also would absolutely not wear any makeup. You do not want to stand out as being noticeably attractive or ugly. Plain Jane is the look you should be shooting for. Any quibbles with any of that?"

Ava replied, "We both prefer being ugly to being dead."

Office Reagor said, "The goal is really not ugly. I want everyday, boring plain. Now let's hear what new names you have come up with. Ava, you first."

"I am suggesting Mary Patricia White," Ava replied.

Reagor thought a moment then spoke, "I would like Mary Sue White better. You should introduce yourself, if need be, as Mary White. OK?" Ava nodded in agreement.

"Now, Woody, let's see how creative you were."

Woody answered, "My choice was Michael Robert Smith."

Reagor shook her head. "I don't like Michael, which will inevitably become 'Mike,' which is a dominant male name. My choice would be simply Bob Smith, but you can have a middle initial 'R' on your driver's license. Is that all right with you?" Woody gave a thumbs-up sign.

"From this point on you are to use the names Mary and Bob at all times. Emblazon them into your brains. Now, Mary, I want to do a little trust exercise with you. Come stand by me." Mary stood up with Reagor behind her.

"Now, Mary, I want you to close your eyes and when I say 'fall,' I want you to fall back into my arms. Got it?" Mary nodded yes.

"Fall!" As Mary started to go backwards, Reagor stepped to the side and tossed a handful of large carpet tacks on the floor where Mary's head would land.

Woody screamed, "No, Ava!" and lunged toward her. Reagor was quick as a cat and stuck out one muscular arm and stopped the fall.

Reagor shook her head. "Woody, you just failed. Regardless of how dire the situation is, you cannot reflexly use Mary's real name. This could be a fatal mistake."

"Now a bit of good news. I have written a credible history for each of you. Most people in your situation cannot create a coherent story that does not have many potential pitfalls in it. In all modesty, I am an expert at this. Here is a typed history of Mary White and Bob Smith for each of you. It is critical not only to know your own story backwards and forwards, but also to know your partner's story perfectly. I will give you an hour to memorize this material, then I will return to test you. Do not disappoint me."

CROSSING THE RIVER STYX

Woody and Ava poured over their own histories as well as the other person's history intently for the entire hour before Reagor returned. They were surprised at the brevity of each document. There was bare bones information with no details.

Bob said to Mary, "This material is child's play compared to the Krebs cycle or learning the umpteen million parts of the cadavers during our brief stint in medical school."

Mary smiled and responded, "Considering that you never really learned the difference between the Krebs cycle and a unicycle, I have to take that statement with a grain of salt. Even with as fantastic a tutor as moi, biochemistry was a real intellectual reach for you."

Bob put his hand to his heart as if in great pain. "That's one of the many reasons why we can never get married and procreate. The kids would inherit my stupid gene."

Mary gave a smile and asked, "Is that a proposal? If so, the answer is 'not a chance, Buddy.' I know that I can do a lot better on the open market. Need I reiterate the fact that you were valedictorian in high school and Phi Beta Kappa in college? So, you are not hopelessly stupid."

Bob walked over to Mary and gave her a kiss on the hand. "Need I point out that a woman who is a high number on the KGB hit list is not exactly a hot commodity on the marriage market? Wasn't it Tolstoy who said, 'A bird in the hand is worth two in the bush?'"

Mary laughed. "Even a slow-witted middle-school student in Russia would know that maxim comes from medieval falconry. Sometimes I think that you are hopeless."

At that exact moment, Reagor came into the room. She shook her head and said, "The last sixty minutes were not designed as a social hour. Please concentrate on the fact that there are very skilled, professional people who will stop at no end to kill both of you. Becoming Darwinian poster children is not a laudable goal. You have night time for hanky-panky. Now let's get back to working to increase the chances that each of you will spend your next birthday above ground and with all body parts intact.

"First, some basics. Do everything you can to avoid any entangling personal relationships with people that you might meet in your new life. If asked a question about your past history, respond with the bare minimum of information. Just like testifying in court, never provide any information beyond a simple answer to the question."

Bob said, "Pardon the interruption, Officer Reagor, but I assume you know that our goal is to isolate in the boonies of the West Texas desert. Our only contact should be my crazy uncle and local prairie dogs. We are counting on not having to deal with strangers."

Reagor said, "Yes, I know your plans in detail. But isn't there a small town twenty miles away which at some point one of you will have to visit for supplies?"

Bob replied, "That is true. But my hope is that my uncle will be the one to go into town."

Reagor replied, "You can hope that things work out that well. But don't count on it. Now, no more interruptions. I am going to fire questions at each of you that should be answered briefly with information from the life histories you were to memorize."

"Mary, what year were you born?"

"1938."

"Where?"

"Stanley, North Dakota."

"What college did you attend?"

"I never went to college."

"Woody, when were you born?"

"1937."

"No! No!" Reagor shouted as she banged her hand down on the desk. "You are not Woody. You are Bob! The correct answer to my question should have been a puzzled look on your face and the questioning response, 'Woody?' I am beginning to think that you may need a keeper."

Mary smiled and said quietly, "Amen."

Reagor continued, "I have never lost a person that I prepared to be in our witness protection program. You two are likely to be an exception. I cannot express too strongly that your best chance for survival is to stay under CIA protection. It is not too late to change your minds."

Bob responded, "With all due respect, the CIA had a major leak that Av— Mary and I helped uncover. But there is clearly another leaker at Camp Peary who threatened our lives. I hate to say it, but we don't have confidence in the CIA protection. We will feel much safer on our own in a remote area of Texas. However, we know that the work the director and you are doing is critical for our surviving to get to our new location."

Mary added, "And we are very, very grateful."

Reagor was silent for a moment, then said, "Understood. I think that you two are intent on crossing the River Styx. So be it."

There was a moment of silence, then Mary asked hesitatingly, "Officer Reagor, you know everything about Bob's and my real backgrounds. Would it be way out of bounds to ask what your college degree was?"

For a moment it appeared that Reagor would explode. Then her face assumed a kinder look. "You both know the rules of confidentiality in the CIA. All I will tell you is that I have a PhD in classics from Harvard. Now back to work. Time is growing short."

For the next two hours Reagor peppered Mary and Bob with a series of questions about their new histories. She tried to trick them in providing incorrect or too much information. Toward the end of the grueling session she abruptly asked, "Woody, are you and Ava sleeping together?"

There was a shocked pause, then Bob answered. "I don't know those people. But I doubt if their personal lives are really any of your business."

Reagor almost smiled and said, "Bravo, Bob. I tried to shock you into a wrong response. You are completely correct. Your personal lives are only my business in terms of trying to keep you two alive as long as possible. You both made progress today. Get some rest and be prepared for a busy day tomorrow."

Reagor ushered Bob and Mary back to their rooms and locked them in. There was a brown bag dinner in each room. The two met in Mary's room and sat on the bed to eat.

Bob looked at Mary and said, "I'm beginning to think…" Mary put a finger to her lips and pointed toward the ceiling.

Bob scooted over close to Mary and whispered, "I'm beginning think that Reagor may not have a penis after all."

Mary shook her head and mouthed, "You are hopeless."

CHAPTER 14

TIME TO RIDE

The next two days passed in a blur of intense drills on past history, solidifying Bob and Mary's new names, and reviewing ways to defeat any possible surveillance. Reagor continued to be a task master and never provided another glimpse into her personal life. On Friday afternoon, she took a face photograph of Mary and Bob to be used to generate North Dakota driver's licenses for each of them.

"I am pleased to see that each of you has followed my advice for changing your appearance. Mary, with your newly chopped off hair and no makeup, it will be difficult to recognize you as the former Ava Volkov. And, Bob, your beard is a work in progress, but your hair needs to be a lot shaggier. Combing it partially down in your face would help."

Reagor closed a lengthy afternoon session on Friday by asking if either Mary or Bob had need to update their wills. Both of them responded that they did not wish to name heirs for security purposes. Reagor suggested that they should get as much rest as possible since Saturday would start a long period of limited sleep.

* * * *

Saturday morning began at 7 AM with a knock on each of their doors. Once again, the two were led to the teaching room. They were given fifteen minutes for a real breakfast of scrambled eggs, bacon, toast and jelly, and very strong coffee. When the hurried breakfast was over, Officer Reagor stood in front of them and began to speak.

"This is my last chance to fill in details and answer any questions. First, about tonight. I will come to your rooms at 7 PM to lead you on a secure route to one of the maintenance garages where the plumbing truck will be waiting. The CIA driver is very experienced and will be armed. The truck is special with a large V8 engine and heavy-duty shocks. I don't expect any trouble en route, but the driver is prepared to handle any situation. If you leave Langley at 7:30 PM, you should reach Staunton just before 10:00 to pick up the VW travel van."

Bob asked, "What about weapons for us as promised?"

Reagor replied, "Patience is a virtue, Mr. Smith. There will be a fully tested Walther PPK pistol in the back of the truck for each of you. This gun doesn't have as much stopping power as some other weapons, but it is easy to conceal. The plan is clearly for you not to need weapons on this trip. I have the baggy travel clothes we discussed before in this bag. You can take them with you when you go to your rooms for lunch. Be sure to be wearing your new apparel when I come for you tonight. The goal is to make you both appear to be harmless, perhaps not too bright, travelers.

"Now, let's talk about Odessa and meeting Bob's friend, Clarke Driver. We vetted him as best we could in such a short period of time. His military record is spotless, and we could find no red flags in his history. However, we did not feel safe to give him the precise coordinates for your drop spot. He was simply told that his old friend and a companion are in government service and needed help doing a practice night jump for a desert survival exercise at a site that is easily in range of his aircraft. The CIA is paying him well for his services. You can give him specific information when you are in the air."

Bob said, "Clarke and I played football in high school. He is a real salt-of-the-earth guy. I trust him."

Reagor dimmed the lights and turned the projector on. "I want to go over the route that we think will be the safest and fastest from Staunton, Virginia to Odessa, Texas. Both of you should memorize this route in detail. I would suggest that you use four-hour shifts of one person driving and the other person sleeping in the back. Any route questions? No? Then I need to broach an unpleasant subject. You both are aware of the horrible torture methods the KGB as well as the crime syndicate have used with their victims. Should one or both of you be captured, what is sure to follow would not be pleasant. I have in this vial two strychnine suicide pills that are very fast acting. To use the pill, one has simply to crush the pill with his or her teeth. Any takers?"

Bob and Mary looked at each other. Finally, Mary said, "I want one."

Bob continued to hesitate, then said quietly, "I'll take one, too."

Reagor had a strange look on her face. There was an almost imperceptible tremor in her hand as she gave Mary and Bob the pills.

"Remember, the fluid inside this gel capsule can be absorbed by your skin, so be careful how you carry the pills. Now that we have that little unpleasantry out of the way, I must reiterate that once you pick up the VW camper, you are really on your own with no CIA protection. I am going to give you a secure phone number that could be used in case of dire emergency, but with no guarantee that help would be sent."

There was a pause before Bob said, "I need to mention that there are no phone lines anywhere near Uncle Wilbur's ranch. The nearest phone will be twenty miles away in Barlow. Our only method of communication from the ranch will likely be smoke signals."

Reagor almost had a tiny smile—almost. She looked directly at Bob and Mary and said, "It's not too late to call this crazy plan off. You may want to reconsider staying somewhere under our protection."

Mary replied, "We know that you and the director have our best interests at heart, and we are very grateful. But Bob and I are in complete agreement that freedom often trumps safety. We want to go."

Reagor slowly nodded her head and said quietly, "So be it. I think that you two are as well prepared as you could be in such a short period of time. I will now walk you back to your rooms and give you a little free time before dinner. My understanding is that you will have another real meal tonight to provide extra calories for your trip."

* * * *

Once Mary and Bob were back in their rooms, they reviewed their new histories again in detail. At 5:30 PM Reagor rolled a serving table into Mary's room. Under the cover was a veritable feast compared to the usual brown bag fare. Neither Bob nor Mary had a great appetite and picked at the food.

Bob took a bite of the dinner roll and said, "My stomach always wants to shut down before something big is about to happen."

Mary replied, "Mine, too. I think they gave us decent food similar to the last meal of a condemned person on death row. I must say that the discussion about suicide pills was not too cheery."

"Mary, you know that we are like cats with nine lives. And the way I count, I have only used four of them. Hopefully, you also have most of your cat lives left since I plan to be around for a long time to annoy you."

Mary frowned and said, "I am really going to miss my Makarov pistol. What Reagor is giving us may be easy to hide, but it would be pretty much a pea-shooter in a real gun battle. Maybe we can get some better firepower from your uncle's weapon collection."

Bob nodded his head and replied, "If we ever are in need of heavy-duty munitions, my isolation safety plan has gone way off of the tracks. What say we put on our new travel clothes and preen around the room. I'm going to my room, but I will return as a different person."

"Yikes!" Mary said when Bob came back. "You look like a homeless person. All that outfit needs is a drop flap in the back of the pants to be perfect."

Bob shook his head and replied, "Talk about the pot calling the kettle black. You could easily be mistaken for a street person yourself."

Mary smiled and said, "If our appearance suggests the Joads leaving the Oklahoma dust bowl and heading for California, then our fashion designer has distinguished herself. But I can't say that I am looking forward to perspiring in these clothes for 26 hours on the road in a hot camper and then for what may be a long trek through the desert before we reach your uncle's posh resort."

Bob responded with a mischievous smile, "I assume by perspiring that you mean sweating. But perhaps princesses don't sweat. Besides, I may like you even more a bit stinky. Remember the message that Napoleon sent to his wife Josephine when he was still in battle. As I recall, it was, 'Josephine, I'll be home in a few days. Don't bathe before I get there.'"

Mary just shook her head. "You are unspeakably crude, Mr. Smith. I'm going back to my room to pack a few things for our trip. Our fearless leader is due here in twenty minutes. Time to ride."

CHAPTER 15

TRANS-PECOS DESERT OR BUST

Officer Reagor arrived at 7 PM sharp to lead Mary and Bob on a circuitous route to a seldom-used storage garage on the Langley campus. In a poorly lit back corner there was a panel truck with the painted sign 'Premier Plumbing.'

Reagor said, "Before you two head off into the wild blue yonder, here are your North Dakota driver's licenses. I must say that neither of your pictures suggest Mensa brilliance. Your new weapons are in the back of the truck. If this trip goes as planned, you should have no need for them. Don't forget that neither of you now has government protection if you have to shoot someone. Be discriminating."

Reagor walked with Bob and Mary over to the panel truck and opened the passenger side door. "Here are your passengers," she said to the wiry driver who appeared to be part Asian. "Take good care of them. Our country owes them a large debt of gratitude for their previous service." The driver nodded his head with no change in expression.

Reagor said, "There is a bench seat in the back for you two. You will note that there are no windows in back. You both must stay hidden for the entire trip to Staunton."

There was an awkward pause, then Bob said, "Officer Reagor, Mary and I are very grateful for all you have done for us. I hope somewhere down the road we can buy you a drink. Of course, if you ever need an upscale vacation, I'm sure my crazy uncle could find a spot for you. Feel free to drop in unannounced."

Reagor actually smiled, then shook hands firmly with Bob. She turned to Mary, hesitated, then gave her a short hug. Reagor offered a quiet "Godspeed," then turned and walked away without looking back.

The driver tapped his wrist watch and signaled for Mary and Bob to enter the truck from the back. Once they were seated, he eased the truck out of the garage and moved with traffic speed until they reached I-66 West. At that point the V8 roared to life and pushed Mary and Bob back in their seats as the truck accelerated. By the time they merged with I-81 South past Front Royal, it was fully dark. There was the mesmerizing click of the large tires rolling over the pavement.

Weekend traffic was light, and Bob and Mary were half dozing. Bob felt the truck suddenly speed up and saw in the rearview mirror very bright headlights closing fast. Quickly, there was the sound of gunfire coming from behind the plumbing truck.

"Sounds like an M-16!" Bob shouted as he reached for his pistol. The driver who was looking in the rearview mirror uttered a command in perfect English. "No guns. I will handle this."

The engine gave a huge roar and the truck leaped forward. For a few seconds the space between the truck and the pursuing vehicle widened, but then it narrowed as there was more gunfire, with one bullet smashing through the back door of the truck and exiting through the windshield on the passenger's side.

Bob and Mary dived for the floor. Mary shouted, "We each just lost one more cat life. I hope that the yo-yo driving this truck is a CIA expert and not just some random plumber's helper."

There was a sudden loud whoosh and the smell of gasoline. Looking in the rearview mirror Bob saw a huge fireball. There was a screeching noise of a car swerving, then a crash sound.

The driver looked back and said, "It's all over. Time for a quick nap. We are about an hour out of Staunton."

Bob said to the driver, "Don't give away any CIA secrets, but it sounded like you released a blast of gasoline then ignited it with a rear flame thrower."

The driver shook his head and replied, "I can't confirm or deny."

Mary looked at Bob and said, "So much for the CIA keeping this little gambit top secret. I wonder if someone at headquarters sold us out or if there was high-class surveillance that thought a plumbing truck leaving Langley at night was very suspicious and tailed us before making a move."

Bob replied, "We'll never know. Hopefully, whoever was tailing us has no knowledge about our VW camper rendezvous in Staunton."

Exactly fifty-nine minutes later the plumbing truck drove into the rear of the parking lot of an all-night grocery just outside of Staunton. He stopped near a tan VW camper.

"Your keys," the driver said with no emotion as he reached toward the back of the truck.

Bob replied, "Thanks for taking care of that little problem on the road. Our little pea-shooter pistols would not have been of much help. Do you have to drive the plumbing truck back to the Langley area?"

"Can't say," the driver responded noncommittally. "Time to get moving."

Bob and Mary grabbed their backpacks and exited from the rear of the truck and shut the door. The plumbing truck was quickly in motion and disappeared into the night.

Bob turned to Mary. "Best not hang around here. What say I take the first driving shift. You can lie down in the back and catch some sleep. Your turn will come soon enough. I'll wake you up."

They both got into the camper, and Mary disappeared into the back. Bob put the key into the ignition switch and turned it. The engine started immediately.

Mary complained from behind, "It's really going to get hot tomorrow when the sun comes up. The tiny fan back here barely moves any air. Let's get rolling and see if we can at least generate some road breeze."

"As always, your slightest wish is my command, your Majesty," Bob said with a deferential head bow as the camper left the parking lot.

Mary retorted, "This is going to be a long trip, so don't start out being a total horse's ass. And speaking of horses, hay might taste better than the snacks the CIA thoughtfully provided for us. Don't get your hopes up."

Bob observed, "Our plumbing truck driver may have had all the personality of a department store mannequin, but he sure knew how to eliminate bad guys in a burst of flames. That was a brilliant defensive maneuver. Our little pop guns would not have been a good match for high-powered rifles."

Mary replied, "I really was attached to my Makarov pistol. There will never be as perfect a weapon again for me."

As the camper picked up speed, Bob said, "Sweet dreams, Mary—and no nightmares. I'm betting that this part of the trip is going to be boring and uneventful."

Mary replied, "Your parents should have named you Pollyanna. Our trip is no longer secret and somebody already made an attempt to take us out."

Bob said, "Let me respectfully disagree. Did you notice all the shots seemed to be low? I think the bullet that passed through the truck was bad aim from a speeding car. Whoever was doing the firing wanted to hit the tires and force the car off of the road so they could capture us. I don't think killing us was their plan. My guess is that the car was a surveillance team that picked us up as we left Langley without knowing where we were going or what our real plans are."

Mary said, not unkindly, "Your little fairy tale has made me sleepy. Please wake me when it's my turn to drive—or when someone new starts shooting at us."

CHAPTER 16

GHOST FROM THE PAST

It was 2:30 in the morning and Bob had been pushing the camper, keeping it as close to sixty-five miles an hour as possible. The forty-horsepower air-cooled engine was noisy, but its sound had lulled Mary to sleep in the back. The front windows were open wide, sending blasts of warm road air into the van. Watching the gas gauge, Bob surmised that the vehicle had been fitted with a gas tank much larger than the standard 10½ gallon size. He mentally calculated that the VW was getting just over 15 miles a gallon.

Mary stirred in the back. She sat up and said, "It should be my time to drive. And if I don't get a bathroom stop soon, I may be even more desirable than Josephine."

Bob laughed and said, "My hormones are surging. We are getting short on gas. I'll pull over at the next quiet highway stretch. You can drive and find a truck stop and visit the bathroom while I hide in the back and become acquainted with the chamberpot. This van obviously has a much larger gas tank than it came with. Someone must have tuned the engine since I can occasionally coax the speed up close to seventy."

A few miles down the road, Bob spotted a place to pull off the highway. There was a very quick change. The van was back on the road in less than sixty seconds with Mary at the wheel.

"My gosh," Mary said. "This van is a toad. I could run up this hill quicker than it can make it to the top."

"Remember, you've only got forty ponies under the hood," Bob replied. "But push it as much as you can. We want to hit Odessa as close to midnight as possible."

Mary looked down the road and said, "Looks like a truck stop ahead. I'm going to pull in and park at one of the pumps. I'll ask the service person to fill it while I use the bathroom. You need to keep quiet and lie low in the back."

The truck stop was a small one and poorly lighted. It was almost deserted. An older man with a ragged beard and shaggy hair came out using a cane. Mary spoke to him. He gave Mary a key to the women's bathroom at the side of the building. When she came out, she stood in the shadows until the man removed the nozzle. She walked back to the man and paid cash. Mary got into the van and headed it back onto the highway.

Once they were away from the truck stop, Bob asked, "Were the bathroom facilities up to your standards?"

Mary said angrily, "A squat toilet would have been an upgrade. It was a hover experience with no toilet paper. But I was prepared."

"You sound really pissed," Bob responded. "Were the facilities that terrible?"

"I'm pissed because after I paid the attendant, the creep patted me on my bottom. I almost converted his cane to a permanent walker. But then I remembered the mantra Reagor gave us—'Blend in, never call attention to yourselves.' I figured that having an ambulance arrive to take care of an elderly man with two broken legs would not be consistent with keeping a low profile."

Bob said, "I admire your restraint. Getting back to practical matters, remember we leave Interstate 81 and get on Interstate 40 before Knoxville. We'll go through Nashville, but since it's Sunday and early, there won't be much traffic. About an hour out of Nashville it will be my turn to drive again, and we will be needing gas. I probably should be the one to use the station bathroom since you seem to be making a habit of getting molested."

Mary snapped back, "Watch yourself, buster. The opera house in Vienna is still looking for muscular men who sing soprano."

Bob smiled and said, "Time for some shut-eye for me. But I guess I better sleep with one eye open."

The road noise quickly put Bob to sleep on the hard bed in the back of the van. He woke up after almost four hours and spoke to

Mary in a high, squeaky voice. "Yikes! I guess I really should have slept with one eye open. Vienna, here I come."

Mary gave a small chuckle and said, "It takes a really talented woman to emasculate a misbehaving man and keep driving at the same time."

Bob returned to a normal voice and asked, "Where are we now?"

"Right on schedule—about 45 minutes out of Nashville," Mary responded. "Memphis is over two hours away. I'll find a good spot to pull over and you can pick the next gas station."

Bob replied, "I'm getting hungry and almost desperate enough to try some of the government-issue food in the back. Let me look and see what is the least likely to poison us. Most of the stuff would make K-rations look good. Fortunately, we still have plenty of water in glass Mason jars."

There was a pause. Then Bob gave a little shout. "Home run! I just uncovered a picnic hamper that has four glass bottles of Coke with an ice pack, several great-looking sandwiches, and a number of Hershey bars with almonds. Bonanza."

Mary said with a puzzled tone in her voice, "Who could have prepared that? I wonder if it's poisoned. Why don't you try a sandwich and a Coke, and let's see how you are doing in 30 minutes…. On second thought, I'm almost starving. Think I'll also risk another of my cat lives with a Coke and a sandwich."

After Mary and Bob had eaten with no dire effects, Mary found a good place to pull off the interstate to change drivers. Bob pushed the VW toward Memphis.

The sun was up, and the camper was growing warmer.

Mary said from the back, "Princesses normally only perspire delicately, but now I am really sweating. These bulky clothes that Reagor put us in would be better for the Antarctic." Mary tapped Bob on his back and said, "Napoleon, get ready for the smelly treat of your life when we reach your crazy uncle's place."

Bob called out, "Truck stop ahead. It looks fairly busy, but we're getting low on gas. Can't risk being stuck on the side of the road." Bob pulled up to a pump and killed the engine. A young woman with bleach-blonde hair and purple lipstick who was wearing Minnie Mouse shorts and a halter top came over to Bob.

"Fill 'er up?" she asked, chomping noisily on a big wad of gum.

Bob went inside the station, which also had a restaurant with several truckers enjoying breakfast, and found the men's room. When he came out, the blonde was still putting gas in the van. Bob looked back toward the building several times while waiting for the woman to finish.

"This sucker has a big gas tank," she observed. "Most of these piece-of-crap VW vans don't hold enough gas to get you from your house to a beer store and back."

Bob paid cash for the gas and quickly got back into the van and headed for the highway, looking frequently in the rearview mirror as he drove.

Mary popped her head up through the curtain and asked, "So, how were the facilities?"

Bob said rather curtly, "Just like the men's rooms in most truck stops—wade in and wade out."

Mary asked, "Why do you keep looking in the rearview mirror all the time like a Nervous Nellie?"

Bob said, "I thought I saw a ghost inside there. There was a big man having a cup of coffee. He was too well dressed to be a trucker. I swear he looked just like Randy Williams, the person who almost succeeded in roasting both of us in the cremation oven in his brother's funeral home. The man stared at me, then quickly looked away. If it wasn't Randy Williams, it was a perfect doppelganger."

Mary replied, "And weren't you the fortune teller who predicted an uneventful trip to Odessa? It looks like the KGB is not the only group interested in our demise. I'll feel a lot better when we are up in the air in your friend's Cessna waiting to jump."

CHAPTER 17

MISSING TEETH

The van kept functioning well despite being driven hard at its top speed. Outside of Little Rock, Mary picked up Highway 30, which would take them through Arkansas and into Texas. Steep hills were a challenge, causing Bob to threaten to get out and push. The van had become a little oven with the summer sun bearing down on it relentlessly.

Mary called to Bob in the back, where he was sitting on the mattress and munching on a Hershey almond bar. "Now that we're through Memphis, we'll need gas pretty soon. Thank goodness it's my turn to use the real bathroom."

"Got it," Bob said. "Just promise me you won't tempt some gray-haired geezer on a walker at the station into trying to molest you."

"Not so funny," Mary retorted.

Bob replied, "Just trying to introduce a bit of levity into our situation. I wish I could get the image of Randy Williams out of my head. If the man at the truck stop wasn't Randy, it had to be his identical twin. If anybody with a fast car and guns wanted to take us out, we would be pretty defenseless."

"Maybe not if I am in the driver's seat," Mary replied. "You forget that I have beaucoup hours of training in pursuit driving and could make this toad-mobile do tricks that you would not believe…. Look, there's a gas station just up ahead."

Mary eased the van off the interstate and into the station that had a faded sign that read, "EDDY'S GOT GAS."

Mary shook her head and said, "Bad choice. This station looks like a real dump."

There was a young muscular attendant with a mullet and scraggly mustache who was tossing a football with an older man who was holding a bottle of beer. As Mary was getting out of the van, the man walked over to the attendant and pointed at Mary and whispered something in the attendant's ear that made him guffaw.

When the man with the mullet started filling the gas tank, Mary walked inside the station to find the ladies' room. She lingered inside the station until the older man, still swigging his beer, came in and went to the cash register.

After Mary handed over the right amount of cash, she started walking quickly back to the van. The young man with the mullet blocked her way.

"I've always had a liking for old women with no makeup and a bad haircut. Maybe you'd like to jump into my pickup truck and go see where I live."

"Not a chance," Mary answered. "I never mess around with children."

The man snarled, "I ain't no child, sweetie. Maybe I need to help you get into my pickup." He grabbed Mary's wrist.

Mary jerked her arm away and said quietly, "You are about to make a huge mistake. If you touch me again, very bad things are going to happen to you in a big hurry."

The man said, "I like 'em feisty," and reached for Mary's arm again. In a flash she butted the man in the mouth and twisted his arm behind his back before shoving him to the ground. He lay there whimpering and spitting teeth out.

The man with the beer came running out of the store and headed toward Mary, but stopped when Mary turned toward him.

"Do you want to be next?" she asked quietly. The man hesitated, then ran back into the store and quickly locked the door.

Mary hopped into the van and headed back to the highway.

"What was that all about?" Bob asked. "It sounded like a fight was going on. Did you tempt another senior citizen to lust after you?"

Mary said, "I tried my best to stay out of trouble, but some smart ass with a mullet tried to drag me into his pickup truck and take me to his house. I was polite at first, but finally had no choice but to knock a few teeth out and rework his shoulder. The thing that really made me angry was when he said that he liked old women with no makeup and bad haircuts. Makes me wish I had cracked a few ribs with a kick before I left."

"Sounds like he and I lust after the same kind of women."

"You're walking on thin ice, buddy."

"You need to work on your sense of humor, my princess. You obviously had no choice but to deck that guy. I wonder if someone took down our license plate number?"

Mary said, "Not a problem. While I was rummaging around in the back earlier, I found two extra sets of license plates from different states. Makes me wonder if whoever left that picnic basket also blessed us with extra plates. Once we hit a quiet stretch of highway, I'll pull off, and you can change the plates and take over and become the pilot."

* * * *

Bob was driving, pushing on toward Little Rock. The van now had Texas plates. Bob called back to Mary, "We're staying right on schedule. If we can hit Dallas before 7 PM, we will be only five hours from Odessa."

Mary replied, "If you promise to be super nice for the rest of the trip, I'll share some really good news with you."

"I promise."

Mary shook her head, "Not good enough. Say, 'cross my heart and hope to die.'"

Bob complied. Mary then said, "You are not going to believe this, but I searched some more in the far back of the van and found a grocery bag that had, guess what, inside."

"More yummy food," Bob answered.

"Much better than that," Mary answered. "Inside the bag was my Makarov pistol and your Beretta."

"Wow!" Bob exclaimed. "I wonder who the good fairy was who seems to have provided food, extra license plates, and, now, some real firepower. I'm feeling better already. You need to grab some sleep. I'll wake you when it's your time to take over."

Mary said impishly, "I don't want to damage your male ego, but I feel safer sleeping with my Makarov than with you."

CHAPTER 18

PLAYING CHICKEN

It was just before 7 PM on Sunday, and the VW had sped along faithfully with no problems. Mary was driving. It was hot and the blast of road air into the van was like sitting in front of a hair dryer. Bob was having restless sleep in the back. He suddenly shouted, "No! No!"

Mary called to him, "Are you having bad dreams?"

Bob set up on the mattress and put his head into his hands. "I was dreaming that Randy Williams was shoving both of us into the cremation oven at the medical school and laughing hysterically. Seeing him or his doppelganger at the truck stop earlier is really playing tricks in my head."

Mary said, "Thank goodness it was only a dream. I have never been interested in becoming a crispy critter myself. The good news is that we are on the outskirts of Dallas and on time for our rendezvous with your pilot friend in Odessa. You've got another hour to rest. We won't need gas until we are past Fort Worth."

Bob replied, "I don't think that I can sleep anymore. Want me to take over driving?"

"I'm going to finish my shift," Mary answered. "Let's urge your friend to fly us to the jump location tonight. The less time we spend in civilization, the safer we will be."

"Agreed," Bob answered.

After a moment Mary asked, "Bob, are you sure that your crazy uncle is actually alive and still hunkered down at his place?"

"Not one hundred percent certain, but based on his age and what he looked like when I last saw him, he should still be ticking. Wilbur's in his late fifties at the most."

Mary said, "Sounds a little uncertain to me. Then, there is the question of whether Uncle Wilbur will actually let us inside his oasis or simply blast us to smithereens with his arsenal of weapons."

"We shall soon have the answer to that question. But I'm betting that Uncle Wilbur will welcome his favorite step-nephew with open arms," Bob replied. "If not, we may have to rely on your feminine charms."

Mary gave a quick, "Ha!," adding, "It's hard to display feminine charms when you are wearing a circus tent."

"Don't undersell yourself. The kid with the mullet obviously saw something he liked."

Mary snapped back with great annoyance, "Has anybody ever told you that you are a royal pain in the ass?"

Bob said, "Time for a truce. We have bigger fish to fry than assessing your ability to function as a male magnet wearing a Barnum and Bailey circus outfit."

* * * *

By 10 PM it was dark. Traffic was light. Bob was driving and keeping the accelerator pushed to the floor. He announced over his shoulder, "We should pull into John's Truck Stop a little before midnight. Hopefully, Clarke and his black panel truck will be waiting. We need one more gas stop."

Mary was sitting up in the back and replied, "This is your turn to visit a real bathroom. I, with my legendary holding power, am doing just fine. But what say a few miles beyond that gas and pee stop that we trade places, and I drive the last stretch. You can get our backpacks ready, stick in a few rations, and make sure our guns have ammo just in case any unexpected problems arise."

"I will let you finish the drive," Bob said. "My legs are getting stiff, and I need to stretch them out."

After the gas stop, Mary took the wheel and kept pushing the van to its limit. Bob got the backpacks ready and passed Mary's Makarov up to her. "Not expecting any problems, but let's carry our weapons and not bury them in the backpacks. They are both fully loaded. I'm actually looking forward to our jump."

"Me too," Mary said. "I'm tired of being beaten up by the road bumps. This van may well have been super serviced before we got it, but somehow, they missed the bad shocks."

Just before midnight Mary said, "There's a truck stop about a half mile ahead. That must be the one. I'll coast into the back lot and keep an eye out for a black panel truck."

Bob pulled back one of the back curtains and said, "I see a panel truck at the very back of the lot. Pull up close to it, and I'll pop out and get reacquainted with Clarke. I haven't seen him since college."

As Mary drove closer to the panel truck, Bob suddenly ordered, "Slow down. There's a Lincoln Continental parked in the shadows at the other side of the back lot. Something doesn't feel right here. Accelerate and run up close to the driver's side of the truck and brake hard to a stop, but keep the motor going. Be ready to haul ass and head straight for the Lincoln as if you plan to ram into it at top speed."

Mary pushed the accelerator pedal to the floor and sped to an area behind the panel truck before whipping the protesting van into a fishtail and sliding to a screeching stop beside the truck. Bob leaped out of the side door and ran to the driver's window and shined a flashlight in.

He jumped back into the van just as Mary popped the clutch and headed straight for the Lincoln Continental whose headlights suddenly flashed on. The big V8 roared to life, and the vehicle lurched forward, spewing gravel as the tires tried to gain traction. The Lincoln raced forward toward the van and was accelerating rapidly. There was a muzzle flash, and a high-powered bullet shattered the van's passenger-side outside mirror.

Bob shouted, "Play chicken with them, Mary! Make them swerve. I'll try to shoot out one of their tires as we fly by. I've got a feeling that our old buddy Randy Williams is in that Lincoln."

At the last second, the Lincoln swerved to the right. Bob and Mary fired simultaneously. The Lincoln braked sharply and spun around behind the van and began rapidly to gain on the van. There was a volley of shots from the Lincoln that missed since Mary was swerving the van from right to left. Suddenly the Continental veered to one side and slowed and came to a halt.

Mary said, "Mercifully, one of us must have gotten a tire. Looks like no jump for us. Was your friend in the truck?

Bob said, "He was there all right—slumped over the wheel with the side of his head gone and brain splattered everywhere. There is no choice now—we have to drive to my uncle's compound. I figure that we can make it by 4 AM if we don't get blown up from behind. We have to hope that the people in the Lincoln won't be very fast in mounting the rear spare tire."

Mary replied, "Ugh. Sorry about your friend. Looks like our secret travel plans weren't so secret after all. The CIA might just as well have posted them on a giant sign in Times Square."

"Why don't you keep on driving, Mary? Anyone who can make this toad-mobile dance like you just did is a car-driving magician. We may need some more fancy evasion maneuvers before the night is over. Take I-20 West to Monahans, then if we are still alive, we will want Texas 18 South toward Fort Stockton."

CHAPTER 19

ANSWERED HAIL MARYS

Mary was pushing the VW to its limit as it traveled southwest on the interstate. It was 2 AM, and there was no traffic except for a few night-hauler eighteen-wheelers. Mary kept looking in the rearview mirror, expecting to see the bright lights of the Lincoln Continental closing fast at any moment.

Mary rubbed her neck with one hand and kept the other one on the steering wheel. "No way this VW can outrun that Lincoln with its huge V8 engine. If I see highlights way back coming up on us, I may need to leave the highway to even the odds."

Bob had moved up into the passenger's seat and replied, "I'm thinking that Randy Williams and his crime buddies may not know our full plans. The CIA never gave my friend coordinates for our drop spot. He was just told that the jump was within the fuel range of his Cessna. I was to give him information once we were in the air so he could use dead reckoning. So, even if the thugs tortured poor Clarke before they blasted his brains out, he would not have the information that they wanted."

Mary said, "Wish I could share your optimism. We both know that Camp Peary was not secure. Langley may well have its own mole problem. Assuming we survive to reach your uncle's place, there may be a welcoming committee waiting for us."

Bob paused a minute, then said, "If we assume that the bad guys don't know about my uncle's place or its exact location, then they would have to guess which way we left Odessa since they were busy changing a tire. Too bad we didn't flatten two of the tires. We had several options leaving the truck stop, including: hunkering down somewhere in Odessa, headed back toward Fort Worth, continuing down Highway 20 toward Monahans, or driving due east toward

Kermit. If Randy and his buddies show up behind us on the road, we'll know that they are lucky guessers, or that we have been completely sold out."

"Don't we have to take a tough twenty-mile goat path out of Barlow across the desert to reach your uncle's welcoming oasis?" Mary asked. "I'm betting that this van is awful in sand."

"Good point," Bob answered. "Not sure that we could survive a long hike in this heat if the van craters or gets stuck. I grew up Catholic and may use a few Hail Marys to ask for a transportation miracle."

Mary shook her head and said, "If you mean finding a camel, don't hold your breath."

It was a full-moon night with a cloudless sky, and details of the landscape around the highway were easily seen.

"Wait!" Bob shouted. "Stop and turn around."

Mary came to a stop and asked, "Have you lost your mind, Woody? Or do you have a bathroom emergency?"

"Neither," Bob relied. "Officer Reagor would be very disappointed in you for getting annoyed and using my real name. You may be the one needing to utter some Hail Marys in penance."

"Cut the bull crap, Bob, and tell me why I need to turn around."

"Head back a few hundred yards and stop in front of the ranch gate and you will see what got my attention."

Mary turned around and drove back to the ranch and stopped. Just inside the gate was a Willys Jeep station wagon that had been painted amateurishly with camouflage markings. There was a large sign that read, '1960 Jeep for Sale.'

Bob said, "Sometimes Hail Marys actually work. If that Jeep is in running condition, with its four-wheel drive, it would be perfect for driving across the desert. I want to buy it and leave this van as a trade-in."

Mary said, "This heat has made you loco crazy. It's in the wee hours of the morning, and the owner is no doubt fast asleep. The gate's locked. Do you plan to climb the gate and just saunter up to the door of the house and knock politely? The owner will almost certainly blow you away before he answers the door."

Bob tapped his head and answered as he opened the van door, "You always underestimate my genius."

Bob climbed the fence and walked toward the house, half expecting a snarling dog to attack him. When he was about fifteen yards from the house, he lay face down in the dirt with his arms extended over his head. Once positioned, he gave a very loud groan. Lights quickly came on in the house. The door slowly opened and a bearded older man holding a shotgun in one hand and the leash of a growling German Shepherd in the other stepped out on the porch. Bob lay completely still.

The man cautiously approached the form sprawled out on the ground. When Bob could hear his footsteps in the sand drawing closer, he remained motionless but said, "Really sorry to wake you, but I need to buy that Jeep. It's an emergency. I'll pay cash."

There was a pause. Then the man said gruffly, "What's wrong with you, you stupid son-of-a-bitch? It's two in the morning. I've got a good mind to blow you away with my shotgun and tell the sheriff that you were trespassing."

Bob said, "Please don't. My wife is out there in the van and is pregnant. My baby's going to need a father."

The man said, "I think that you are lying. If you really have a wife out there, call her to come join us and let me see her hands at all times."

Bob called out loudly, "Honey, this man needs to see you. But don't try to climb over the fence in your condition…. Sir, could I please sit up? I'll keep my hands over my head."

The man replied, "Do it slow and easy."

Mary got out of the van and called out, "I can get over this fence. No sweat."

She carefully reached the top of the fence and gently lowered herself to the ground and walked toward Bob and the man with the shotgun and dog.

Bob said, "Sir, I don't have time to tell you everything, but we are needing to head out into the desert for a religious ceremony to bless our future child, and our old van won't be worth a darn in the sand."

The man glared at Woody and said, "I have never heard so much bullshit in all my life."

Mary said, "Sir, what he says is true. What my husband wants to do is pay cash for your Jeep and drive it off tonight. We will leave our van, and you can do anything that you want with it. The van is not stolen and runs perfectly."

Bob slowly stood up with his hands still in plain sight. "Is your Jeep in good running condition? Does it have gas in it?"

"I drove it a few miles yesterday. The Jeep belongs to my grandson who just left for the Army. He is a good mechanic and put an overdrive kit on the Jeep to give it better top end. But only an idiot would buy your story. I think that you two are con artists."

Bob said, "Just on the off chance that we are real customers and not con artists, would $2200 interest you?"

The man replied cautiously, "My grandson was wanting $2500."

Bob answered, "I have $2600 cash in my pocket. If you will open the gate, my wife can drive the van in for you to look at. And, if you will kindly start the Jeep and let me look at the motor and listen to it, I'm sure we can make a deal."

The man was clearly undecided. He finally said, "No tricks or I'll turn my dog loose on you. He's trained to go for the throat."

The man called, "Vera, come out here."

A woman in a housecoat came out on the porch.

"These people want to buy Buddy's Jeep—at least they say they do. But I don't trust them. Please get the Jeep key and drive it here up to the house. I'm going to keep a close eye on these people."

Vera went back into the house and returned to walk to the gate and open it. The Jeep gave a nice little roar when it started. She drove it slowly back toward the house.

The man looked at Mary and motioned for her to go get the van. Once the van was close to the house, he peered inside while keeping the shotgun handy. "Race the engine," he ordered Mary. She complied.

He listened for a moment, then said, "What about papers of sale on the cars? Do you have a title to the van?"

"No," Bob said. "But the car's not hot. If you just keep it for the ranch, there will never be any problem. I'm not interested in getting a title for the Jeep. If you will let me get my backpack out of the van, I will give you the cash."

At that moment, Mary gave a little groan.

Bob said with seeming alarm, "Honey, what's wrong. Are you having contractions?"

Mary shook her head and answered, "The baby just kicked me. No problem. I think she wants us to get back on the road."

The expression on the face of the woman in the housecoat softened. "Sweetie, when are you due?"

Mary smiled and replied, "I'm just six months along. With these travel clothes, I don't show very much."

The man looked toward the highway at rapidly approaching headlights. There was a loud roar as a car sped by.

"Damn fool," said the man. "That looked like a fancy Lincoln Continental. That idiot was going at least 95 miles an hour. He's going to end up in dead in a ditch."

The man looked at Bob and said, "My grandson was afraid that I would have trouble getting a fair price for his Jeep with all the camouflage paint on it. If you've really got the cash on hand, I'm gonna do this deal."

Bob went into the back of the van and came out with both his and Mary's backpack. He reached into the side pocket of his backpack and took out a wad of hundred-dollar bills. He counted twenty-six of them into the old man's hand and said, "You will never know how much my wife and I appreciate your selling us your grandson's Jeep. I hope that the van serves you well."

Bob and the man shook hands. Then Bob and Mary got into the Jeep and passed through the gate back onto the highway.

The vehicle slowly accelerated to 65 miles as Bob shifted through gears.

"That's about it," he said to Mary. "Even with overdrive, this wagon is more of a rock climber than a race car. And it has almost a full tank of gas."After a brief pause, Bob looked at Mary and said, "You played the mother-to-be role perfectly. That groan was pure theatrical genius."

"We dodged a bullet for sure," Mary answered. "Randy and his gang blew by the ranch like a bat out of hell. But now they are somewhere ahead of us. Let's pray that they are not fireballing to your uncle's compound."

Bob responded, "That Lincoln won't be much good on sand. We are much better off in this four-wheel-drive Jeep wagon. Randy won't be looking for us in a Jeep. If we meet bright headlights coming back toward us, duck down so it won't look like there are two people in the Jeep."

A few miles down the road Bob looked over at Mary and said, "I'm still waiting."

Mary looked puzzled and said, "Waiting for what?"

Bob smiled and replied, "Waiting for you to admit that I am a certified genius."

Mary reached over and pinched his thigh very hard and said, "I going to insist on separate bedrooms at your uncle's place. From this point on you will have to provide your own bedtime entertainment."

CHAPTER 20

IN HOT PURSUIT

There were lightning flashes in the west as Bob and Mary reached the outskirts of Monahans. The temperature was still in the low 90s, but the humidity was less oppressive. So far, the Jeep station wagon had performed flawlessly, but it topped out at 66 miles an hour. Any attempt to milk out a few more miles an hour resulted in an ominous high-pitched engine whine.

Bob, who was still driving, looked over at Mary and said, "We have over a half tank of gas left, but this Jeep eats fuel. I want to be certain that if trouble breaks out down the road there is plenty of gas left for you to perform your dazzling evasion techniques. So, let's fill up here if we can find a station that is open and let you take over driving."

Mary replied. "Since Randy and his crew are ahead of us, we still need to be careful not to be seen together. There have been very few cars or trucks on this remote stretch of highway, so pull over soon and let's change drivers. Then I will be the one to get the real bathroom. Outside of town, we can find a Mesquite bush or cactus for you."

Bob shook his head and replied, "For shame, Miss Mary. Really high-class women would not talk so coarsely. You must have cut the classes in social deportment in finishing school. You have to promise me that you will be on your best behavior at Uncle Wilbur's place and not embarrass me."

Mary snapped back immediately, "You could use a little social decorum yourself."

Bob smiled and said, "I was just yanking your chain. Try not to be so sensitive."

Mary replied ominously, "You know that I can be a violent woman, and you won't be happy if I become the yanker and you become the unfortunate yankee." She then turned to look down the highway and said, "There's a wide area just off the road ahead. Let's make the driver change there."

After a quick switch, the Jeep was back on the road with Mary driving and Bob sitting in the back.

The lights of a small truck stop came into view. Mary guided the Jeep to one of the two pump stations and cut the engine. Nothing happened for a couple of minutes, then a young woman with bleached-blonde hair came slowly outside, wiping the sleep from her eyes.

When Mary returned from the bathroom, the female attendant was still filling the tank. "Sorry the pump is so slow. You're getting about all that's left. We are expecting a tanker truck early in the morning."

"Slow night?" Mary asked.

"Sure enough. The only other business since when I came on at midnight was a really fancy Lincoln Continental with three men inside. One of them was a big guy with expensive clothes. He showed me a picture of two people who he said were running from the law in a stolen VW camper van. The man asked if I had seen the people and if I could tell him when they were here and what direction they were going, he would give me a fifty-dollar bill. I could use the fifty, but I didn't want to lie to him. He seemed really mean."

Mary said nonchalantly, "That's really interesting. Do you think that the man was a law officer of some kind?"

"Could be," the attendant replied. "But it seemed weird for law people to be in a Lincoln Continental. Once there was a full tank, the Lincoln blasted out of here, heading down Highway 18 toward Fort Stockton. That car must suck a lot of gas."

Mary paid the woman and climbed back into the station wagon. Once she and Bob were back on the highway, Mary related the conversation to Bob. "We now know that Randy and his friends got to Monahans. What is uncertain is whether they know about Barlow."

Bob said, "Let's hightail it down 18 as fast as this Jeep will go and try to reach the turn off for Barlow before Randy and his buddies decide to come blasting back this way. The small highway sign for Barlow was falling down when I was here several years ago. It's going to be easy to miss at night. About five miles beyond Grandfalls, slow down and keep your eyes peeled."

Mary kept the Jeep speedometer pegged at 65 miles an hour. Just before Grandfalls, bright headlights of a fast-moving car were seen approaching.

She said, "Hit the floor, Bob. Here come Randy and his henchmen."

When the Lincoln was about a hundred yards away, it slowed down as it approached the Jeep. Suddenly a blinding spotlight was trained on the Jeep that made Mary almost run off of the highway. The Lincoln then accelerated quickly and headed back toward Monahans.

Bob said, "Don't think that they recognized you. They are bound to still be looking for the VW camper."

There was a pause. Then Mary said, "Oh, no! Big trouble. I hope that the old man parked our van behind the house or in his barn. If not, Randy and his boys may spot the van as they fly by. If so, they are going to make life difficult for that old couple."

"Ugh!" Bob said. "Unfortunately, we may have given those people a death warrant. We can only hope and pray that the van was not left in front of the house or that the Continental was moving too fast for the van to be seen. If the poor couple got tortured for information, the crime boys are bound to know what we are now driving."

Mary pushed the Jeep along. After a few minutes she announced, "We are over four miles past Grandfalls. If you blinked, you probably missed it."

Bob said, "Put your high beams on and slow down. I'll watch, too. Wait, there's the Barlow sign. It is almost lying on its side. Make a right just ahead."

Mary slowed down and turned into a narrow, two-lane gravel road. The Jeep tires started kicking gravel up, causing metallic pings from the undercarriage. "Not exactly the German Autobahn," she said.

Bob replied, "Actually, it is the Autobahn compared to the drive out of Barlow across the desert. It's only eight miles from the Fort Stockton highway to Barlow, then there is the twenty-mile goat path of shifting sand to Uncle Wilbur's compound. I'll be happy to drive out of Barlow."

The Jeep moved along the uneven gravel road, bouncing the passengers up and down. By 3 AM the lights of Barlow were seen across the desert. The gravel road ended at Barlow just off the main square of the town. The caliche streets of Barlow were a modest upgrade over the gravel road.

Bob looked around as they drove through the town and marveled, "Barlow has sure changed since I was last here. The small hotel has been enlarged and upgraded, and there are now three bars. I wonder why there are so many pickup trucks parked in front of the hotel. And, look, there is a really nice hardware store, as well as what looks like a decent grocery store. I can't imagine what draws people out here."

Mary said, "Let's not loiter while you take a nostalgic trip down memory lane. We don't want to be seen. Let me drive until we are out of town. Where is the magic road that leads to Uncle Wilbur's enclave?"

Bob said, "Hook a left into the field at the end of town and then head due east across the desert."

Mary slowed down and asked, "What is that thing over there that looks like a small arena?"

Bob replied, "Very interesting. It looks like a cock-fighting pit. Highly illegal in Texas. Maybe that helps explain the growth of this remote town. People aren't going to drive way out into the boonies just to get liquored up. But I wonder if the cock fighting is only the tip of the iceberg."

Bob paused, then added, "But none of that is our business or concern. Once you get a little further into the desert, I'll take over. We are going to keep going straight east. Good thing we have a compass since there are almost no landmarks at night. And, Mary, throw on some lipstick and fluff your hair up just in case we have to play the sexy older woman card to convince my uncle to let us in."

Mary slammed on the brakes, causing Bob to lurch forward and barely miss bouncing his head off of the windshield. She glared at him and said, "Watch your mouth, Buster."

CHAPTER 21

AN UNPLEASANT SURPRISE

The Jeep station wagon handled the desert sand well, occasionally sliding to the side before the four-wheel drive brought the rear end back in line. Periodically, there were faint vehicle tracks in the sand ahead that were illuminated by a full moon and the Jeep headlights. Occasional clumps of stunted netleaf hackberry trees stood silhouetted against the dark skyline.

Mary was holding a compass in her hand and navigating. She turned toward Bob and said, "We're still on a due east course. I hope that those tire tracks aren't from a Lincoln Continental."

Bob replied, "Those are old tire tracks and certainly weren't made by a vehicle as heavy as a Lincoln Continental. When I graduated from high school, my parents gave me a 1955 Pontiac station wagon that had been rebuilt after a wreck. It was baby vomit green and really ugly, but the price was right. It was a heavy vehicle with big tires. I used the search for my step uncle as a rite of passage into adulthood. My mother had vague directions about where he was living. She was not keen on her son heading out into a desert wasteland."

Mary said, "If your old Pontiac handled the desert drive, why couldn't a newer Lincoln Continental do the same?"

Bob replied, "The only way I was able to do it was by loading the back of the station wagon with bags of rocks to give more traction on the rear wheels. And even with that, I occasionally bogged down in the sand and had to rock the car back and forth to get going again. It was a long, slow trip coming and going. You are correct in thinking that a new Lincoln Continental could do the same, but it would not be easy and would take a long time."

The Jeep continued, occasionally reaching 25 miles an hour before the thermostat in the dashboard showed a rising temperature.

Bob commented, "I can't push the Jeep too fast or it will overheat. If the radiator boils over, we've got real trouble."

After 45 more minutes of driving, always with a watchful eye on the thermostat, Bob announced, "I think that we are heading right and getting closer. But, if we don't see the walls of the compound in another four or five miles, we may have to backtrack."

Mary said, "If your calculations are right, we should be arriving pretty soon, but I doubt if Uncle Wilbur will be happy to have guests in the dead of the night."

Bob replied, "There is just starting to be a hint of pink in the east. Sunrise will be before 5 AM. Let's hope that Wilbur has chickens and gets up early to feed them."

Ten minutes later high walls could be discerned off in the distance. "Bingo!" Bob shouted. "We are closing in on Shangri-La."

After another mile of desert sand, the Jeep pulled up to the front wall of the compound. There were high stone walls with concertina wire on the top. The wall enclosed an area of several acres. There was a watch tower that rose twenty feet into the air beside the large gate.

"Time for Uncle Wilbur to rise and shine," Bob said as he started honking the Jeep horn. There was no immediate response. After waiting a few minutes, Bob honked again with a long staccato series of loud blasts.

Suddenly an angry female voice shouted from the top of the tower, "You bastards are never taking me back! I'll blast you to hell first!" The head of a young woman appeared above the wall of the tower platform. She pointed a shotgun toward the Jeep.

"I'm counting to three, then wiping you miserable pieces of shit off the face of the earth! One…"

Bob jumped out of the Jeep and shouted, "I'm Bob Smith, and Wilbur is my uncle. He is expecting me and my girlfriend. Please go let him know that we have arrived."

There was a moment of silence. Then the young woman called back, "Liar. I know why you are here. How much are they paying you to drag me back to Barlow?"

Bob answered, "I have no idea what you are talking about. Who are you, anyway? I thought Wilbur always lived by himself and was something of a hermit. I visited Wilbur several years ago. He will know who I am. Go ask him, please. I know that he will let us in."

"I'm still deciding whether to shoot you or not. You say you've got a woman with you. Let's see her."

Mary got out of the car slowly and walked over to Bob.

The young woman asked suspiciously, "Are you one of the hotel girls sent to trap me?"

Mary shook her head and replied, "Bob and I have been on the road for over 24 hours and are really exhausted. Some water and food as well as a bed would be really nice."

"Fat chance of that," the girl answered. "We're not running a youth hostel here. I was super smart in school until I ran away, and you can't fool me. I know the story of the Trojan horse. You two are coming inside over my dead body. Now get your asses back into that Jeep and head back to Barlow before I blow your heads off."

Bob took a different tack. "My girlfriend's pregnant, and she really needs some water and a place to lie down. Please at least be kind enough to go ask Wilbur about his favorite nephew."

The girl in the tower gave a little laugh. "Your girlfriend's knocked up and doesn't even have a ring? Somebody's pretty stupid here. Haven't you folks heard of the pill? I've put up with enough of your bullshit. For the last time, haul ass out of here pronto if you don't want to be a statistic."

The woman repointed the shotgun at Bob and Mary and began counting again, "One…."

Bob said, "OK. We're leaving. Uncle Wilbur is going to chew your butt for sending us away." He and Mary got back into the Jeep and headed slowly away from the compound.

Mary looked at Bob and asked, "What now, genius?"

Bob shook his head and replied with a half-smile, "Never doubt a wannabe Mensa charter member. Stay tuned. We'll be inside that compound having a nice breakfast with my uncle before you know it."

Mary replied, "Not to doubt you, but I won't believe it until I see it. By the way, who is that young girl? She doesn't look older than sixteen. I thought that your uncle was a crazy loner. And what's all this stuff about people coming to take her back to Barlow? Maybe she has paranoid schizophrenia like your uncle, and they hit it off."

"A definite mystery," Bob replied. "It's hard to believe that Wilbur would take a stranger in to live with him. Maybe that's something we can ask him while we sip after-breakfast coffee here shortly."

CHAPTER 22

A FRESH GRAVE

Bob drove slowly away from the compound and headed toward a clump of hackberry trees 200 yards in the distance. The sun had not yet risen, but the east sky was starting to brighten. Once the trees were reached, Bob pulled the Jeep behind the trees to conceal it.

Mary said, "I am all ears. Please share your brilliant plans to breach the walls of the castle. The only thing that this compound lacks is a moat full of alligators."

Bob said, "You are going to be the star in this assault strategy. I will have only a minor part. First, let's gather some of these dry branches on the ground. Then you will drive us to the east wall and park snug up against the stone wall. There is no way the girl can fire at us there unless she throws a ladder up from the inside. I will start lighting branches and throwing them over the wall to get her attention. She will be almost certain to come running to the fire scene."

"So far, so good," Mary said. "When does my starring role begin?"

Bob replied, "Once I get a few fire branches heaved over the wall, you can hug the wall and walk around to the gate. You may have noted that there is a small gap in the concertina wire where the guard tower abuts on the wall. Big-time design flaw. There is a twenty-foot nylon rope with a small hook on one end in my backpack. You can use it to grab onto the wire mesh just to the side of the gap. Then, you can scale the wall and drop down on the inside."

Mary shook her head and said, "Great plan, but you are forgetting one thing. It's not safe for pregnant women to be scaling walls."

Bob smiled and answered, "You and the baby may have to take a hit for the team. Which reminds me, I never asked if you are on the pill."

Mary said enigmatically, "That's for me to know and for you to find out. There's one other little problem with your plan. What if a snarling Rottweiler is waiting for me inside and decides to have me for breakfast?"

Bob replied, "I'm sure you heard the dog barking while we were at the gate talking with the girl with the shotgun. The barks came from farther back in the property and never got closer. So, I'm betting that there is only one guard dog that is penned up somewhere. If the dog is loose, you may have to shoot it as a last resort."

Mary said, "Let's get the show on the road. I'll drive us to the east wall and start some zigging and zagging if there is gun fire."

The Jeep reached the wall with no shotgun blast. Mary and Bob unloaded the dry Hackberry wood. Mary started working her way toward the gate as Bob began throwing fire branches over the wall.

A dog began to bark ferociously, followed by the sound of something bumping on the wall from the inside. The girl's head and torso appeared above the wall followed by the shotgun.

"You're a slow learner, you dumb ass," she said angrily. "Trying to burn us out is a crime. Now I can blast your sorry butt away, and it will be legal."

Bob stared calmly at the girl and pulled his Beretta out. "You're not the only person who has a gun, and I'm a hell of lot better shot than you are." He fired a shot above the young woman's head. She screamed and lost her grip on the shotgun, which fell to the ground at Bob's feet.

A woman's voice was heard from behind the wall saying, "Come on down, Sweetie. Everything is going to be OK. We are not here to hurt you or take you anywhere."

Bob called out, "Mary, open the gate, and I'll get the Jeep in. It's almost breakfast time."

∗ ∗ ∗ ∗

Bob and the girl were sitting at a wooden table in the kitchen while Mary was scrambling eggs at the propane stove. The young woman had been crying and was still wiping her nose with a small towel.

Bob looked at the girl and said kindly, "Let's go over this again. You said my uncle is not here. That's hard to understand since his old truck is in the barn."

The girl looked at Bob and started crying again. She finally answered between sobs, "He's here, but he's not here. I don't want to get in trouble. They'll make me go back to El Paso or give me to the horrible people at the hotel."

Mary sat a plate of scrambled eggs in front of the girl and Bob, then she placed a hand on the girl's shoulder before sat down to eat with them. Mary then reached across the table and took the young woman's hand. "My name is Mary, and this is Bob. You never told us your name."

The girl sat silent, then answered, "My real name is Leta, but back at the hotel I was called Candy."

Mary said, "Tell you what. Let's just eat and not worry about anything for now. Bob and I are just like you—we are running away from people, too. When you are ready, we can share stories."

The girl looked up. "Is the law after you?"

"Not exactly," Bob replied. "It's a lot worse than that."

Mary and Bob were starving and finished all of the scrambled eggs and had several pieces of toast.

Bob asked, "Where do the eggs come from—and the bread?"

Leta answered, "There are a bunch of chickens out back. I make the bread." Then she asked, "Is Mary really pregnant?"

Bob smiled and answered, "Better not be."

Leta's eyes teared up. Then she said haltingly, "I was pregnant several months ago and got beaten. They made me have an abortion by some quack doctor. The pain was awful. I bled for almost a week." After a pause she added, "I'm telling you way too much."

Mary asked gently, "Leta, how old are you?"

Leta wiped her eyes and answered softly, "I'll be seventeen in September."

Mary suggested, "Leta, let's you and me clean up the kitchen. Then Bob and I really need a shower and a chance to catch up on sleep."

Bob said, "It's really amazing that this place has running water and flush toilets. Uncle Wilbur was always something of a mechanical genius. I'll get a few things out of the Jeep. Leta, Mary and I will use the far back bedroom that seems to be unoccupied if that's all right with you."

Leta shook her head yes.

Bob went out to the back porch to walk to the Jeep, which had been pulled into the barn to make certain that it could not be seen. As he walked, his eyes swept the extensive property. Then his eyes caught something that made him stop and give a small gasp. There appeared to be a fresh grave in the back west corner of the compound.

CHAPTER 23

RUNAWAY

Bob and Mary were exhausted after their long trip and crashed for several hours. Mary woke up first and made her way back to the kitchen. Leta was stirring a huge pot at the stove. When Mary spoke to her, she turned around with a startled look on her face.

Leta said, "You scared me. I'm not used to having people in the house. You look so different."

Mary smiled and answered, "A nice shower, some sleep, makeup, and getting out of that gunny sack road dress has made me a new person. What are you cooking?"

Leta replied, "I figured that you folks would wake up hungry. I'm making some stew. Bob's uncle has a huge storeroom of food, including a generator that runs a freezer. He told me that there is a giant propane tank underground that will last at least a year. It runs the lights, the freezer, the refrigerator in the kitchen, and the water pump."

Mary said, "That stew really smells good. Once Bob gets up, I'm sure he and I will be eager to have some. It is so thoughtful of you to make it."

A quick smile crossed Leta's face, but was immediately replaced with a worried look. "You folks aren't going to turn me in, are you?"

Mary shook her head, "What in the world would we turn you in for?"

Leta teared up and suppressed a sob. "Wilbur had an accident. He's not here anymore. But it wasn't my fault," she added quickly. "He's the only man who has ever been nice to me in my whole life."

Mary said quietly, "Everything is going to be all right, Leta. Nobody's going to blame you for anything. You can trust Bob and me.

Why don't you tell me how you ended up living here with Uncle Wilbur."

Leta wiped her eyes and blew her nose. "There's not much else bad that can happen to me. So, I might as well tell you everything."

"I was born in El Paso. My mother got pregnant by a man I never knew. She worked as a clerk in a grocery store during the day. My grandmother Sarah kept me while my mother was working. I loved her. She read wonderful stories to me and taught me how to play games. I always hated it when my mother came to pick me up.

"By the time I was five, my grandma had taught me how to read. When I started school the next year, after a few days I was moved up to the second grade. My mother didn't have much time for me, so I ended up being at my grandmother's house frequently. She checked out all sorts of books for me from the library, and I read for hours on end. When I was eleven, my mother started seeing a man named Bart, who drove a big truck. Before long he was staying at our house when he came back off of the road. The man drank a lot and was never very nice to me. I was happy when my mother suggested that I move in with my grandmother.

"I continued to do very well in school and had a few close friends. When I was fifteen, my grandmother had a stroke and had to go to a nursing home. There was no choice but for me to go back home. The trucker man at first was angry that I was back in the house. But that all changed when I started turning into a young woman. The man was often at home when my mother was at work. Before long he would come to my room, and…."

Leta started crying again and began hyperventilating. Mary walked over to her and said, "I understand, Leta. You don't have to say anything more. But how in the world did you ever get from El Paso to here?"

Leta struggled to regain her composure, then the words came out in a torrent. "One day my mother was working late. I was reading in my room with the door locked. Bart banged on the door demanding to come in. He had been home drinking all day. When I didn't respond, he kicked the door in and tried to grab me. I had hidden a kitchen knife under my pillow. When Bart started trying to rip my clothes off, I grabbed the knife and stuck it in his stomach. He gave a scream and went to the floor. I grabbed a small bag that I had prepared and ran from the house."

Leta paused to catch her breath. "I had a plan and had managed to save seventy-five dollars. The Greyhound Bus station was only three miles away from our house. I walked there and bought a ticket to Pecos, Texas. Since I looked much older than sixteen, nobody questioned me. Once I got to Pecos, I was able to get a job as a maid at a motel which paid me just enough to rent a small room at the motel and eat at the restaurant. I was scared to death that I might have killed Bart, and that the law would find me and send me to prison."

Mary said angrily, "The man was a predator and deserved to be killed just like a rabid animal. What you did was self-defense. There's no way that you would ever be found guilty…. How did you ever get from Pecos to the hotel in Barlow?"

Tears filled Leta's eyes. "It's not really a hotel—it's a whorehouse." She wiped her eyes again and continued. "One day as I was cleaning rooms at the motel, a man came down the hall and stopped when he saw me. He said, 'Hey, you look like Leta Mitchell, the girl who stabbed that man in El Paso. I saw your picture in the paper. Girl, there's a reward out for you. I figure for murder they'll lock you up for the rest of your life.'"

"I broke down in tears and started shaking. The man came over to me and put a gentle hand on my shoulder. He said, 'I can help you, Leta. I'd hate to see a pretty girl like you rot away in prison for the rest of your life. You need to find a place way off the beaten path where you will be safe until this all blows over.'"

"The man was kind with me and seemed so nice. He was well dressed and smelled good. He told me about a small town out in the desert where he owned a hotel. He promised me a job in the kitchen where I could stay out of sight. The hotel would pay me seventy-five dollars a week and provide a room with free meals. The offer sounded almost too good to be true."

Mary shook her head and commented, "And no doubt it was too good to be true."

Leta nodded and said quietly, "Yes."

At that moment Bob walked into the kitchen and said cheerily, "I slept the sleep of the dead. But after a shower and clean clothes, I feel like a new man." He sniffed and asked, "What smells so good?"

Bob then saw that Leta had been crying and asked quietly, "Am I interrupting a private conversation?"

Mary shook her head. "Leta has been telling me things that you also need to know. But she made some great stew for us. Let's eat first and then let Leta tell us the rest of her story so we can see how we can help her."

CHAPTER 24

LIGHTS OUT AT BEDTIME

Bob and Mary ate Leta's stew with relish, while Leta sat at the table with her head down staring at her cup of coffee with a worried look on her face. Suddenly she looked up and blurted out, "Promise me you won't turn me in or take me back to the hotel."

Mary said, "Leta, you can trust us. We will keep you safe. Were you planning to stay here all by yourself?"

Leta nodded affirmatively. "I'd kill myself before I would go back to the hotel."

"We told you that Bob and I are running away from some bad people just like you are. Let me give Bob a summary of what you have told me so far, then we both want to learn how you came to be here with Bob's Uncle Wilbur."

Mary recounted Leta's story of El Paso and Bart's abuse, which forced her to flee to Pecos, and how a nice man took her to Barlow with the promise of a job in his hotel. Then Mary said, "Leta, I know that it's hard for you to talk about what must have been an awful experience at the hotel, but please tell us a bit about that and how Wilbur came into the picture."

Leta said, "I think that I can talk about it now that I know that I'll never have to be in that horrible place again." She paused, then began her story hesitatingly. "The man who offered me the job in his hotel had me pack my small bag and leave by a back door and go to the alley. He drove up in the shiniest black Cadillac that I had ever seen. The man said that his name was Mike and that I had to be one of the prettiest girls in Texas. It only took a little over an hour to get to the dirt road that led out into the desert to Barlow.

"Once we got to the hotel, Mike took me in a side door and introduced me to a heavy-set woman named Sadie who was wearing a low-cut dress and smoking a cigarette with a jeweled holder. Mike said that the woman would take care of me, then he left.

"We walked down the hall into the back of the hotel where there were a number of small rooms. Sadie led me into one of the rooms and locked the door. She began asking me a lot of personal questions such as whether I had ever been with a man and if I had ever had a disease of my female parts. When I asked her why she needed to know that, she got very angry and slapped my face hard. Then she said that she knew about my past and what happened to Bart, and that if I did not do just what she told me to do, she would call the police. Sadie said that I was working in a gentleman's club. My job was going to be making customers extremely happy.

"I was given two days to learn how to apply makeup, how to flirt with men, and how to convince them to pay money to come back to my room. Sadie gave me three dresses that didn't cover up very much. She said that I would be in big trouble if one of the dresses got ripped or stained. I was told that a record would be kept about how many drinks my customers bought. The goal was to convince them to buy a lot of drinks for them and for me. My drinks would not have any alcohol in them. Once back in my room, the idea was to satisfy the customer as quickly as possible, then find another mark. Sadie said that the best girls could take care of several men each night. She said that any tips we got had to be turned in to her."

Mary said very sympathetically, "How awful. Taking a young woman and forcing her to work as a slave in a gentleman's club."

Leta quickly corrected Mary. "It was not a gentlemen's club—it was a whorehouse. There was big money coming in every night and not just from drinks and sex, but also from a private gambling room."

Bob asked, "Were you the only young woman working there?"

Leta replied, "Sheree and Amber are just about my age. They are also runaways. We were told that if we tried to leave the hotel, we would be beaten. Sadie made a point that there was no place to escape to except the desert, and that she would track us down with dogs."

Mary asked, "Were there any older women working there?"

Leta replied, "There were several older women who were professionals. They seemed to be there by choice and got a share of the money they generated.

"Each Sunday afternoon Sheree, Amber, and I were paid fifteen dollars. Sadie and a man with a scarred face named Carlos would take each of us separately to the general store later in the afternoon and give us ten minutes to spend the money.

"They stayed right by our sides at all times to make certain that we didn't try to run."

Mary shook her head and said, "I'm sick to my stomach listening to what you had to go through. Can you tell us how you came to live here with Bob's uncle?"

Leta tensed up and had a slight shudder. "For sure you're not going to turn me in?"

Bob and Mary said, "No," simultaneously.

Leta took a deep breath. "One Sunday afternoon when I was at the general store with Sadie and Carlos for my ten minutes of shopping, Wilbur came into the store. He had wild hair and a bushy beard and was talking to himself crazy-like. He brushed against Carlos as he walked past him. Carlos shoved him and shouted, 'Watch out you crazy old coot!' Wilbur suddenly got a strange look in his face like he was listening to something no one else could hear. Suddenly he punched Carlos in the face and knocked him down. Before Carlos could move, Wilbur jumped on top of him and smashed his head into the floor several times. Sadie kneeled down to help Carlos. I saw my chance and dashed out of the store.

"There was a pickup full of supplies behind the store. I jumped into the back and hid under some bags. When the truck started driving away, I stayed hidden. I figured nothing could be worse than going back to the whorehouse. It was a long bumpy road back to Wilbur's place. Once he found me in the back of the truck, I started crying and begging him not to take me back. I told him who Carlos and Sadie were and that I was a prisoner in their whorehouse. He listened, then said, 'I should have killed Carlos.'"

"To make a long story short, Wilbur took me in. I started cooking and taking care of the cleaning. He seemed less crazy the longer I was there. Wilbur taught me to play chess. He was always very kind to me. The only bad part was at night when he would start crying out in his sleep about people dying all around him. It sounded like he was back in battle and being tortured. One night he kept on yelling so loudly that I went to his room and sat on the edge of his bed and talked to him and held his hand. From that point on, whenever he had a really bad night, I would go calm him down. One night after he stopped crying out, he started shaking so bad like he was freezing that I crawled into bed with him. Occasionally, I would spend the entire night with him. Nothing bad ever happened. But one night after a particularly bad dream, he kept sobbing. I snuggled up close to him. One thing led to another, and we got to know each other a lot better before morning."

Leta stopped talking and started to choke up. After a pause, she continued with a soft voice. "Wilbur made no demands on me, but I wanted to be close to someone who was kind to me and wanted me as a woman and not a cheap hired body. We continued our physical relationship from that point on." Another pause and a small sob. "A week ago, right in the middle of lovemaking, Wilbur gave a huge gasp and slumped over in my arms. He had no pulse. I hit him on the chest and breathed into his mouth—but it was quickly apparent that he was not coming back."

Mary said, "How terrible!"

Leta took a deep breath. "I panicked. My first thought was to take Wilbur's truck and run. But then I stopped to realize that with people looking for me after stabbing my mother's live-in, I was bound to be recognized and caught at some point. It made more sense to drag poor Wilbur's body to the back of the lot and bury him and hide here as long as possible."

Bob said, "I saw that grave out back and felt certain that Wilbur had been buried there. But I would never have guessed how he died. There are sure worse ways to go. Leta, you know that you could have just told us that you found Wilbur dead in bed one morning, and we would have believed you."

Leta shook her head. "I couldn't keep what happened inside me much longer. I was feeling too depressed and guilty that I seriously thought of shooting myself." She burst into tears and sobbed, "Now I've killed two men."

Mary got up and put an arm around Leta. "You don't know for sure that Bart died, but if he did, he sure deserved it. And you didn't kill Wilbur. It was his time to go. You obviously made his life better while he was alive."

Leta looked up at Mary and said, "Promise me that Bob and you won't leave me alone here."

Bob said, "This is the only safe place for us now. We plan on being around for a long time."

CHAPTER 25

THE COMPOUND

Leta seemed greatly relieved after telling Mary and Bob her story. She suggested giving them a tour of the compound. The house was more extensive than it appeared from the outside. The kitchen spilled over into a den with a hairhide couch and chairs. A huge storage room could be accessed from the backside of the kitchen and was stocked with an immense amount of food and staples. There was a large freezer and a refrigerator, both of which were humming away.

Mary said, "The generator that runs the house must be very large."

Leta nodded her head and said, "The generator is 40 kilowatts and liquid cooled. It runs on propane. There's a huge buried propane tank behind the house that gets filled once a year. Wilbur and I had a lot of free time. He taught me a great deal about this compound and how to maintain and fix things. I actually can work on the generator almost as well as he could."

Leta continued, "Let's go down into the basement first. You can learn one of the secrets of this place."

Bob asked, "Secrets?"

"Yes, secrets," Leta replied. "Wilbur may have been strange, but he was a genius as you will soon see."

Leta walked to a large wall of shelves in the storage room that were loaded with bags of flour and sugar. She removed one of the flour bags and exposed a combination dial which she twirled. It was then possible to swing one end of the panel open and reveal stairs leading downward to a large basement that was full of weapons and boxes of ammunition.

"Wow!" Bob exclaimed. "You could outfit a small army with all these guns and explosives."

Leta said, "Wilbur was very paranoid and was convinced at some point that a large force of Germans would storm the compound. Very few people ever wandered this far out into the desert. But if anybody did come close to this place, he would fire warning shots in their direction. People learned to stay away a long time ago. He was teaching me to shoot before..." Leta teared up and stopped mid-sentence.

Mary said kindly, "Leta, stop beating yourself up. Bob and I have done our share of taking care of bad people, and we don't torture ourselves about doing what was right. If the rapist man in El Paso died, I say good riddance. Accidents can happen at any time, including during sex."

Bob added, "If Wilbur's in heaven, he's probably still grinning."

Leta forced a smile and said, "The generator's outside behind the house. It's under a roof to minimize heat in the summer. There's also a swamp cooler constantly blowing on the generator in hot weather."

Mary had a puzzled look on her face as she asked, "What in the heck is a swamp cooler?"

Bob answered, "A swamp cooler is an old-fashioned term for an evaporative air conditioner. You may have noticed a large evaporative unit on top of this building. It doesn't take much electricity to run one of them. And since the climate is so dry, the system is actually quite efficient."

Next, Leta led Mary and Bob outside to walk around the four-acre walled compound. There were chicken coops toward the back as well as a small garden that was irrigated with pipes from the water pump. They walked over to a wire-fenced off dog area and were met by a snarling Rottweiler. Leta patted the dog through the fence.

"Wilbur named the dog Avenger and trained him as an attack dog. If you two will walk up slowly and let him sniff your hands, he will get to know you and only bite you occasionally." Leta smiled and added, "Just teasing, of course. I let Avenger out at night so he can guard the property, but he likes dining on chickens, so I have to be certain no chickens are out of their pen."

Next the three walked over to the barn. Leta swung the double doors open. Inside were tools, bags of chicken feed, and two trucks. One was an old four-wheel drive Dodge Power Town Wagon with chipped black paint. The other vehicle was a vintage Army deuce-and-a-half truck with two flat tires.

Leta volunteered, "The Dodge has large tires with deep tread and does well in the sand. That is the truck that Wilbur would take into Barlow every month or so for supplies. I don't think that the Army truck has been driven for a long time."

* * * *

Bob, Mary, and Leta were sitting around the table after supper having coffee. Mary had made dinner by raiding the refrigerator and freezer.

Leta said, "That was a great meal, Mary. Maybe you can teach me how to cook like that."

Mary replied, "It looks like all of us will be here for a while, so there will be plenty of time to polish your cooking skills. But I think that there will be things for you to learn that will be much more important in your life than food. Bob and I cannot tell you too much, but we both have been in work that demanded excellence in defense and with weapons. In all modesty we are experts. We are going to teach you how to take care of yourself."

Bob added, "Leta, there are enough armaments in the basemen to start World War III. My goal is to make you more than proficient with weapons. Mary is an incredible fighter and can teach you to take care of goons likes Carlos."

Leta thought a minute, then said, "If I really get good at all of this, I'm going back into town to rescue my friends Sheree and Amber at the whorehouse. Every day they are being pawed over and forced into sex with nasty, drunk animals. Then they get abused by Sadie and Carlos."

Mary exchanged a worried look at Bob. "Leta, right now the last thing you need is more trouble. There are some very mean people at the hotel. You would end up being killed or being forced back into the same terrible work. Let's put your heroic plan on the back burner for now and wait to see how quickly you can learn to take care of yourself before you start trying to be Super Woman."

CHAPTER 26

SPY IN THE SKY

The next morning Bob was up early walking around the grounds, thinking about how best to defend the compound if the heavies from the hotel came calling looking for Leta or if Randy and his thugs or some KGB agents showed up. The stone walls topped with concertina wire would be a deterrent, but the single observation tower would not be of any strategic value if an attack came from the sides or rear. Bob knew the best defense was to lie low and not become a place of interest for ill-intentioned people.

After becoming very familiar with the land inside the fence, Bob went back into the house and used the combination code that Leta had given him to take the stairs to the basement that served as an armory of sorts. He was amazed once again at the number of rifles and pistols with boxes of ammunition. There were also several shotguns as well as hand grenades and a Thompson machine gun.

Bob ascended the basement stairs, closed the concealed door, and headed for the kitchen hoping to find some coffee. Mary and Leta were at the stove together. Leta looked up and said, "Mary is teaching me to make a fancy omelet."

Just as Bob finished saying, "Sure smells good," the sound of a small plane in the distance was heard. As the plane grew closer, Bob said urgently, "Stay away from the windows. That's got to be somebody looking for Mary and me. Thank goodness all of the vehicles are in the barn." There was a loud roar as the plane buzzed the compound and rattled the dishes on the table. It came back for a second very low sweep, then headed east.

Bob asked Leta, "Do you know if there is any type of landing field near Barlow?"

Leta replied, "There is a strip outside of town. Some of the men who patronize the whorehouse actually fly small planes in. I heard Sadie telling the owner Mike that men like this can easily drop a thousand dollars for drinks, a woman, and gambling."

Mary said, "The plane most likely was hired by Randy Williams. He is determined to get Bob and me."

Leta looked puzzled and asked, "Who is Randy Williams, and why is he after you two? Is he a policeman?"

Mary responded, "Leta, we can't tell you everything, but Bob and I were involved trying to bust a criminal enterprise that Randy, his son, and some big-name mafia people were running. There was a gunfight, and Randy's son was shot and later died. The crime people would like nothing better than exacting some revenge on us."

Leta asked, "If they caught you, what would happen?"

Mary looked at Bob for approval, and he nodded yes.

Mary said, "They would torture us, then kill us."

Leta had a shocked look on her face. "Really?"

Bob answered, "Really and truly. But Mary and I are extremely well trained and can take care of ourselves. We plan to keep you safe also. But if we are going to live here together, you have a lot to learn to help us all stay safe. Starting today Mary will begin to train you in self-defense, and you and I will work on handling weapons."

Mary asked, "Leta, do you know how to drive?"

Leta replied, "Wilbur taught me to drive his pickup truck in the desert. I can handle a stick shift well."

"That's a good start. "I plan to give you some graduate courses in tactical driving."

Bob said, "Speaking of driving, I want to see if I can get that old deuce-and-a-half in the barn running again. I have a feeling that at some point we are going to need it. We are pretty certain that the bad guys know that we were driving the Jeep station wagon that is now hidden in the barn. It won't be safe to use it again."

Leta said, "I am ready to get started on my training. It is really hard for me to feel OK about being safe here while Sheree and Amber are being basically raped every day by smelly low-life men. Customer hygiene is not a top priority for the owner Mike and his madam Sadie."

Mary looked at Bob then said, "Leta, we hurt for your friends, but at this point we have to worry about staying alive. Being with us puts you at more risk. Give us time to get settled in here, and at some point we can discuss if there is any possible way of helping Sheree and Amber without getting us all killed."

The distant sound of a plane was heard approaching. Once again, the plane swept low over the compound with an ear-splitting roar. On a second sweep a blazing flare was dropped that barely missed the barn.

Bob said, "They want to start the barn burning as a way to force us out of the house so they can see if Mary and I are here. We can't let that happen."

Bob rushed out of the kitchen and quickly returned with an M16 from the basement. "Time to see if that plane can fly without gas."

The plane made another pass, much slower, trying to land a flare on the roof of the barn. Bob had run to the covered back porch and managed to get several shots off as the plane passed.

"We'll know quickly if I managed to hit the fuel tank."

The small plane made a turn and headed back in the direction of Barlow.

"Bingo!" Mary cried. Leta started applauding.

Bob shook his head and said, "Too early for praise. The chances of hitting a plane with a weapon such as an M16 requires a lot of luck, even if the plane is flying low and fairly slow. Aerial surveillance is not a good turn of events. Our only hope is that the people in the plane think that Wilbur was the one shooting at them. If they suspect Mary and I are here, they will be back. We have to always be alert for the sound of a plane and run for cover before the plane gets in sighting distance."

Leta was silent thinking, then slowly said, "I may have a good idea. What if Bob gets some of Wilbur's work clothes and one of his large hats. If the plane comes back later or another day, Bob can run outside and wave his fist in the air and start shooting. Everybody knows that Wilbur was never shy about taking shots at anybody who came close to the compound."

Mary said, "Great suggestion, Leta. Did Wilbur have a large beard that was gray?"

Leta replied, "It was speckled gray and bushy, but just before Wilbur went into town the last time, he had me trim it fairly short."

Mary looked at Bob and said, "Your beard is growing pretty fast. I think that I can bleach it and make it look almost gray. Your idea is really good, Leta. As long as we can keep people thinking that the only person at the compound is Wilbur, we should be safe—maybe."

A THUMP ON THE ROOF

The plane that had buzzed the compound earlier in the day did not return for another pass, which gave at least some hope that Bob may have hit the gas tank or damaged some other important part of the aircraft. Bob went outside and climbed a tall ladder to look at the top of the barn after the plane hightailed it to the east. He tapped on the edge of the roof and heard a metallic ting. Although the appearance of the roof suggested wood, Bob discovered that the roof was actually steel that had been processed to simulate wooden planks. He went back inside the house to update Mary and Leta.

"Good news. The roof of the barn is metal. No way any flare is going to set it ablaze. I am amazed how Wilbur ever managed to get this compound built way out here in the desert."

Leta said, "Wilbur and I had a lot of time to talk before he…" Leta teared up, then she cleared her throat and resumed talking. "Wilbur told me that when his father died, he left Wilbur more money than anyone could ever spend. With this money, he was able to hire a large crew to come out into the desert and build the compound. That happened at least twenty years ago. Wilbur didn't trust banks. He said that the money is now all in cash and is in the large safe down in the basement."

Mary said, "I noticed the safe when we were looking at all the guns earlier, but I didn't think much about it. Leta, do you know the combination?"

Leta shook her head no.

Mary looked at Bob and said, "You are a master lock picker and safe cracker. Do you think that you could open the safe? There could be something more important than money in it."

Bob replied, "No time like the present."

The three of them went down into the basement and walked to the safe which was installed into the wall. The safe was five feet tall and resembled a bank vault. Bob looked at the combination dial for a moment, then began slowly turning the dial trying to hear or feel a slight click. After a few tries he said, "Wilbur paid the big bucks for a really good German lock. This may take me a little while." After several more minutes he said, "Pretty sure I have the first two numbers. Hopefully, this is three-number lock and not a four-number."

After another few minutes Bob exclaimed, "Eureka!"

Leta asked with a smile, "Aren't you supposed to run around the house naked now like Archimedes?"

Mary laughed and said, "No way Bob will have a clue what you are talking about. He's just a dumb football player with too many hits to his head."

"Au contraire, ladies. I am very familiar with Archimedes and how he solved the problem of determining the purity of the gold in the king's crown by observing water displacement while soaking in a public bath. And, yes, he allegedly did shout 'Eureka' and leaped out of the bath and ran naked down the street—something I do not plan to emulate."

Leta smiled and said, "Thank goodness. I've seen enough naked men's bodies to last me a lifetime."

Bob swung the large safe door open and gasped. Inside were huge stacks of hundred-dollar bills. "Zowie! There's enough money here to pay off the national debt of most small countries."

Leta said, "Wilbur told me that his father was very successful as a lawyer, but that most of the family money came from the sale of hundreds of acres of tobacco land in North Carolina. Apparently, your uncle was an only child."

Bob commented, "Wilbur was actually my step-uncle. The only time I ever met him was when I drove across the desert to see him the summer before I started college. We really hit it off. He let me shoot several of his guns."

Mary peered into the open safe and observed, "Lots of money for sure, but I wonder what's in that big manila envelope way at the back."

Bob reached into the safe and pulled the envelope out and held it up to the light. "Weird. The envelope has my name on it."

Inside were two sheets of paper. Bob took the top piece out, looked at it, and had an immediate look of surprise on his face.

Mary smiled and said, "I bet it's a treasure map."

Bob hesitated, then replied, "The paper is actually entitled 'The Last Will and Testament of Wilbur Wilbanks.' It was hand written in print and was signed and dated shortly after I visited my uncle six years ago."

Mary urged, "Don't keep us hanging in suspense. What group is the lucky beneficiary? Maybe the VFW?"

Bob replied very seriously, "My uncle left every penny to a woman named Ecstasy."

Leta observed, "That sounds like a stripper's name."

"Cut the bull," Mary said.

Bob shook his head slowly. "Wilbur left everything he owned to me."

There was a moment of shocked silence, then Mary asked, "Is a handwritten will valid in Texas?"

Bob replied, "There are a number of states where handwritten, or holographic, wills are definitely legal, and Texas is one of them. The money in the safe sure gives us some working capital."

Leta asked, "What about the second sheet of paper?"

Bob took it out and studied it carefully. "It is an elaborate map of this property with a multitude of notes penned in. At first glance it appears that there is a great deal about this compound that is not readily apparent."

Leta said, "Wilbur told me that there were plenty of secret surprises here that he would show me in time. Early on after we started sleeping together he showed me the false wall that opens into the weapons area."

The conversation was interrupted by the sound of an aircraft approaching. The plane made a low pass.

"Guess I wasn't as great a shot as I thought," Bob said wryly. "I don't think that there's much damage they can do with flares. Unless they start shooting, let's just stay hidden."

The plane came back for a second very slow pass. Suddenly there was a loud thump as if something heavy had been dropped on the roof of the house. The plane then picked up speed and flew away.

After a few minutes Bob said, "Should be safe to come out now. I'm going to grab a ladder and see what the plane dropped on the roof. The house has the same metal roof as the barn, so I don't think there is any danger of fire."

Mary said, "Leta and I will make some sandwiches for lunch while you go roof exploring. Come on, Leta. Time for us to put on our chef's hats."

After a few minutes Bob came back to the kitchen and looked shaken. He walked over to Mary and put an arm around her waist. "Just awful, just awful," he said quietly.

Mary took Bob's hand and said with concern, "You look worse than when people are shooting at you. What in the world did you find?"

Bob shook his head, then replied. "There's a large canvas bag on our roof with blood stains, and I bet I know what's in it."

CHAPTER 28

BODIES FROM HEAVEN

There was a moment of silence, then Bob looked at Leta and said, "There is a great deal that you do not know about Mary and me. Being with us is growing increasingly dangerous. Do you want us to see if we can find a way to safely get you to a relative's house somewhere far away where no one will be looking for you?"

Leta shook her head emphatically, no. "You and Mary promised to teach me how to take care of myself. I'm not going anywhere until I can go back to the hotel and settle some scores and also bust Sheree and Amber out of there. Besides, I don't know any relatives other than my grandmother who had the stroke. Mike told me when he took me away from Pecos that the law was after me for stabbing Bart. I'm staying put regardless of what you two say."

There was a moment of silence, then Mary said, "Let's all sit down for a moment and think rationally. Then we can deal with the canvas bag on the roof."

After they sat down, Mary looked at Bob who said, "You go first."

Mary began, "Leta, the first thing that you need to know is that Bob and I recently worked for the U.S. government breaking up a criminal enterprise that was also supported by clandestine Russian agents in this country. American secret operatives who worked for the CIA were being kidnapped, tortured for information, then murdered and incinerated in a cremation oven. A number of people were killed during this operation. Bob and I are wanted by both the Russian KGB and a large crime syndicate."

Bob continued, "Mary and I changed our names and identities and drove a long way to reach my uncle's compound. Our belief was that we would have a better chance of staying alive if we could hide way out in the desert for a number of months. Of course, we had no idea that Wilbur was dead or that you were living here. We don't want to tell you everything about our training or past since it would be safer for you not to know too much."

Mary said, "Leta, as previously discussed, if we all stay together it will be very important for you to learn as much as we can teach you about weapons, surveillance, and hand-to-hand fighting. The bad problem now is that at least one of the groups looking for us is suspicious that we may be at the compound. The goal of the attempts to light the barn on fire or dropping the canvas bag on the roof was to get us to rush out of the house so that our enemies can confirm that we are indeed here. As of now, they have no proof that anyone other than so-called crazy Wilbur is living at the compound."

Leta said, "Nothing that you have said spooks me. I've lived through some awful times, and I am not afraid. Please keep talking and tell me about the blood-stained canvas bag on the roof."

Bob said, "We drove a long way in a VW camper that would have great difficulty making the drive from Barlow to the compound across the unusual shifting desert sand. Somewhere south of Monahans we saw the Jeep station wagon now in the barn for sale and traded the VW and some cash for the Jeep. Unfortunately, the people chasing us knew that we were driving the VW. My guess is that the man who sold us the Jeep and took the VW left it out front of his house. The bad guys who were speeding up and down the highway looking for Mary and me saw the camper and stopped to torture the man and his wife trying to learn where we were going. I'm almost certain the unlucky couple is in the canvas bag."

"Yikes!" said Leta. She paused, then said, "But count on me to help you do whatever is necessary."

Bob said, "I'm going back on the roof. I'll drag the bag to the edge and try to lower it down toward the ground. Leta, this is not going to be very pleasant. Do you want to stay in the house?"

"Nope. I'm going," she replied firmly. "Remember—I had to drag poor Wilbur all the way to the back of the compound and bury him. Digging that grave took me at least five hours."

Bob climbed the ladder and walked across the roof to the canvas bag. He dragged it to the edge, leaving a small trail of blood and body fluids. Then he got back on the ladder and slid the bag to the edge. Bob tried to hold one end of the bag and lower it down to the ground, but the bag slipped from his grasp and hit the ground and split open, spraying fluids on Mary and Leta.

Mary gasped, "What a horrible smell! Shower time, for sure!"

Inside the bag were the old man and his wife who were starting to bloat in the desert heat. Both of them had missing fingers as well as cigarette burns on their body.

Bob shook his head and said quietly, "Mary, we set these poor people up for this. Remember that we told them that we were going out into the desert for a religious ceremony to bless your supposed pregnancy. No doubt Randy and his thugs extracted this information from them very quickly, then just started torturing them for sadistic kicks."

Mary nodded in agreement. "I think if we get the law involved in this, we will be sitting ducks for both the crime guys and the KGB. It wouldn't surprise me if the KGB has offered a big reward to the mafia people to track us down."

Bob had a grim look on his face. "You and Leta can clean up while I put these bodies into the big wheelbarrow in the barn and roll them out back. I'll need to dig a deep grave."

Leta interjected, "As far as I know, I'm the only one here with grave-digging experience. I can help. It's not too hard digging down, but the problem is keeping the sand from sliding back into the grave. But at about two feet you get into firm soil that is easier to deal with."

Mary wrinkled her nose. "Those poor folks really smell awful. Leta and I will clean up, then join you out back. We can all help dig."

Bob said, "I don't know about you, Mary, but this horrible killing changes things for me. Sometimes offense is the best defense. If I were Randy Williams and his crime buddies, I wouldn't count on seeing old age."

CHAPTER 29

A NEW GRAVE

Bob started digging the grave in the back of the compound near Wilbur's resting place. Once Leta arrived, she insisted on helping. She was strong and tall for a nearly seventeen-year-old woman and took the shovel with grim determination and made the sand and dirt fly. Leta's face was pretty, the kind that made people look twice. However, her face had etched-in sorrow lines beyond her years.

Once the grave was almost six feet deep, Bob pushed the wheelbarrow to the edge. He hesitated, then said softly, "Folks, Mary and I are so sorry that we set you up for such a terrible death. We feel awful. I swear to God that your deaths will not go unavenged."

Then Bob lifted the handles of the wheelbarrow, and the canvas bag fell to the bottom of the grave with a squishy thud. Mary brought two more shovels from the barn. With three people working, covering the bodies was much quicker than digging the grave.

After the burial was finished, Mary, Leta, and Bob walked slowly back to the house and sat down in the kitchen. Nothing was said for a few minutes, then Bob spoke.

"I think our most important goal right now is to do everything we can to convince people that Wilbur is here, alive and alone, and that Mary and I have disappeared into the desert. The biggest threat to us is air surveillance. My guess is that the crime people gave a lot of money to hire the plane and the pilot to drop the bodies on the roof. It would be hard to believe that the pilot was totally unaware of the pay load, particularly if he had a normal sense of smell. There had to be someone else in the back to push the bodies out. We need some way to make flying over the compound so risky that no one will want to try it."

Leta said, "Wilbur let me fire one of the Thompson machine guns once. Could you hit a plane with that?"

Bob replied, "Unfortunately, it is close to impossible to use hand weapons to hit a plane flying even several hundred feet up in the air. An M16 with automatic fire has a better chance than a small machine gun. I don't think that weapons from the ground are the answer."

Mary said, "One important advantage we have is that we can hear a plane coming, which gives us time to get out of sight. But I think that it would make sense for Bob to pretend to be crazy Wilbur and run outside and fire at the plane."

Bob said, "I see no good option but for me to make a night-time visit to the Barlow airfield. If the plane that carried the bodies suddenly goes up in flames, that should be a deterrent for anyone else thinking of hiring out to Randy and his thugs. When I was firing at the plane before, I had a pretty good look, and I think that I can recognize the plane if I see it again."

Mary asked, "Leta, do you know anything about the airfield outside of Barlow? Is it just open field?"

"I heard Sadie talking with one of the customers who had flown in. The landing area is just open desert where the ground is a lot less sandy. There are no lights marking a runway, so taking off or landing at night would be dangerous. The customers who fly in usually spend the night at the hotel."

Bob asked, "What is the least busy night for the girls at the hotel?"

"Sunday night is never busy. We often got free time on those evenings."

"Another question please. When was the last time Wilbur took his desert pickup with large tires into town?"

"He went into town about two weeks ago and bought some meat for the freezer as well as milk and some cookies that I requested. Wilbur has an underground tank, not the propane one, that is smaller and holds at least 200 gallons of gasoline. I'm not sure how it gets re-supplied, but Wilbur only drives to town and back once a month. So, he doesn't use much gas."

Mary had a concerned look on her face. She looked at Bob and asked, "Are you sure going to the airfield is a good idea? If you go, you're sure not going solo. My Makarov and I are not about to stay home."

"Fair enough," Bob replied.

Leta immediately said, "I want to go, too."

Mary shook her head. "This is not going to be a safe outing. If something goes wrong, you need to be here guarding the compound. You and I need to start working on your hand-to-hand combat skills tonight. Tomorrow Bob can begin your shooting lessons. Life has really been tough for you, Leta. The best thing Bob and I can do is to teach you how to take care of yourself so you never end up being abused again."

Leta stated with determination, "Once I get good at all of this, I want to rescue Sheree and Amber."

"That won't be easy, but I am working on some ideas," Bob responded.

Mary said, "I find it hard not to keep thinking about your friends at the hotel. You told us that they are runaways. Do you know where they are from?"

Leta shook her head affirmatively and replied, "Sheree is from Amarillo and Amber is from Albuquerque. Both of them had abusive fathers with terrible home situations. Each day now is a living hell for them."

"We fully understand," Bob agreed. "But first things first. Our most urgent job is to eliminate aircraft surveillance of the compound. Next Sunday night I plan to use Wilbur's pickup and find the airfield in the wee hours of the morning and arrange for the plane that Randy has been hiring to have an unfortunate fire."

Mary said, "Bob, I'm curious about the map that was in the safe with the will. Any surprises there?"

"I need to study it in detail. But my immediate thought was that there are areas connected to the house that we haven't discovered. I also think there may be at least one other weapon cache. Why don't you go start teaching Leta how to beat up bad guys while I sit down with the map? Then we can fashion a gourmet dinner out of the freezer and the store room."

CHAPTER 30

COW CORN FLAKES

The next morning Bob was up early and was sitting at the kitchen table with a cup of coffee when Mary came in. He was intently studying the map of the compound that had been in the safe along with Wilbur's will.

Mary asked, "Any startling revelations?"

"And how," Bob replied. "On the back of the map there are all sorts of notes about defense plans when the Germans try to take the compound. Clearly, my uncle was convinced that at some point some of the Germans he fought in World War II would try to overrun this place. There is at least one substantial weapons area that we haven't discovered that appears to be part of a safe bunker underground. The map doesn't show where this area is. However, there seems to be weird clues of some sort."

"Like what?" Mary asked.

Bob said with a puzzled look on his face, "At the bottom of the map there is a note that reads, 'Bunker/Weapons: Cow Corn Flakes.'"

Mary responded, "Bizarre."

Leta came into the kitchen and got a cup of coffee and sat down at the table. "I had a dream last night that Sheree and Amber were being chased by an ugly man that looked like Carlos. The girls were running and screaming. Just as the man was about to catch them, I suddenly woke up drenched in sweat and with my heart pounding."

Mary said, "What an awful dream. Bob and I really want to help your friends. But it's going to take time to make a plan that won't get all of us killed."

Bob looked at Leta and asked, "Did Wilbur ever talk about German soldiers trying to break into the compound and kill him?"

"Oh, yes," Leta replied. "He would mumble in his dreams about soldiers firing at him. Then he would scream, 'To the bunker! To the bunker!'"

Mary asked, "Leta, do you know if there really is a bunker in the compound?"

Leta shook her head. "Once I asked Wilbur about it, and he replied, 'That's for me to know and for you to find out.'"

Bob asked, "Were there ever any cows on this place?"

Leta replied, "The only animals I know about are the chickens and the watch dog Avenger. There are some empty animal stalls in the barn, but there is nothing to suggest that they were ever occupied."

In the distance there was the faint sound of an airplane. Bob said, "That sounds like the bad guys are coming back for a look. They will certainly see the new grave in the back and figure out that someone buried the people in the canvas bag. But I wonder what they thought when they saw the first grave when the plane initially flew over. Hopefully, they assumed that a large farm animal, and not Wilbur, had been buried there."

Bob jumped up and quickly stepped into a pair of Wilbur's work overalls. He put on one of his uncle's large hats, then rushed to the back porch with the M16. As the plane flew over, Bob ran into the yard and fired a volley of shots toward the plane which stayed safely at more than a thousand feet. When the plane turned and came back toward the compound, Bob fired again, then began shaking his fist at the plane which sped up and flew back toward Barlow.

"Good show," Mary said when Bob returned to the kitchen. "Hopefully, the people in the plane were up high enough not to get a perfect look at our pretend Wilbur."

Bob said, "At least they didn't drop any dead bodies or incendiaries on us this time. Unless you girls want to suffer through my lack of cooking skills, I plan to go look around the barn while one of you super chefs whip out a four-star breakfast."

* * * *

When the group sat down for breakfast, Mary asked Bob, "Did you learn anything in the barn?"

"Afraid not. I just can't make heads or tails of how Cow Corn Flakes can be a clue to where the hidden bunker might be."

Leta wrinkled her forehead in thought, then said, "Corn Flakes are a type of cereal…"

"True," replied Bob. "But that doesn't help much."

Leta thought again, then suddenly blurted out, "Unless it's a homophone."

Mary laughed. "No chance that Bob understands that word after all of his head injuries. He probably thinks a homophone is a pay phone in a gay neighborhood. You and I know that a homophone is a word that sounds just like another word but has a different meaning."

Bob frowned. "You ladies should stop demeaning me. Deep down inside I am really very sensitive. So, what's a homophone of cereal?"

Leta said, "How about serial, like a serial number on a piece of equipment."

Bob stood up quickly. "I'm really tempted to shout 'Eureka!' and shed my clothes as I run back to the barn. Leta, I think that you have unraveled part of the mystery."

Bob announced over his shoulder as he rushed back to the barn, "Keep on stuffing your faces. I'll be back in a minute."

CHAPTER 31

COUNTDOWN

Bob walked back into the kitchen and appeared to be deep in thought. Mary looked up and said, "Must not have been a Eureka moment since you are still fully clothed. Don't keep us in suspense. What did you learn?"

"There's only one thing in the barn that has a serial number and that is an old John Deere tractor. The serial number is 69474. But I have no idea how that is a helpful clue toward finding the mysterious bunker."

Leta started figuring on the table with her finger. "I think I may have it," she said. "But first, was there anything unusual about the serial plate on the tractor?"

Bob hesitated, then said, "Well, it almost looked like someone had altered the numbers on the plate. I figured that it was just a mis-stamp at the factory that was corrected with an over-stamp. Why did you ask?"

"I watched carefully when you were picking the safe lock downstairs. The combination was 47-49-6. And, strangely enough, the altered serial number on the tractor is that same number backwards."

Mary said, "Leta, you are just too smart."

Leta said modestly, "I took an IQ test at school. The counselor said I tested very high, but it was best for me not to know the score. But, if you want to talk about smart, Wilbur may have been disturbed and paranoid, but he was absolutely the most intelligent person that I have ever been around."

Bob commented, "I can believe that. My mother said that Wilbur was accepted at MIT when he was sixteen and graduated summa cum laude in theoretical physics in three years. He volunteered for the Army right after college and went into the infantry."

Mary asked, "So how does knowing that the serial number of the tractor is the safe combination code backwards help us find the mythical bunker?"

Bob replied, "My guess is that it means that there is something else in the safe that we missed. Let's finish this incredible gourmet breakfast of Spam and scrambled eggs, then go look in the safe again."

Mary glared at Bob. "Well, your Majesty, Leta and I will let you put on a frilly dress and morph into Betty Crocker. Then we'll see what you can whip up out of the survival food choices in the store room and freezer for the next meal. And there better be candlelight and a harpist playing in the background."

Bob smiled slyly and said, "Must be that special time of month that makes someone here so sensitive and crabby."

Mary grabbed her coffee cup and splashed Bob in the chest with the hot coffee.

Bob winced and shouted loudly, "Call in the chopper! I need to go to the closest burn unit!"

Mary replied, "Just be glad that I didn't aim a lot lower. Poor baby—I think that you will survive without a skin graft."

Leta laughed. "Looks like I'm the only adult at the table. You children need to calm down."

After breakfast, Mary, Leta, and Bob trooped to the storeroom and opened the concealed door to get back into the weapons room. Bob went to the safe and carefully dialed in the three numbers, but to everyone's surprise, the door to the safe would not open.

"That's really weird," Bob exclaimed. "I know that I put the correct numbers in."

Leta said, "I have a crazy idea. Try the backward numbers from the tractor serial plate."

Bob seemed very dubious. "I see no way that the combination could change from one day to the next. But, let's give it a shot." He dialed in the backward numbers, hesitated for dramatic effect, then shouted, "Shazam!" The safe door slowly swung open.

Mary patted Leta on the back. "You, my dear young lady, are clearly Mensa quality."

Suddenly, a raspy recorded voice began to speak. "German thieves get blown up. If you don't know the code, you will soon join your cowardly brothers in hell.… Twenty-four, twenty-three…"

Bob ordered, "You two need to get out of here now! I'm going to try a couple of things. If neither is right, I'll be running right behind you!"

Mary and Leta turned and dashed up the stairs into the storage room. Bob was feverishly turning the safe dial. The initial code was a failure as was the backwards set of numbers.

"Eleven, ten…"

Bob was wracking his brain and about to bolt for the stairs—then he rapidly began dialing again.

"Four, three, two…" Miraculously, the countdown stopped.

Bob shouted to Mary and Leta, "Should be safe to come back down now."

The two women slowly descended the stairs.

Mary said, "How did you stop the countdown? We heard it get down to two."

Bob replied, "I tried the original numbers and the backwards one, but they did not work. Then a sudden idea came to me, and I dialed in Wilbur's birth date—6-6-24."

Mary asked, "How in the world did you know your uncle's birthdate?"

"Actually, pretty simple. I visited Wilbur in early June just after I graduated from high school. We shot some of his guns on June 6th, and my uncle mentioned that it was his birthday and also the date of the Normandy invasion in 1944. We talked a little, and I learned that my uncle was 20 when he waded ashore in Normandy off one of the early landing crafts. A little simple head math told me the date had to be June 6, 1924. Fortunately, 6-6-24 were the magic numbers."

Leta asked, "Do you think that there really are some rigged explosives?"

"I sure didn't want to find out," Bob said. "But Uncle Wilbur obviously knew a great deal about blowing things up. With his physics background, I have no doubt that he could set up a countdown clock hooked up to a hand grenade or dynamite."

"What next?" Mary asked.

"Let's take all these stacks of money out and see what might be behind them. I think that we may be close to finding the location of the secret bunker. Supposedly there are more weapons in the bunker. If by chance we find a mortar tube, we may be able to scare the surveillance plane off and cancel our risky arson trip to the Barlow airfield in the dead of the night."

CHAPTER 32

CLAUSTROPHOBIA

There was an amazing amount of cash in the vault. As the stacks of hundred-dollar bills were removed, there was room enough to walk inside. Mary and Leta could stand up, but Bob had to bow his head. Once all of the money had been stacked on the floor outside the vault, the back wall could be seen.

"Oh, no," groaned Bob. "Not another combination lock."

There was a circular, metal door about waist high in the wall with a large combination dial. Bob got down on his knees and began slowly moving the dial.

"Another tough one!" he exclaimed in exasperation after several minutes of work.

Leta asked, "Is it feel or sound, or both, that lets you know when you are on a proper number?"

"It's usually a slight resistance that is felt. But it can be really subtle."

"I asked because I could hear an occasional, very faint sound as you moved the dial. Were you or Mary able to hear the sound?"

Both Bob and Mary shook their heads no.

Leta continued, "My hearing is really acute. I'm the only person I know who can hear a dog whistle. Turn the dial again slowly, and I'll say 'stop' when I hear the sound."

Bob slowly resumed turning the dial. "Stop," Leta said. "You were at 42 in the dial when I heard the sound."

Bob spun the dial and stopped on 42. "I heard the sound again there," Leta said.

Once Leta had pinpointed a number, Bob could feel a very slight hesitation of the dial. In five minutes all three numbers had been identified. After entering the last number, Bob opened the door to reveal a dark tunnel that was only three feet in diameter. The walls were corrugated metal like a large drainage pipe.

Mary asked, "Anyone here have claustrophobia? That's going to be a pretty tight fit. Wonder how long the tunnel goes?"

Bob replied, "No fear of small places here. Leta, would you run up to the kitchen and get the flashlight by the sink?"

Once Leta returned, Bob shined the light into the tunnel. He said, "There's a bend in the tunnel about ten feet in. No telling how much longer the tunnel is after the bend. But before we all clamor to see who can be the first junior explorer, I'm going to run to the kitchen and get a broom, and…"

Before Bob could finish the sentence, Leta was dashing back upstairs to the kitchen. When she returned, Bob took the broom and sent it bouncing down the tunnel with a hard shove.

"Clang!" There was a loud metallic sound as a guillotine blade dropped down from the top of the tube about six feet into the tunnel. The blade sliced the broom handle in two.

Mary exclaimed, "Thank God one of us didn't blunder into the tunnel and lose our heads!"

Bob wedged himself into the tunnel and started crawling slowly forward. When he reached the blade, Bob flattened it on the floor of the tunnel.

Mary winced and asked, "Are you sure, Wood… I mean Bob."

"I'll be OK, Mary," Bob replied. "I'll keep throwing this half of the broom handle ahead of me to check for booby traps."

The light from Bob's flashlight bounced off the tunnel walls until he reached the bend. Mary and Leta could hear the broom hit the wall of the tunnel one more time before Bob and his light disappeared. There were scraping sounds followed shortly by a soft thump. Then there was silence.

Suddenly Bob shouted back, "Holy crap! You won't believe what's here! Come join me. You need to know that after the bend, the tunnel goes straight down for a short distance. You'll have to brace yourself with your feet and hands on the wall of the tunnel. When the tunnel ends, there's a five foot drop to the floor. It's pitch black down here except for my flashlight. I'll shine it on the floor so you both can see where to land."

CHAPTER 33

UNDER THE TARP

Mary and Leta followed Bob's path down the narrow tunnel. Using his flashlight spot on the floor, they both made the drop without difficulty. Once they were standing by Bob, he used the flashlight to sweep the large space. There was a huge supply of weapons and shells as well as a number of metal storage cabinets and shelves.

Bob said, "We need some real light in here. There's bound to be power since when I shine the light up, I see sodium vapor lamps on the ceiling." Bob searched the wall near the spot where the tunnel ended.

"Found a switch. Here goes. Hope that this is not a trip switch to a bomb that will blow us all up." He paused, then said loudly, "Let there be light." A reddish glow began emanating from a number of bulbs on the ceiling. Slowly the reddish color gave way to monochromatic yellow light that illuminated the entire area.

The three people slowly looked around the space with awe. There were weapons of all sorts. On one extensive wall there were shelves of canned foods and dry goods as well as several hundred Mason jars of water.

Mary said, "Just take a look—the walls and ceiling are all reinforced concrete. This bunker could probably withstand bombing from the air. How Wilbur could engineer something like this way out in the desert is beyond me."

Bob replied, "Money talks, and Wilbur must have had more cash than a New York bank."

Leta spoke up and said, "Is anybody but me wondering how all the weapons and supplies got down here in the first place? No way that they could have come down the tunnel."

Bob replied, "I was just wondering the same thing. There has to be another entrance somewhere that is very well concealed."

Mary started wandering around the bunker looking for a possible exit. "Hey, look," she said. "There's a large tarp covering something way back in the corner."

All three of them walked over to the corner. Bob pulled the tarp off and gave a little gasp. Under the tarp was a large, sand-colored dune buggy that appeared to be in pristine condition. There were armor plates on the side and back. The tires were inflated and showed almost no wear.

"Yikes!" exclaimed Bob. "Uncle Wilbur was well prepared if he had to make a sudden getaway. That buggy has a Corvette engine that probably has been souped up. It also has heavy duty shocks. I bet that baby can really go."

Mary asked, "But how in the heck would he ever get out of this bunker if he needed to exit in a hurry?"

Bob asked himself, "I wonder if that buggy will run." Bob opened the door and sat in the driver's seat. "Hmm. No key. But I can hot-wire anything on the road." He reached under the dash and began to fiddle. Suddenly, the engine came to life with a throaty roar.

Mary said, "That's great, but don't run it too long and asphyxiate all of us."

Leta chimed in, "When Bob turned the lights on, I heard the faint sound of a motor. There are several vents in the ceiling. There must be an exhaust fan somewhere."

Bob killed the engine. "This dune buggy would be perfect if we have to make a nighttime visit to the airfield. We have to find an exit or we'll all have to climb back up the tube."

Bob walked over to where there was a pile of military equipment. "Great! Here's a mortar tube as well as a few shells. There are two that have been labelled with white paint 'Flash/Frag.'"

Leta asked, "So, what does that mean?"

Bob answered, "Mortar shells usually explode on impact, but some shells can be set to go off at a certain distance. These shells are unusual since when they explode, there is a blinding flash as well as small pieces of metallic flak that cover a large area. Hitting a plane up in the air is nearly impossible, but if a plane were moving slow enough, I might be able to lead it and give the pilot such an unpleasant experience that he wouldn't want to come back. If that plane buzzes the compound again, I plan to give it a try."

Mary said, "We need to discover how to get out of this place without hoisting ourselves back up the tube. There has to be a concealed door somewhere that the dune bubby could fit through."

Bob walked over to the tube and started to grasp it to see how hard it would be to pull himself up when Leta shouted, "Stop!"

Bob hesitated and asked, "What's the problem?"

Leta responded, "I just saw a funny reflection from the end of the tube that made me think of razor blades."

Bob looked closely at the tube and said, "Leta, you saved me from getting my hands sliced up. There are a series of sharp blades welded to the outside of the tube for the first foot or so. Getting back inside this tube is going to be tricky. I wonder if there are any other nasty surprises."

Bob reached above the blades and tested his weight on the tube. There was a small staccato blast, and the tube separated at the bend. Bob fell to the floor with the bottom part of the tube. He got up and said, "This may be like one of those old B-grade horror movies with a spooky hotel that you can check into, but you can't check out."

Mary said, "Let's get to work and find the hidden exit. I'm not wanting to celebrate a lot of birthdays down here."

CHAPTER 34

THERMOSTAT MAGIC

Bob looked up at the end of the tube which was left after the lower part of the tube separated with the explosion and fell to the ground. "Even if we found a way to get high enough to reach the remaining part of the tube, it would do no good. The incendiary melted the end of the tube, and it has collapsed. There is no way we could pry it open. We need to find the other exit or we will be singing Happy Birthday multiple times to Mary."

Leta said, "There has to be a space big enough to accommodate the hot-rod dune buggy, or Wilbur would have had no way to escape from here in case, as he often feared, the Germans launched a massive attack on the compound."

Mary said, "Agreed. And I think that wherever the exit is, it most likely ends up somewhere inside the compound. We need to walk around down here and look carefully for anything that suggests a fake wall."

Bob headed toward one of the side walls and began tapping, but could not elicit a hollow sound that might indicate a fake segment of wall. "Nothing suspicious here," he announced. "But, wait. Here's something very odd. There is a thermostat on the wall higher than I can reach. This bunker is far enough down in the ground that it would not really need heating or cooling."

Bob moved three of the wooden shell boxes near the wall and stacked them on the floor. Standing on the boxes he was able to reach the thermostat. "The reading on the thermostat is 37.1 degrees Celsius—that would be 98.8 degrees Fahrenheit. No way that's the correct temperature."

"I bet that you have to plug in a specific temperature to make an exit open up," Leta ventured.

Mary responded, "Ugh. It could take forever to stumble onto that magic number."

Leta thought for a minute. "The current number is 37.1, so it's probably safe to assume that we need three numbers. Now all we have to do is figure out what Wilbur's wily brain would have chosen. He told me once that the compound had lots of secrets that would be hard to figure out, but there were a few easy ones. Let's assume for a minute that this one is easy."

Mary said, "What about something related to the word 'out?' If we use the three letters and give them a number related to their position in the alphabet, that would give us the sequence—15-21-20. Now the trick is to reduce it to three numbers. What do you think, Bob?"

Bob answered, "Let's use the first one of each number pair which would give us a temperature setting of 12.2 degrees. Here we go." Bob reset the temperature, but nothing happened. He next tried 51.0, using the second number in each alphabet position couplet. For the next few minutes, he plugged in various combinations of the six numbers, but to no avail.

Leta suggested, "I have another idea. Let's take the first three letters of 'dune' and convert them to alphabet sequence numbers. D would be 4, U would be 21, and N would be 14. Bob, try 42.1 degrees." Nothing happened.

Bob said with irritation, "This is like trying to calculate how many angels can dance on the head of a pin!"

Leta responded, "I think that we are on the right track. Try 42.1 backwards, which would be 12.4 degrees Celsius." Nothing. "How about taking the last three letters of 'dune' and convert to alphabet numbers—which would be 21-14-5. Bob, please try 21.5 degrees."

Bob replied with exasperation, "I'm about ready to use some of the heavy-duty weapons here to blast a hole in the wall. Here goes 21.5 degrees." Bob moved the thermostat. There was a moment of quiet, then there was a slow rumbling sound.

"Run!" Bob shouted. "It sounds like something's about to explode!"

All three of them sprinted away from the wall and just escaped being hit with pieces of concrete as part of the wall disintegrated, sending a cloud of concrete shrapnel in all directions. Fortunately, none of the large pieces struck them. When the dust cleared, there was an opening in the wall that revealed a car ramp that led upwards to a concrete platform.

Bob, Mary, and Leta walked up the steep ramp carefully and discovered an underground tunnel large enough to accommodate the dune buggy. Bob took the flashlight out of his pocket and shined it ahead of them as they followed the passageway for about thirty yards before it began to ascend and dead ended in front of an iron grate.

"The road to nowhere that ends in a portcullis like the ones guarding feudal castles," Mary said.

"That thing is bound to move up, down, or sideways," Leta commented.

Bob replied, "Frankly, I'm getting fed up with my uncle's puzzles."

Leta added, "If Wilbur were fleeing from some mythical Germans who were overrunning the compound, he would not want to delay here having to do something time consuming before hauling ass across the desert."

"Great thought," Bob said. "I bet when the dune buggy approaches the gate, the portcullis gets an infrared signal from the vehicle that causes the gate to open. I'm going back down the little roadway and will drive the dune buggy up and see."

A few minutes later, Mary and Leta heard an engine sound approaching. The headlights of the dune buggy came into view. The passageway was too narrow for them to press to the side, so they stood in front of the iron gate as Bob slowly inched the dune buggy closer. Just when Mary and Leta thought that they would have to jump on the front bumper of the vehicle to keep from being sardined, there was a mechanical sound, and the gate moved to the side to reveal a wall of bales of hay.

"We're about to end up in the very back of the barn," Leta said. "I don't think that Wilbur ever had any livestock, so I always found these hay bales to be a mystery. If we move them, Bob can drive the dune buggy right into the barn."

Bob said, "Well, Mademoiselle Mary, looks like you won't have to celebrate even one birthday in the secret bunker. Now it's time to make plans for the future. If the snooper airplane shows up again, I want to try a couple of flash/frag mortar shells to see if that closes down the airspace. But if that is not a successful deterrent, then we need to plan a late-night visit to the airfield near Barlow and arrange for an unfortunate fire. The dune buggy will be perfect for the trip."

CHAPTER 35

DOPPELGANGER

The dune buggy was parked in the barn behind bales of hay ready for a possible arson trip to the airfield. Leta was very insistent that she go along if the surveillance plane continued to fly over the compound. Bob and Mary were reluctant to let Leta be put in possible danger, but relented after she agreed to work even harder on her combat and arms skills. Leta was not only smart, but was very athletic and had cat-like reflexes. She had a gift for weapons and soon was hitting targets at 20 yards routinely with a pistol.

Two weeks later Bob and Mary were sitting in the kitchen early one morning after Bob had done his routine 200 setups and 200 pushups and Mary had finished thirty minutes of agility and stretching exercises. Bob said, "No question that Leta is exceptional in many ways. I still feel like we may be corrupting a minor teaching her to fight and shoot."

Mary said, "It's hard to corrupt someone who has been raped multiple times ever since they were fourteen. Leta and I have had some private talks. You cannot imagine what abuse she and the other young girls have been put through. I'll spare you the awful details and simply say that no body opening was off limits for the customers willing to pay enough. Leta overheard Sadie tell one man who had asked how old Leta was, 'If they're old enough to bleed, they're old enough to screw.' We need to make Leta able to protect herself from the slimeballs of the world."

"Ugh. Makes you sick to your stomach. We really have to get Leta's friends out of that whorehouse hell hole."

In the distance the drone of a plane engine was heard. "Oh, oh," Bob said. "Time for me to go into action. I've got one of the mortar tubes and two flash/frag shells on the porch. You and Leta need to stay out of sight. I'll put on my big Wilbur hat and overalls and get ready to send a little welcoming message skyward if the plane comes close."

Bob quickly transformed himself into a poor man's Wilbur doppelganger and waited near the porch. He squeezed off a couple of AK-47 rounds and shook his fist as the plane passed overhead at 200 feet. The pilot did a brief wing waggle as he flew off as if to say, "Screw you! I'm not afraid of your little pop gun." Then the pilot made a turn over the desert and returned to swoop even lower over the compound. Bob was waiting and dropped the first shell into the mortar tube, trying to lead the plane. The shell exploded well ahead of the plane with a huge flash and cloud of flak.

With an engine roar the plane climbed steeply until it went into a stall. The pilot expertly pointed the nose of the plane downward and picked up air speed and descended rapidly, heading straight for where Wilbur stood. At the last second the pilot aborted the dive and climbed off to the east and disappeared.

Bob walked back into the kitchen. Leta had joined Mary at the kitchen table. "That last pass sounded like a kamikaze pilot was about to crash into the house!" Mary exclaimed. "I heard the mortar explosion. Did you get close to the plane?"

Bob replied, "I was way ahead of it since the plane slowed down a lot after I dropped the shell into the tube. The pilot didn't seem fazed by the flash or the flak shrapnel. The way he stalled the plane on purpose then dive-bombed the house makes me think the pilot almost has to be ex-military."

Leta smiled and said, "Looks like your flash and flak plan is not going to work. When do we fire up the dune buggy and head for the airport?"

Bob replied, "I need a little time to plan and consider unexpected problems and how to deal with them. For example, what if there is a vicious guard dog patrolling the airfield, or even a human guard? And how would we handle a plane or planes being locked up in a hangar? Can we identify the correct plane if there are in fact more than one?"

Mary said, "Leta, Bob is trying to teach you the importance of careful planning before going off on a mission that may entail real danger. Do you know the difference between strategy and tactics?"

Leta replied quickly, "Easy peasy. Strategy is an overall plan, and tactics are decisions made pretty much on the fly as occasions arise."

Bob nodded his head and said, "Correct, Leta. Now, I have a little homework for you. I want you to be prepared to tell us tomorrow at breakfast what strategy you would plan for three possible situations that we might encounter at the air field at 2 AM:

"Number one—There is an armed guard at the field.

"Number two—There are three planes parked, and they all look alike.

"Number three—We decide to commit a little arson to knock the plane out of commission. What is the safest and quickest way to do this?"

Leta said with assurance, "I am on it."

$* * * *$

The next morning Leta was up early and had scrambled eggs and hot cakes ready for Mary and Bob. Mary sat down at the table and said, "Smells good, Leta. Among your many talents, Leta, you can cook. One day you'll make a great wife for some lucky guy."

Leta started to tear up, then sat down at the table, put her face into her hands, and began to sob. Mary got up and walked over to Leta and put a hand on her shoulder.

Between sobs Leta gasped, "I'm too dirty. I could never marry a nice man."

Bob came into the kitchen and saw Leta crying. He started to speak, but Mary put a finger to her lips and motioned for him to leave. Then Mary sat down by Leta and began to stroke her hair. "Wrong thing for me to say, Leta. I am so sorry." There was a moment of silence, then Mary said softly, "I know what it's like to be raped. That happened to me in college, and I never wanted to be with a man until I met Bob. One day down the road, you will also meet the right man, and your past will no longer be very important. I promise you this."

Leta lifted her head. Mary took a paper napkin and wiped Leta's eyes. "The problem for you in the future will continue to be how pretty and well-shaped you are. People like you and me are male sleaze-bag magnets. But Bob and I will make certain that you can take care of yourself."

When Bob no longer heard sobbing or female voices, he came back into the room and said, "I'm hungry enough to eat a horny toad."

Leta managed a little smile and said, "Not to correct you, Bob, but the correct term is horned toad. A horny toad is one that is oversexed."

"My bad," Bob answered with a smile. "Let's eat, and then we can see how well you can handle the three scenarios that I presented for you to consider."

CHAPTER 36

IMPORTANT QUESTIONS

Once breakfast was over, Bob refilled his coffee cup and sat back down at the table. "OK, Leta, let's see how well you did your homework. First off, let's assume that we reach airfield and see an armed guard walking the perimeter. What would you do?"

Leta hesitated, then said, "Shoot him."

"Bzzzz!" Mary interrupted. "Wrong answer, Leta. First, we would never take out a person who was not threatening our lives. Second, getting close enough to the guard to have a sure kill might be difficult. Third, the sound of a gunshot might bring other bad guys to the scene."

"I was planning to use a silencer on the pistol."

Bob joined in, "The sound of an average pistol firing is around 160 decibels. A silencer at best only knocks the sound down 20 decibels. So, the gun fire could still be heard for quite a distance."

Mary said, "Bob and I would likely choose to immobilize the guard by luring him out into the dark and overpowering him. Then we would tie him up and use a gag. But if the guard shot at us, we would fire back with the intent to disable or kill."

Bob continued, "Let's move on to the second problem of there being more than one plane of the same type. How would we know which plane to eliminate?"

Leta responded, "Now that's a question for dummies. Just look for the registration number on the plane near the tail."

Bob replied, "Not so simple. You would have to know the identification number of the plane that has been buzzing us."

Leta tapped her head with a smile and answered, "The tail number of the plane that has been flying over is N-XQE4. I peeked out the kitchen window once using one of Wilbur's binoculars."

Mary laughed and said, "Touché! Leta gets a perfect score on that question."

Bob agreed, "Good call, Leta. Now let's move on to the problem of making the plane unable to fly again. Perhaps by fire, or maybe by another means."

Leta said, "The first thing that I have to know is whether the destruction of the plane has to look like an accident or not."

"Perfect question, Leta," Bob answered. "It would be very difficult to make any sort of fire look like an act of God or nature. So, let's say, all we want to do is eliminate the plane in the best way possible."

Leta thought a minute, then responded, "Why not just poke a hole in one of the wing gas tanks, drip a big puddle on the ground, throw a match, and run."

Mary chimed in and said, "No way that we would want to be anywhere near the plane when it goes up in flames. Ideally, we should be several miles away."

Bob said, "Let me give you some help, Leta. In the bunker there are all sorts of war salvage weapons, including several satchel charges. These are dynamite devices. In a perfect world, a satchel charge is detonated remotely with a radio signal, but all the ones Wilbur acquired have fuses. We need a way to light the fuse when we are long gone."

Leta looked puzzled, then said, "How about using a punk stick?"

Bob replied, "Good thought, but I'm going to show you something more reliable. When I was here several years ago, Wilbur allowed himself one filter cigarette a day. Do you know if there are any still around?"

Leta answered, "Wilbur stopped smoking cigarettes when I came here since the tobacco made my eyes burn. There are several cartons left in the pantry. I'll go get a pack."

When Leta returned, Bob took a cigarette and used a toothpick to poke through the filter and into the tobacco for a half inch. "Here's what to do, Leta. I will push the satchel fuse through the filter and into the tobacco, then use a piece of duct tape to secure the fuse. Once the end of the cigarette is lighted, we should have several minutes to jump back into the dune buggy and head for home. Of course, a wind could make the cigarette burn faster, so we would want to shelter the cigarette from the wind."

Leta nodded and said approvingly, "Neat. So, what night will we send the plane to aircraft purgatory?"

Mary said, "There will be a new moon in three days when the moon is totally dark. That should be a perfect night. But Leta needs more work on Krav Maga before we let her join us. She has really made fast progress. Come on, Leta, let's you and me knock out the dishes while Bob moves hay bales and goes back to the bunker to bring up a satchel charge. After our kitchen labor we can work more on how to disable opponents and leave them hurting."

CHAPTER 37

THE BEST-LAID PLANS...

It was shortly after midnight, but no one at the compound had been to bed. The modified dune buggy was parked in front of the barn. Bob had carefully placed the satchel charge in the back of the vehicle. He and Mary had checked their pistols out carefully. Both of them, as well as Leta, were wearing dark clothes and had blacked their faces with burned cork. Leta had insisted on going on the mission, and Bob and Mary had reluctantly agreed on the stipulation that she stay in the dune buggy while they slipped onto the airfield.

Shortly before 1 AM, the three of them drove out of the compound. Leta jumped out to close and lock the gate. With no moon it was very dark on the desert. Mary held a compass and was the navigator. Bob pointed the buggy due east. He commented, "Once we get closer to Barlow, there should be enough lights from the town to keep us on course. This machine with the big tires just eats the desert sand up. I don't think any normal vehicle could begin to keep up with us in a race in the desert."

A sudden wind blew up, spitting shards of sand in the faces of Bob, Mary, and Leta. Mary said, "Worse luck to have to head into a mini-haboob tonight. The particles really sting. I should have kept my mouth shut since my teeth are now gritty."

Bob said, "Actually, a good stiff wind is our friend. These huge tires make a big imprint into the sand that would leave a trail from the compound to the airfield and back. But if the wind keeps gusting this hard, blowing sand will cover up our tracks."

The only sound for the next few minutes was the noise of the Corvette V8 engine effortlessly turning over. Leta asked, "The motor in this thing is pretty loud. Won't people hear us coming at the airfield?"

Bob answered, "Wilbur's mechanical genius and attention to detail is nothing short of amazing. He put a bypass in the exhaust system to have full engine power when needed. If we want to be in a stealth mode, I can simply flip this lever here and close the bypass which routes the exhaust through the muffler, and—Voila!—very little motor noise."

Mary squinted her eyes in the darkness and said, "In the distance you can now see a faint glow from the lights of Barlow. Bob, if you just head for the lights, we can put the compass away."

The buggy kept churning effortlessly through the sand. Near Barlow, Bob closed the exhaust bypass, which made the engine very quiet. He said, "I'm betting that the airfield is close to town so that the esteemed brothel clientele who fly in won't have to schlep too far across the desert."

Leta said, "No schlepping at all. The whorehouse has its own fancy limo. The big bucks gamblers and party boys are very well taken care of."

Bob said, "Let's head north about a mile before reaching town." He slowed down so that there was very little engine noise. "There's a light ahead that I'm guessing is part of the airfield." After slowly driving another hundred yards, Bob killed the engine. He and Mary quietly got out of the dune buggy. Bob took the satchel charge. The two of them separated themselves by thirty feet and began to carefully walk toward the field.

When Bob and Mary got closer, they saw a high metal pole that had a sodium lamp on top that gave out a sickly, yellow light that pointed toward two small aircraft parked and tethered on the field. There was no obvious guard and, so far, no snarling watch dog as they drew closer. The single light was bright enough to dimly illuminate the fuselage of each plane. Bob looked at the identification on the tail of each plane and then pointed to one of them.

Mary stayed back with her Makarov pistol drawn as Bob approached the plane. He knelt down beside the aircraft and set the satchel charge underneath one of the wings. Quickly Bob inserted the fuse into the filter of the cigarette. Just as he was about to light the improvised delay fuse, he heard muffled screaming. Mary immediately dashed back toward the dune buggy. As she approached the vehicle, she was blinded by a bright light.

A harsh voice shouted, "Don't move or I'll shoot this little bitch who escaped! Drop your pistol, now!" Mary let her Makarov fall to the sand. "Put your hands above your head and walk very slowly toward me. Any tricks and I'll blow this little whore's brains out."

As Mary walked closer, she could see that the man had Leta in a one-arm chokehold with a gun jammed against the side of her head. He had a large flashlight in the hand of the arm around her neck.

Mary looked at the man and said, "You must be Carlos the chicken-shit coward who abuses little girls."

The man snarled and pointed his pistol at Mary. "Say goodnight, Sweetheart." Just as he pulled the trigger there was a loud explosion that caused his hand to jerk and his shot to whiz by Mary's head. Leta suddenly lunged forward very hard and used one leg to trip Carlos, causing him to stumble and lose his chokehold and drop the flashlight. He regained his balance and began firing wildly in the darkness toward where he had last seen Mary.

Mary crawled back to feel for her pistol in the sand as a hail of bullets danced around her. There was a sudden burst of light as Carlos recovered his flashlight and rapidly swept the ground to find Mary. Just as he pointed his pistol toward her, there was the loud roar of engine approaching very fast. Carlos turned quickly and got only one shot off before the dune buggy struck him. There was a loud thud as he was lifted ten feet into the air. He came tumbling back to earth and landed on a large rock, which split his head wide open with a burst of blood and brains.

Leta slammed on the brakes, and the dune buggy slid to a stop. Mary ran to the vehicle and jumped in. Bob sprinted in out of the darkness and slid into the back seat.

"Hit it, Leta! Time to haul ass! But kill the noise!"

Leta closed the exhaust bypass, and the engine gave a small growl as she popped the clutch. The wheels spit sand, and the buggy sped off into the desert.

Bob said breathlessly, "Sorry that I couldn't help you, Mary. It was so dark that I was afraid to fire for fear of hitting you or Leta."

Mary replied, "I fully understand. At least that rat Carlos is dead. And judging from the flame in the background, the surveillance plane is toast. Great job, Leta, in knocking Carlos off balance and causing him to drop the flashlight."

Bob asked, "Leta, how in the world did you know how to hot wire the dune buggy?" Leta answered simply, "I saw you do it once."

Mary asked, "How did you learn to drive so well?"

"Wilbur taught me, and I drove his pickup truck around the desert a lot practicing."

Bob said, "We still have big gusts of wind with blowing sand. That should do a nice job of covering our tire tracks. Once things settle down, we need to decide how to rescue your friends, Leta. Things are likely to get pretty hot in Brothel City when Carlos and the burned-out plane are found. My guess is the man who owns the hotel and gambling establishment will want to bring some heavies in for protection. We'll need to lie low for a few days."

CHAPTER 38

VAN GOGH IN THE DESERT

The return trip to the compound with Leta driving and Mary using a compass to help navigate in the pitch black was uneventful except for the continued swirls of blowing sand. Bob was sitting in the back and kept looking toward Barlow to make certain that they were not being followed. "I think we made a clean getaway," he said loudly to overcome the noise of the engine and the wind. "But it won't take a Harvard scholar to figure out that Uncle Wilbur's compound must have been involved in the plane explosion and the demise of Carlos."

By 2:30 AM the dune buggy was safely ensconced in the barn, and Bob, Mary, and Leta were in bed. Mary and Leta enjoyed some catch-up sleep, but Bob was up early to exercise and to look at Wilbur's deuce and a half. There was an air compressor in the barn that allowed Bob to pump up all six tires on the Army truck. He checked the oil level and was amazed to find that the dipstick showed only one quart low out of the standard 22 quarts of oil in the huge crankcase. There were a number of cans of 30W oil lined up on a shelf in the barn that made topping off the oil easy.

Bob climbed up into the cab and tried to start the diesel engine. There was a brief grinding sound, then nothing. The twin 12-volt batteries both had corrosion on the terminals. Bob cleaned the terminals then hooked one battery up to a charger.

Later in the day with both batteries charged, Bob was able to start the deuce and a half and drive around the compound and out into the desert. Mary and Leta took turns learning to handle the truck and soon mastered all of the gears.

Bob was watching as Mary stopped the deuce near the barn. Mary said, "It takes off like a herd of constipated turtles, but once it gets going, it can hit 65 miles an hour. It's kind of fun to work through all of the gears and play with the low and high range shifter. Do you have any idea how far it can go on a full tank of diesel?"

Bob thought a minute, then responded. "The tank holds 50 gallons, and with an average of 10 miles a gallon, a range of 500 miles would be reasonable. I can think of no definite plans for the truck right now, but I have a feeling that at some point this monster may help keep us alive."

For several days all was quiet at the compound. Bob and Mary kept expecting unfriendly visitors and kept a sharp surveillance. The guard dog now knew Mary and Bob and was no longer ever kenneled. He served as an early warning system twenty-four hours a day with his keen hearing and sense of smell.

Bob decided that the safest vehicle to take to Barlow when shopping needed to be done was Wilbur's old Dodge Power Wagon pickup. He and Mary had kept the extra set of plates from the VW van that were not used. The plates were from Chihuahua, Mexico. Bob replaced the Texas plates with those from Mexico. He then found a power sander and removed all loose black paint from the Power Wagon. In the barn he found several cans of white lacquer paint. It took him several hours, but he repainted the Dodge, not trying to be perfect.

The following morning the paint was dry. Bob found that the Power Wagon started immediately and ran well. It had large tires that were perfect for driving on sand. After breakfast Bob had Mary and Leta stand on the back porch while he drove up in the repainted van.

Mary said, "Yikes! It looks like some slow-witted person with a bad tremor did the color change from black to white."

Leta added, "That thing looks like a first-class trash mobile. It's going to stand out like a sore thumb if you ever take it to town."

"Oh, ye of little faith," Bob responded. "It is now good for one trip into Barlow. If it ever needs to make another trip to town, it will be dark green, not white, and it will have Texas plates again. Just call me the Vincent van Gogh of car styling."

"Oh, goodie!" Leta exclaimed. "I want to be the one to cut off your left ear!"

"No way, José," Bob replied. "I like my body parts just the way they are, thank you."

Later in the day Mary signaled Bob to follow her to their bedroom. Once they were inside, Mary closed the door. Bob smiled and asked, "Is this an invitation for a quick afternooner?"

"You wish. No, this is something serious. Leta confided in me earlier today that she is spotting, and that she is certain that her periods are about to resume. When she and her two friends were being rented out at the whorehouse, Sophie the madam made them take Enovid birth control pills which are so high in estrogen that they shut down the girls' menstruation and kept them in service at all times. The bottom line is that Leta is going to need some tampons."

Bob said, "I think that I can make myself disheveled enough that I can safely slip into town driving the reconfigured Dodge Power Wagon and find some tampons at the grocery store. If there is anything else you want, just make me a list."

Bob walked to the kitchen and found Leta making sandwiches for supper. She looked up when Bob entered and said, "Prepare yourself for gourmet fare tonight—Vienna sausage sandwiches. Yum. But I am also going to serve some nutritious canned spinach as well as some chocolate chip cookies that I am going to whip out."

Bob replied, "Beats K-rations. I'm going in to town tomorrow morning for a little shopping. Let me know if you need anything from the grocery store."

Leta hesitated, then said, "Well, there is one thing…"

"Say no more," Bob answered. "I can read your mind and am a specialist in feminine hygiene products."

Leta's face got slightly red. She asked, "How is it possible that a person who has been through all I have can still be sensitive about having periods?"

Mary entered the kitchen in time to hear Leta's question. "We still live in a Victorian society where discussing normal body functions is taboo. Bob knows exactly what you need."

Bob said to Leta, "Tomorrow's Monday. I want to go to Barlow early while most people are still at home. Do you know what time the grocery store opens?"

"Unless the time has changed, the store opens at 7:30 AM. There is a small pharmacy inside the store that may not have a pharmacist until 8:00."

Mary looked at Bob and asked, "Do you want me to ride shotgun?"

"Not a good idea for us to be seen together. Randy and his henchmen are likely still around and will be looking for a man and woman together. I'll go armed and be very careful. If all is quiet, I may take a look around the hotel to help decide how we can rescue Leta's friends. The best plan may be for me to go there at night and pose as a customer looking for some fun with young women."

CHAPTER 39

TAMPON TROUBLE

Bob left the compound the next morning at 6:45 AM in the repainted Dodge Power Wagon. He had not shaved since leaving Langley and had grown a bushy beard. His hair was unkempt and covered his ears. The Dodge did very well in the sand, and Bob arrived in Barlow several minutes before the grocery store opened.

The weathered sign out front read, "Dalton's Grub and Gear." There was a stocky, middle-aged woman waiting outside the door. Bob decided to join her.

The woman gave him a suspicious look and said, "I was here first, so don't try to get ahead of me."

Bob conjured up a friendly smile and replied, "Not a chance, Ma'am. I'm in no hurry. You're out pretty early for shopping."

The woman's face softened a little. "I run the kitchen at the hotel. We were so busy over the weekend that I need some emergency food supplies."

Bob said, "I'm new around here, actually kind of passing through. Barlow looks like a quiet little town. Is there ever any excitement around here?"

The woman nodded her head and replied, "There's a lot that goes on in Barlow. A few days ago, someone blew up a small plane on the landing field in the middle of the night. One of the hotel guards apparently was run over at the field. They found him dead with his head busted open and his brains splattered everywhere."

"Oh my," Bob said. "Who would have done such a terrible thing?"

The woman shook her head and said, "We've got a rinky-dink sheriff who couldn't find his butt with both hands on a dark night. Everything has been kept awful quiet. But one thing changed in a hurry. The hotel just hired some big guy and two of his friends to work security at the hotel. They rolled into town in a big honking Lincoln Continental."

The door to the grocery store suddenly opened. The woman said, "Nice talking with you," as she hurried into the store and grabbed a small buggy. Bob followed slowly behind her and also took a buggy. He pulled a shopping list out of his pocket and slowly walked up and down the aisles finding the articles that Mary and Leta had requested. The store had an amazing variety of goods for such a small town.

The lady from the hotel filled her buggy quickly. She paid for her items and hastened out carrying two large bags. Bob located the sanitary napkins, but there were no tampons. No other customers had yet arrived. Bob went up to the clerk at the cash register and asked, "Where can I find tampons for my wife?"

The clerk appeared to be in his early sixties. He was heavy set with a pot belly that hung over his western belt. The man had thin, sandy hair that had seen its better days. His face had small residual scars from adolescent acne many years ago. The clerk appeared startled by Bob's question.

"We can't stock tampons on the shelf—city ordinance. You'll have to get them from the pharmacy in the back. The pharmacist is due any minute."

Bob said, "City ordinance? That's strange. How so?"

The clerk hesitated a minute and looked intently at Bob, as if deciding whether to continue the conversation or not. Then he answered slowly, "Yeah, it is a strange deal. You see there is only one church in town, and it's primitive Baptist. The members believe that only married woman should be able to get tampons. They think tampons cause unmarried women to lose their virginity. The pastor of the church is also the mayor. He and two other people make up the town council, and they make the rules. Only the pharmacist can sell tampons."

Bob shook his head and said, "Never, ever heard anything like that. Out of curiosity, who else is on the council?"

"Sadie, the lady who manages the hotel, is one member. She is in church on the front row every Sunday morning and is as fine a Christian woman as you could ever hope to meet. The third member was Carlos, who was in charge of guest services at the hotel. But he was recently killed in a tragic accident at the landing field in the middle of the night. Carlos was a little strange, but he often came to church with Sadie. Rumor is that Sadie always places a check for a thousand dollars in the collection plate every Sunday."

"Wow," Bob said as he looked up to see a man enter the front door and walk to the back of the store.

The clerk nodded his head. "That's Clem the pharmacist. He can be a little crabby some days."

Bob walked to the back of the store and arrived just as the pharmacist was raising the metal guard that covered the counter. He looked up at Bob disapprovingly. "We don't fill any prescriptions for narcotics or sedatives."

Bob smiled and replied, "Understood. I just need to buy some tampons for my wife, please. It's that time of the month for her."

The pharmacist looked intently at Bob again with obvious disapproval. "We take only cash at the pharmacy. No hot checks."

Bob answered, "No problem." He pulled a hundred-dollar bill out of his pocket.

The clerk said, "I need to see that bill up close."

Bob handed him the bill. The pharmacist held it up to the light, then tried to stretch it. He eyed Bob again. "I'll need you to sign a statement that the tampons are for a married woman. How many boxes do you need?"

Bob answered, "Me and my wife travel a lot, so how about several boxes."

Still holding the hundred-dollar bill, the clerk said, "Tampons are in short supply way out here. They are going to be very expensive. I only have five boxes."

Bob pulled out another hundred-dollar bill and gave it to the pharmacist. "How about two hundred dollars for the five boxes. Would that be fair?"

The clerk nodded and replied, "Not much profit for me in that deal, but I'll take it. And I think that we can forget about your needing to sign a statement." With a sly chuckle he added, "If your wife will be using these, looks like you'll be sleeping with mother thumb and her four daughters for a few days." The clerk reached under the counter and got the tampon boxes and put them into a paper bag. Just as Bob was placing the bag in his grocery cart, he looked up and saw a large man approaching him who was several inches taller than he was. The person was wearing expensive boots and had a black Stetson hat on with a rattlesnake band.

As Bob started to push his buggy away from the counter, the man said, in a deep voice, "Not so fast, sweetie. Are you trying to monopolize the tampon market for West Texas? I bet that those pussy sticks are for you and not for your whore wife. You're going to have to give all of the boxes except one back to Clem unless you want me to smash your face in."

Bob looked up at the man and said quietly, "Cowboy, I didn't come in here looking for trouble. Are you sure that you're big enough to mess with me?"

The man gave a deep throaty laugh and said, "Are you serious, asshole? I'm bigger and tougher than you could ever hope to be."

Bob looked at the man with a hard stare and said, "Last chance before you get hurt really bad, cowboy."

The large man launched a haymaker punch that Bob parried with his forearm and then delivered a fist to the man's abdomen that doubled him over. Almost instantly the cowboy recovered and stood up, but not before Bob grabbed one large arm and yanked it behind the man. The cowboy gave a loud groan as his shoulder separated with a loud crack. Cursing loudly, the man used his other hand to pop Bob's head back with a vicious slap to the face. Bob was momentarily staggered, which gave his opponent time to pull a razor blade knife out of his waist and start slashing wildly at Bob.

Bob was able to duck, but one slash opened his shirt in front and drew blood. He grabbed a can of peaches out of his buggy and rifled it at the cowboy, hitting him in the mouth and knocking several teeth out and causing him to drop his knife. Bob kicked the knife across the floor away from the man. Spitting blood, the man slumped against the wall.

Bob walked up close to him and said, "Life is full of choices, Cowboy. You just made a really bad choice. Now here's the next choice for you, either sit down on the floor and stay there until I am gone, or I'll need to send you to the hospital. You have exactly three seconds to make the right choice."

The man slowly sat down on the floor. Bob looked down at him and said, "In case you're wondering, yes, I am armed, and I am an expert marksman. Following me out would be your very worst possible choice of the day."

Bob rolled the buggy to the front and put a hundred-dollar bill on the counter in front of the wide-eyed clerk, then quickly bagged his groceries and headed out to the parking lot. Bob put the groceries in the back floorboard and drove east out of Barlow back toward the main highway. After a couple of miles, he veered off the road and into the desert and turned back toward the compound, giving a wide berth to Barlow. "Just another routine shopping day in Barlow," he mused to himself as the Dodge ate up the desert miles.

CHAPTER 40

MENAGE A TROIS

Bob drove up to the gate of the compound and honked his horn. In a moment Leta looked out a peep hole in the gate and muscled it slowly open. Bob steered the Dodge Power Wagon to the back porch and hopped out. Mary came out onto the porch and asked, "Any problems at all?"

Bob shook his head no and began to unload groceries.

Mary frowned and said, "Liar, liar, pants on fire. You've got a big bruise on your face. You didn't try to pinch some LOL's butt in the grocery store, did you?"

Leta walked up at that moment and asked, "What the heck is an LOL?"

Bob laughed and said, "It stands for 'little old lady.' And, Mary, the answer is that it was not an LOL—it was some super-stacked honey who works at the hotel."

Mary shook her head and said, "If that's true, you better wash your hand really well...." Then Mary stopped short and looked at Leta. "Sorry, that wasn't a nice thing to say."

Leta answered, "I'm not offended. All the sex workers got checked once a week by a sleazy doctor who seemed to enjoy his work a little too much. I never had a problem, but some of the older women got treated with penicillin for gonorrhea. Sadie always urged the clients to use condoms."

Mary said, "Leta, it sounds awful, but please spare us any further details."

"Sorry, Mary. Working in a whorehouse really dehumanizes a woman in a hurry."

Bob said, "Not to change the subject, but let's get all of the groceries into the house. Then I can tell you about what happened in town and about the little love tap on my face."

Once the groceries were stored, Bob, Mary, and Leta sat down at the table for coffee and some sweet rolls that Bob had brought home. Mary pointed at Bob impatiently and said, "Leta and I are waiting with bated breath for the gripping details of your adventure. Just don't embellish it."

Bob took a sip of coffee and said, "Let's see where best to begin.... After I ducked into a phone booth and stripped out of my suit and adjusted my cape...."

At this point both Mary and Leta began to hiss. "Stick to the facts, Pinocchio, before your nose explodes," Ava admonished.

"Just adding a tiny bit of embellishment," Woody replied. "But here is the straight scoop. I got to the grocery store a few minutes early and was waiting with the woman who manages the kitchen at the hotel. We chatted a bit, and I learned that a plane had been blown up at the airfield a few days ago, and that one of the hotel security men was found there with his brains scattered about. Now, here comes the important part. The hotel immediately beefed-up security by hiring three heavies that rolled up in a Lincoln Continental."

Mary said, "Well, at least we no longer will have to guess whether Randy Williams is still lurking in the area. If he was the one chartering the plane that kept buzzing us, he and the plane owner have to be super pissed."

Leta asked, "Did the lady at the grocery store say anything about a search for whoever blew the plane up and may have done Carlos in?"

Bob replied, "She commented that it was strange that no outside law officials had been called in to investigate the explosion or the death of Carlos. The woman also commented that the town sheriff couldn't find his butt with both hands in the dark. I think it's plain that the last thing the hotel people want is outside law people sniffing around."

Mary interjected, "Time to 'fess up, Bob. Who messed your face up and why?"

Bob smiled and said, "You ought to see the other guy."

Mary shook her head. "Enough of your hyper-testosterone bragging. What really happened?"

Bob replied, "I think I met one of Randy's men at the grocery store. Just as I finished convincing the pharmacist to sell me several boxes of tampons, a really huge guy wearing fancy boots and a black Stetson cowboy hat got in my face and said some things to me that are best not repeated. We had a little disagreement, and he made the mistake of taking a swing at me. He ended up on the floor with a dislocated shoulder, spitting out blood and teeth."

Leta said with alarm, "Bob, I just noticed that you have a cut in your shirt with some blood stains. You haven't told us about that."

"I forgot to mention that the big guy whipped out a razor blade knife and tried to impersonate a whirling dervish before his mouth ran in to a fast-moving can of peaches."

Mary said, "Looks like we can't trust you to go into town and stay out of trouble. I may need to take over the shopping chores."

There was a break in the conversation, then Bob said, "I think it's time to work on a plan to extract Leta's friends Sheree and Amber out of the whorehouse. Having Randy and heavies likely living in the hotel does complicate things, however."

Mary asked, "Leta, what are your friends' real names?"

"Sheree is Linda Kay and Amber is Ryn."

Bob said, "We need some place safe for them to go if we can get them out. Any chance that they would want to go home?"

"No chance in hell," Leta replied. "The girls, like me, ran away since they were being sexually abused at home by their fathers."

Bob asked Mary, "Do you still have the number that Officer Reagor gave us to use only in case of a dire emergency with no guarantee of CIA help?"

Mary replied, "I memorized it. Let me write it down on this napkin for you."

Bob put the napkin in his pocket and said, "There's a pay phone in front of the grocery store. If I slip into town in the wee hours of the morning, I bet that I can make a call without being seen. My guess is that beneath her stern exterior, Reagor would be interested in helping sexually abused young girls who have been forced into prostitution."

Mary shook her head and said, "Remember, you're that guy who was convinced that Reagor was too mean for a woman and probably had a penis."

Bob replied, "True, but toward the end she started to mellow just a tiny bit. I'm betting that it was Reagor who arranged for the edible snacks in the van as well as the return of our pistols. I think that early one Sunday morning while the town is still asleep would be the perfect time to slip in to Barlow and use the pay phone."

Mary asked, "Bob, what are your thoughts about how to get Linda Kay and Ryn out of Sadie's clutches?"

Bob hesitated as if pondering the question. Then he spoke slowly. "I don't think that we can go in guns a blazing like John Wayne without a lot of people getting hurt, including us and likely the girls. My best idea as of now is for me to go to the hotel posing as a patron and flash large bills and ask to hire both girls at the same time. Then I'll figure a way to slip them out."

Leta said, "I never was involved in a ménage a trois like that. To tie up two workers at the same time Sadie would likely want a bundle of cash."

Bob responded, "Why do you and Mary delight in using words and phrases that are above my pay grade? Is a ménage like a menagerie?"

Mary smiled and said, "Leta, we need to dumb down our conversation for Bob. Ménage is a French word for household and trois translates as the number 'three.'"

"So," Leta interrupted, "A ménage a trois is a group of three people in a domestic relationship. The term is really not precise for what you propose purchasing from Sadie. 'Threesome' would be a better word."

Bob smiled and said, "I am humbled to be in association with two future Mensa candidates. Alas. One less concussion and I also might be a potential member. Now, if you two superior intellects will excuse me, I need to go do some dummy work on the deuce and a half."

CHAPTER 41

CALLING HOME

Bob's mental alarm clock went off just before 2 AM on Sunday morning. As he started to slip out of bed and not wake Mary, she said, "I was having the nicest dream until you interrupted it. Some incredibly handsome man had just asked me to marry him. Before I could answer, your movement woke me up."

Bob said, "Well, the handsome man in the dream couldn't have been me. I for sure am going to wait for some sweet little virgin who thinks that the missionary position is a Bible outreach effort in Africa."

Mary gave a little shriek and slammed her fist in Bob's crotch. "Ugh!" he moaned. "You for sure won't have to worry about getting pregnant now. That's third world birth control for sure."

"Serves you right, you bastard," Mary snapped. "I, myself, am waiting for a man who has much more impressive masculine gifts than you do."

Bob gave a little laugh and reached over and gave Mary a kiss. Then he said quietly, "I wonder if Trigger is already spoken for?"

Before Mary could respond, Bob leaped out of bed and dressed hurriedly. After a quick trip to the bathroom, he slipped out of the door by the back porch and headed for the barn. Soon he was heading across the desert with just enough light from the moon to stay due east. There was not much wind, so he knew that the dune buggy tire tracks would not quickly be obscured by shifting sand.

Once Bob was within two miles of Barlow, he veered to the south and circled Barlow widely so he could enter heading west. With the exhaust cut-off closed, Bob purred into town past the hotel and made a right turn to reach Dalton's Grub and Gear. The store was dark, as was most of the town. Bob slipped out of the dune buggy quietly and entered the pay phone booth. He dialed the number that Reagor had given him and Mary for emergency use.

After a few minutes a synthesized voice said, "Please deposit two-dollars and seventy-five cents for three minutes." Bob was prepared with a pocket full of coins and dropped eleven quarters into the phone slot. The phone rang only once before it was answered by a voice that sounded wide awake. "This is Officer Reagor."

Bob said quickly, "Officer Reagor, this is Bob Smith in Texas. I would never bother you, particularly in the dead of night, unless it were urgent. This is not about Mary and me. We can always take care of ourselves."

Bob then continued to give the CIA officer a quick update, including the story of the two girls being held as slaves in the Barlow whorehouse. He said, "Mary and I want to free those poor girls, but I need somewhere safe to send them. Is there any way you could arrange for someone to meet me and the girls some night at the highway turnoff to Barlow? I'm pretty sure that I can get them out of the hotel and drive them there."

There was a moment of silence. Then Reagor said, "Give me a time and date."

Bob replied, "I need a few days to plan things. The best night will probably be a Sunday since that's a slow time at the hotel according to Leta. She just told me yesterday that my crazy uncle was a ham operator with a general license. There's a big antenna in back of the house. Any chance there is a secure CIA shortwave band that I could use to send the information to you rather than risking coming into Barlow to use the pay phone?"

Reagor paused before replying, "My husband is an experienced ham operator and I know how to use his equipment. I'll give you his call and band information. If we make the contact very brief, there won't be any danger of anyone locating your transmitter. Use the modified third version of the CIA interoffice code to give me a date and time. I will have someone waiting in a black Suburban just off of the highway. I'll plan on hearing from you at 8 PM next Wednesday on the radio using the following information."

As soon as Reagor had given the shortwave numbers, she immediately hung up. At this point the operator voice said, "Please deposit one dollar for another minute of time or you will be disconnected."

Bob got back into the dune buggy and drove slowly down the alley behind the hotel. There were several covered parking spaces. In one of them was a shiny Lincoln Continental with modified gold-spoked wheels. Bob mused to himself, "That for sure has to be the Randy mobile. I'll need to disable it before I go into the hotel to get the girls. A sharp razor knife should do the trick with the tires."

Bob headed east on the road out of Barlow for a mile. Then he turned off of the road and went two miles north across the desert before heading back toward the compound. Once the dune buggy was safely back in the barn, Bob looked at the luminous numbers on his watch and saw that it was 4:30 AM. He slipped back into bed and gave the sleeping Mary a kiss on the back of her neck. She stirred. Bob whispered in her ear, "Now, about that missionary position…"

CHAPTER 42

NIGHT PLANS

At breakfast the next morning, Bob gave Mary and Leta an update on his nocturnal trip to Barlow and his phone conversation with Officer Reagor. He then turned to Leta and asked, "You mentioned that Wilbur was a ham operator. There's a big antenna out back, but I have never seen a shortwave radio. Is it hidden somewhere?"

Leta responded, "Wilbur was absolutely convinced that secret German agents had infiltrated the country and were plotting to attack the compound and capture and torture him as payback for his killing so many Germans in the war. Apparently, your uncle was in an early attack wave at Normandy and miraculously escaped the withering machine gun fire and singlehandedly blew up a German machine gun nest at the top of the beach. He turned the machine gun on the Germans and wiped out a large number of them."

Mary asked, "How does being on his shortwave radio tie in to all of that?"

Leta replied, "Wilbur was constantly roaming the shortwave bands listening for clues that German agents had discovered the compound and were closing in on him. He never broadcast at all for fear that his transmitter would be traced. We had a lot of free time together, and he taught me how to operate his equipment."

Bob joined in, "But that doesn't answer my question about where Wilbur's radio equipment is. I've been all over the compound and have never seen it."

Leta said, "I think that there are still lots of secrets in this compound that none of us has discovered. But finding the radio equipment is not much of a challenge. It is in the octagonal weather tower on the top of the barn. There is a disguised trap door in the ceiling below that opens to a short staircase that leads to a small room that contains the radio and a telegraph key for Morse code. There are small glass windows all around that let Wilbur search the desert with binoculars. He could see for miles around up that high."

Bob said, "I was interested in ham radio in high school and actually got a technical license. My Morse code is still pretty good. Which reminds me, Mary. The first time I was ever in your posh apartment near the medical school, I was snooping around and discovered a shortwave radio hidden behind a tambour on your desk. It later disappeared. How much do you know about shortwave?"

Mary gave a thumbs up and replied, "In all modesty, I am close to being an expert. In my training I spent a large number of hours learning how to stay in touch with other agents through scrambled shortwave communication. I can certainly get a message to Reagor Wednesday night as planned."

Bob said, "Great. That solves one problem. Now we need to strategize how best to bust Leta's friends out of their prison. I still think my going to the hotel posing as an affluent brothel customer and asking for a kinky session with the two young women may be the best approach. Then there would need to be a huge disturbance to give me cover to escape with them."

Mary said, "Sounds pretty risky with Randy and his two heavies living in the hotel. The man with the missing teeth and injured shoulder would recognize you immediately. I assume that you will be driving the hot rod dune buggy. Do you think that you can outrun Randy's Continental on the road from Barlow to the highway to meet the pickup person?"

Bob replied, "Maybe not me, but you're going to be the getaway driver. You can make a car do more tricks than a trained pony. Also, the dune buggy is much lighter than the Continental, which weighs over 5000 pounds. I think that the Corvette engine in the dune buggy is a 1957, which had 290 horsepower before it was modified. I'm betting that in the light dune wagon that engine will turn 0 to 60 in under five seconds and hit a top end higher than the 120 miles per hour which is the max for the Continental. But keeping the flying dune buggy from jitterbugging off of the road at high speeds will take an expert, i.e., the legendary race driver, Miss Mary White."

Mary said, "Not to be dismissive, but your plan sounds a little sketchy to me. Have you accounted for the fact that people may be shooting at us?"

Bob answered, "If you have a better plan to propose, I am all ears." Then with a little smile Bob added, "The only other idea I had was for you to go to the hotel and present yourself as an experienced prostitute looking for a job. You would immediately be queen of the place."

Mary scowled and gave Bob a death stare. "Sometimes you are so full of it! But let me improve on your plan. Why not immobilize Randy's Continental early on so he and his thugs could not use it to chase us? Sounds pretty elementary to me."

Bob agreed, "I had thought about slashing the Continental's tires before going into the hotel."

"Dummy," Mary replied. "I saw some flash grenades in Wilbur's bunker when we were down there. Why not just have one of us roll a flash grenade under the Continental once you are inside the hotel? They ought to have people pouring out of the establishment pulling their drawers up and also put the Lincoln out of commission."

Leta's face brightened. "You said 'one of us.' That means that I get to go, yes?"

Bob nodded yes. "I think that we will need you. But there is going to be some real risk for all of us, including your friends."

Leta replied, "I know that my friends and I all considered committing suicide early on after we got to the whorehouse. Staying there would be worse than death. I am all in."

Bob said, "One strange request, Leta. I need to be sure to get one of your tampons before we leave on our mission."

Leta had an impish look on her face and replied, "New or used, Bob?"

Mary shook her head. "Leta, you are beautiful and super smart, but you could do with a little refinement. We need to work on that together. Tampon, Bob? I shudder to think what crazy idea you may have."

Bob smiled and replied, "That, my dear Mary, is for me to know and for you to find out."

CHAPTER 43

LIKE LOT'S WIFE?

The next morning both Mary and Bob got up to exercise just after sunrise. The desert sand made for poor foot traction, but Wilbur had surfaced the inside of the compound with decomposed granite with some type of stabilizer, which provided a good running surface. The inside perimeter of the four-acre enclosure was just over one-third of a mile and was good for a fast pace. Bob and Mary ran together for several laps. Then Mary shouted, "Bell lap!" and broke into a fast sprint. It took Bob almost the whole final lap to catch her.

They both were standing by the porch breathing hard when Leta came out of the house. She smiled and said, "Bet I can outrun either one of you. Bob, after you catch your breath and have some water, what say I take you on for a lap?"

Bob looked at Leta and asked, "Are you serious? I have never seen you do any sort of aerobic exercise since we've been here except for martial arts with Mary. You can't be in great shape. Maybe if I hopped on one leg it would be fair."

Mary volunteered, "Leta, Bob ran track and played football in high school. I think that you would be overmatched."

Leta said with pretend seriousness, "Would it make any difference if I told you doubters that I waxed everyone in my homeroom potato sack race in the third grade?"

Bob and Mary both laughed. Then Bob said, "My breathing is close to normal. Let me have another swallow of water, then we'll see how fast you are. One lap from the pole over there by the fence. But don't you need to put some shoes on first?"

"Nope," said Leta. "I, like Mercury, already have wings on my feet. Mary, you count down for us."

Bob and Leta lined up by the pole. Mary called out, "Three, two, one, go!"

Leta immediately burst into a full sprint and moved with gazelle-like speed covering the yards in long, fluid strides. Bob was quickly several yards behind. Leta lengthened her lead at the halfway point, but Bob gritted his teeth and began to close the gap. Close to the finish line, Leta suddenly spun around and ran the last few yards backwards. She beat Bob by only a few feet.

Bob was bent over with hands on his knees breathing hard. "Smart ass," he gasped between breaths.

Mary exclaimed, "My gosh, that girl can fly!"

Leta was not breathing very hard. She said, "Sorry, Bob. Running backwards at the end was a cheap stunt. My apologies."

Mary said, "Bob and I need to shower. Leta, can we talk you into scrambling some eggs and maybe whipping up some pancakes while we clean up. I'm really hungry."

Later at breakfast Bob said, "Sunday night will be here before we know it. Let's talk strategy. The first critical thing is to disable Randy's wheels so he and his buddies can't chase us as we streak to the highway with the girls. Number two is to create a massive explosion to rattle the windows and scare the bejesus out of the customers so that they all race for the door. After the plane at the airport got blown up and Carlos had his brains scattered around, workers at the hotel have to be a bit nervous."

Mary said, "I like the idea of throwing a flash grenade under the car to take care of objectives one and two at the same time. The explosion will be around 180 decibels, loud enough to wake the dead."

Bob countered, "The problem with a flash grenade under the car is that there may not be enough concussive force to make it undriveable. How about dumping the flash grenade right inside the Lincoln? That would blow out the windshield and windows and likely start a fire. The downside is that one of us will have to get entrance to the car without making enough noise to alert people inside. I'm sure that I can pick the door lock, but someone else will have to heave the flash grenade at just the right time."

Mary said, "I can certainly take care of that."

Bob replied, "You really can't be the trigger person since you will need to stay in the dune buggy and keep it running so we can make a quick exit. Also, you are by far the best driver if we get in a highway chase."

Leta said, "Yes! That means that I get to be the flash grenade delivery person."

Bob nodded and said, "Agreed. You will have to throw the grenade and then sprint for the dune buggy. You can blow your hand off if you don't know how to handle a flash grenade. We need to take some of Wilbur's flash grenades and go out into the desert for a training session this morning."

Later in the morning Bob and Leta went behind the compound with three flash grenades. Bob showed her how to pull the pin and how to be absolutely certain to keep the handle pushed in until the grenade was thrown.

Bob said, "Leta, once you release the handle, the grenade will go off in four seconds. There will be a blinding flash and an incredibly loud noise. Sunday night you will have to lob the grenade in the car, then run like hell with your fingers in your ears. And absolutely do not look back."

Leta asked coyly, "If I look back, will I turn into a pillar of salt like Lot's wife in the Bible?"

"No, wiseass. You will be blinded and won't be able to find the dune buggy. A flash grenade generates 11 million candelas of light, which is enough to knock out a person's vision for several minutes. Now, let's see if you are smart enough to arm this flash grenade and get rid of it fast enough not to deafen and blind both of us. Remember, try throwing the grenade at least 20 feet away, then stick your fingers in your ears and turn away with your eyes closed."

Leta successfully deployed all three flash grenades. Then she said with a smile, "Now I'm a certified flash grenade expert. I can hardly wait for Sunday night."

Bob cautioned, "Sunday night will be a lot trickier. You'll be dumping the grenade in the car, only a few feet from yourself. And there will be shards of glass flying everywhere. It will probably be best for you to take a couple of quick steps, then hit the ground with your fingers in your ears and your eyes closed. Once the blast is over, hot foot it to the dune buggy as fast as possible. I should be coming out of the back of the hotel with your friends in tow."

Leta replied, "I won't disappoint you. Linda Kay and Ryn will think that they have died and gone to heaven. I will be so happy for them."

CHAPTER 44

GOING DOWN?

The following morning after breakfast and exercise time, Leta showed Mary and Bob how to find the hidden trap door in the loft of the barn that led to the octagonal search tower with Wilbur's shortwave radio equipment. The three of them stood looking out of the tinted glass windows.

"Heck of a view," Bob said. "From up here Wilbur could see for miles in all directions. It would be hard for anyone to slip up on him as long as he was watching. If he was in danger of being overwhelmed, I wonder if his plan would have been to rush to the arms room and blast his way out in the dune buggy."

Leta said, "I really doubt that he would have run without a big fight. He told me once that he could hold off a small army from this tower. But I don't see any weapons."

Mary frowned as if in deep thought. After a moment she said, "Something doesn't add up quite right. The roof of this room is flat, but you can see a large cupola on the tower when you look from the ground. There has to be a significant space above this radio room."

Bob reached up high and tapped on the ceiling. "It sounds hollow all around this light fixture, which is some sort of a weird chandelier." He grasped the chandelier and pulled hard. A small segment of the ceiling folded down to reveal a wooden ladder leading up.

Mary turned to Leta and said, "You knew about this tower and the radio, so you get the honor of going up the stairs first."

Leta scurried up the stairs quickly. There was a moment of silence, then she said in a shocked voice, "Wow! You guys have got to see this for yourselves."

Mary followed Leta up the stairs with Bob right behind her. The three found themselves in a small space that had port holes all around the perimeter with gun mounts. There were several AK-47s stacked against one wall with several cases of ammunition.

"Holy crap!" Bob exclaimed. "With this view Wilbur could pick off anyone approaching the compound. He must have really believed the Nazi secret service would eventually find him."

Leta was silent a moment, and then said, "I see one big problem here for defending the compound. If the supposed Germans got inside the compound, Wilbur would be trapped in the tower with no way to escape. He was way too smart for that."

Mary asked, "Leta, what are you suggesting?"

Leta answered, "There has to be some way for a quick exit ending up with access to the dune buggy. And the fastest way down is obvious—a fireman's pole."

Bob shook his head and said, "Leta, I think that you've been getting too much desert sun."

"Perhaps, but let's go back to the radio room. There is a small closet there that we did not look in."

The three descended the stairs, and Bob pushed them back up, closing the space in the ceiling. Leta went to the door of the closet and opened it. "Oh, ye of little faith," she said triumphantly. "Take a look here."

Mary and Bob peered into the closet and shook their heads. There was a hole in the floor and a brass pole leading downward.

Leta said, "I'd bet a whole lot that this pole ends up somewhere in the barn near the car ramp. Wilbur's bound to have had a way to get into the secret arms room without blowing out the wall."

"I agree," Mary said. "I think that the exploding wall was most likely a defensive measure."

Bob said, "Sunday is fast approaching. Let's get back to business and make certain that you two can work the radio so I can give Officer Reagor the critical rendezvous information on Wednesday night. Then we need to sit down in the kitchen and strategize some more about the possible scenarios for our rescue plan."

It was quickly obvious that Mary would have no trouble making shortwave connections with Wilbur's equipment. "Piece of cake," Mary said.

The three people left the barn and walked back to the kitchen and sat down at the table. Bob began the discussion by addressing Leta, "Tell me about the layout in the hotel. There must be a way to screen people before deciding if it is safe to let them into the girls' area or into the gambling room."

Leta answered, "When you enter the hotel, there is a main lobby that looks very ordinary and innocent. But there are not many people who come in that are not looking for sex or gambling. But for the few that do, there are several rooms down a hall that can be rented for the night. Men who are looking for a playmate are screened, then admitted to another hallway that ends up in a fancy parlor. There are pictures of the women available. Sadie negotiates a price based on how long a customer wants services provided. Once that is done, the woman comes down for drinks with the customer before their play time in a room upstairs."

"Carlos used to provide security and would escort the customer and the woman upstairs while explaining the whorehouse ground rules. But now that he hopefully is frying in hell, there has to be somebody new doing the job."

Bob asked, "If I show up at 8:00 Sunday night and ask to have Linda Kay and Ryn in a kinky trio, will Sadie agree to this?"

Leta replied, "Show Sadie enough money and she'll agree to anything. Sunday night is usually very slow. It's likely that neither girl will be engaged."

Bob said, "Do the rooms where the customers are serviced—sorry to say it that way—have windows?"

"Yes," Leta answered, "but they all have heavy dark-out shades."

Bob asked, "Can you see light around or through the shades?"

"Well, headlights from the parking lot can be perceived as a blurry light source. Why do you ask?"

"That's very important since I need some way to tell you when Linda Kay and Ryn are with me in the room. The signal will mean for you to go ahead and throw the flash grenade. My plan would be to turn the room lights on and off twice when I am ready."

Leta said, "That will work, particularly if you use your hand and pull the shade slightly back."

Bob queried, "One other important thing. Is there a back door that the girls and I can use to escape?"

Leta responded, "There is one back door and one side door." She took a napkin and made a quick sketch of the floor plan of the hotel. "Those doors are always locked from the outside, but you can open them from the inside. The large back door opens to a loading dock in the alley and is used mostly for bringing in food and supplies. Employees enter and leave by a side door just south of the building. There is a keypad on that door."

Bob said, "I think that we all need to take a late-night trip to town to scout out the hotel so we don't make a fatal mistake in planning. What say we hit the bed early tonight and head for town at the bewitching hour of 2 AM?"

CHAPTER 45

NOCTURNAL FORAY

At 2 AM the dune buggy left the compound with Bob at the wheel and Mary in the suicide seat. There was a half-moon that showed faint tracks remaining in the sand that made navigation easy. Leta sat in the back and reviewed her role in the upcoming rescue operation. Bob piloted the vehicle across the desert with the exhaust wide open. Once again, he gave Barlow wide berth and entered the town from the east, driving slowly with minimal engine noise and the headlights off. The hotel was dark except for outside lights. There were only a few parked cars in front.

Bob eased the dune buggy into the alley behind the hotel and passed by the loading dock. On the south side of the building there was an employee parking lot. Close to the side door there were several covered parking spaces. The Lincoln Continental occupied the space closest to the door. Bob quietly circled to the front of the hotel and then headed back east of town before opening up the exhaust cut-off and turning west toward the compound.

By 3:30 AM the late-night explorers were back in bed. Bob had trouble sleeping since he kept mulling over the best way to extract the trafficked girls without getting anyone killed. Finally, Mary nudged him and asked, "Your wiggles are keeping me awake. Do you have restless leg syndrome? Or maybe you just need to go visit the cactus squat potty out back that you told me about."

Bob said back, "Very funny. I'm restless since I keep perseverating over the safest way to get Leta's friends out. If Randy and his two criminal sidekicks are all bunking in at the hotel, that means three potential shooters to deal with. I sure don't want to get Leta or one of her friends killed."

Mary pinched Bob's arm and said sharply, "But I guess it's OK if I get gunned down."

Bob said, "Of course not…. But you're a big girl and can take care of yourself. Tell you what, let's get some sleep and continue this scintillating conversation in the morning. I think that the Sandman is about to arrive for me." Soon both Mary and Bob were sound asleep.

When Mary came into the kitchen the following morning, Bob was already sitting at the table having coffee. When Mary sat, Bob stood up and walked over to her. He kissed her head and said with a smile, "Looks like Miss Lazy Butt is finally up. I've already put my two miles in while you were slumbering."

Mary replied, "Princesses require more rest than plebeians like you. I went to sleep in a hurry last night, but some uncouth person woke me up wiggling around in the bed like someone with a terminal neurological disorder. Then, when I got back to sleep again, I had awful dreams about Randy and his thugs chasing the dune buggy across the desert, firing at us with a machine gun."

"Yikes!" said Bob. "No wonder you needed a little extra bed time. I'll grab a cup of coffee for you—then let's review our plans for Sunday night."

Once Mary had her coffee, Bob continued, "I am worried that the explosion in the Lincoln may not be enough to create immediate chaos. For me to spirit Linda Kay and Ryn out, I really need a mass panic reaction. Any ideas?"

Mary thought a minute, then asked, "Did you notice the power supply to the hotel last night? It looked to me like there is one feed into the side of the hotel near the employee exit. I think if we could kill all the lights in the hotel just after Leta deposits the flash grenade into Randy's Lincoln, that would really terrorize people."

"Great idea," Bob replied. "But that has to be 220 volts coming into the hotel. I don't think Leta could snip the wire without being electrocuted."

"True," Mary replied. "But I sure could do it with no sweat. If the dune buggy is waiting in the parking lot, near the electric line, I could cut the wire. Then Leta would immediately deposit the flash grenade into the Lincoln and run to jump into the buggy with me so we could pick up you and the girls when you come running out."

Bob said, "I think the best exit for us will be the loading dock door. It would be logical for the employees to head for their own exit, while any customers will likely run for the front door where they came in. We would have to hope that Randy and his two buddies use the employee exit. They are not likely to be in a friendly mood when they see Randy's car smoldering."

Mary said, "I'm not as good as you are at picking locks, but I feel certain that I can jimmy the lock on Randy's car. Car locks are usually pretty simple. I can unlock the door first, then stand by to cut the electric feed line."

"Good morning one and all," Leta said as she came into the kitchen.

Bob said, "Leta, our plans for the jail break Sunday night have changed a bit. If you need some coffee, get a cup and let us fill you in."

Once Leta was seated, Bob looked at Mary and said, "Your good idea, Mary. You explain things to Leta."

Mary nodded and began. "Leta, Bob and I both think that we need something more than just the flash grenade explosion to scare people into a mass exit from the hotel. My idea was to cut the power line to the hotel just after the explosion. The sudden darkness will cause more fear, as well as give some cover for Bob and your friends to escape. The trigger for you to deposit the grenade in the car will remain the same—a light flash on and off from the room where Bob and the girls are."

CHAPTER 46

'SMUTTY' EDWARDS

The ham radio connection with Officer Reagor was quick and efficient Wednesday night. Mary had no trouble working Wilbur's shortwave equipment. The entire transmission lasted less than thirty seconds. Mary said to Bob and Leta, "Done deal. Reagor knows to have someone at the highway cut off to Barlow at 9 PM this Sunday night. Now we just have to be sure that our plans for the extraction Sunday evening don't get blown up like Randy's Lincoln."

Bob looked out of one of the octagonal windows across the desert toward the west and the setting sun. "What a gorgeous view with all the rainbow colors in the sky. I can now understand how people fall in love with this area."

Mary gave a little frown and said, "Yes, almost perfect—all it lacks are trees, water, outside air-conditioning, a first-class hair and a nail salon, a real grocery store, a first-class symphony—need I go on?"

Leta quickly said, "Mary, this may not be heaven for you, but if you had been a prisoner in a whorehouse for several months like me, Wilbur's compound would be as close as one can get to nirvana in this world."

Mary took Leta's hand and said softly, "Understood."

Leta regained her composure and said, "I came up here by myself yesterday and left a flashlight and some nylon rope. It's time to see where the fireman's pole ends up. If I tie the rope around my waist, you two can hang onto the end while I slide down the pole slowly using the flashlight. If I get in trouble, you can hoist me up."

Bob and Mary looked at each other silently, then Mary said, "Let's give it a try. But be very careful. Knowing the paranoia of Uncle Wilbur, there may be a booby trap."

Leta opened the closet and shined the light down the shaft. "There is a bend after about ten feet, and you can't see beyond that. But the pole seems to follow the bend."

Bob used the rope to make a shoulder harness for Leta. She leaned into the opening and grabbed the pole and began to slowly slide down with the light of the flashlight playing off of the walls before her. Soon she disappeared around the bend in the shaft.

After three or four minutes, Bob shouted down the shaft, "Leta, we are about out of rope. You need to come back up."

Leta shouted back, "OK. I'll need to walk a short distance back to the pole. When I start shinnying up, I'll yank on the rope."

Leta's head emerged from around the bend in the shaft as Mary and Bob pulled on the rope hand over hand. When she was back in the radio room she said, "Just as I thought. This shaft provided a quick way for Wilbur to access the dune buggy for an emergency getaway. The pole ends at the level of the barn floor, then there is a narrow passageway that leads toward an area above the arms room and the buggy. We ran out of rope, but I feel certain that at the end of the passageway there has to be another shaft and pole that drops down near the escape vehicle."

Mary said, "Good intuition, Leta. It makes me wonder how many other Wilbur mysteries this compound holds. Too bad we can't bring him back from the dead and question him."

Leta started to tear up. "I still feel like I killed poor Wilbur after he was so nice to me."

Bob said with a smile, "Trust me, Leta, there are few better send-offs to meet your Maker."

Mary shook her head and said, "Leta, just ignore Bob. He is a hopelessly insensitive ex-football jock whose main area of thought processing is below his waist."

Leta smiled.

Bob shook his head and retorted, "My ego is mortally wounded. However, we have much more important things to worry about. Which reminds me, Leta, does Barlow have a police department?"

Leta nodded. "There's some fat old guy named Smitty Edwards who is the entire police department. He clearly covers for the people who run the whorehouse and gambling enterprise. Smitty is a disgusting pervert who is rewarded by Sophie with occasional 'freebies.' Fortunately, he likes the more experienced professional women. The ladies all call him 'Smutty.' Apparently, he sometimes shows up at church and sits up front with pious Sadie."

Mary said, "He sounds like a prince of a guy. Has he been in Barlow a long time?"

"I have been told that Smitty and his wife Ellie showed up in town a year or so ago. Smitty had been an MP in the Army, and the hotel people gave him a nice salary to be the police chief."

Bob said, "Does Smitty have a police car?"

"Just before I escaped from the whorehouse, I heard Sadie talking to Smitty one night about the new Ford Galaxie 500 that the city had just bought him. It's supposed to have a big engine. Why do you ask?"

"Simple," Bob replied. "If we knock out the Lincoln, I want to know if there is any other car that Randy might commandeer to chase after us."

Mary interrupted, "It's almost bedtime for princesses. My vote is to go back to the house and break out Wilbur's Scrabble board that I saw on one of the shelves in the main room. A little mental break would do us all good as we wait to start the Sunday night count down."

"Great idea," Leta said. "Wilbur and I often played Scrabble at night. In all modesty, I usually beat him."

Bob said, "I was known as the Noah Webster of my junior high school. You ladies are in big trouble competing with a world-class entomologist such as myself."

Mary and Leta burst into laughter. "You mean etymologist, don't you? Entomology is the study of insects."

Bob recovered quickly and said, "Just trying to see if you ladies were really listening."

Mary said, "Bob, if you were Pinocchio, you would be having a gigantic nasal erection right now. Talk is cheap. Leta, let's go find out if Bob can walk the walk or just talk the talk. This is going to be just like stealing candy from a baby."

CHAPTER 47

FINAL PLANS

It was late Sunday afternoon. Bob, Mary, and Leta were having a small supper of bologna sandwiches and Dr Peppers. Mary wrinkled her nose and said, "The only thing more revolting to put into a human's mouth than bologna is Vienna sausages. This is not exactly the gourmet food that Bob promised when he lured me out into this endless desert."

Bob smiled and said, "Mary, you know the only assurance I gave you was that coming out here gave us both the best chance of staying alive for a few more months. And, I even had my fingers crossed behind my back on that one."

"I was just teasing you, Bob," Mary replied. "As I have said before, there is no one I would trust more in a fight than you. I am just a little edgy thinking about what could go wrong with our plans for tonight. A gun fight would not be my first choice for Sunday night entertainment."

"Agreed," Bob said. "Which reminds me, Leta, you need to bring the pistol that you have been practicing with. The chances are small that you will need it. But if all hell breaks loose, try not to shoot Mary or me. And remember, if you need to use your gun, shoot to eliminate people—not just to wound them."

"Roger," Leta answered. "And I know that it's better to aim for the chest than the head since the chest is a much larger target."

Bob looked at his watch and said, "It's now 6:00 straight up. We need to head for town in exactly one hour. My goal is for both of you to be positioned by 7:45 PM. I want to enter the hotel around 8 PM. First, I will have to pass muster as a paying customer with plenty of cash to get into the whorehouse parlor. Then I will need to negotiate with Sadie to agree to letting me have two girls at the same time."

Leta said, "Bob, Sadie is going to insist that you have a few over-priced drinks in the parlor and meet the girls before you go back with them."

Bob replied, "Money talks. I plan to flash enough large bills to make Sadie willing to violate whorehouse meet-and-greet protocol. Leta, review with us what happens next."

Leta replied, "Once you are in the room with Linda Kay and Ryn, you will pull back the black-out shade just an inch or so and flash the room light twice. By this time Mary will have picked the door lock of the Lincoln. I will simply open the car door, pull the pin on the flash grenade, and lob it onto the front seat and run like hell for the dune buggy with my fingers in my ears. Just as soon as the blast is over, Mary will cut the power line to the hotel and jump back into the dune buggy. We will speed to the loading dock to pick up you and my friends and hightail it to the highway."

Mary said, "All perfect, Leta. But what happens if we pull up to the loading dock and no one appears?"

Leta looked puzzled and replied, "I'm not sure."

Mary answered her own question. "You will slide into the driver's seat of the dune buggy and keep the motor running while I go inside to find Bob and the girls. Keep your pistol ready in one hand and shoot anyone who approaches the dune buggy except Bob, the girls, or me. Got it?"

"Yes," Leta replied. "I can handle it." After a pause, Leta turned to Bob and said, "Please be gentle with Linda Kay and Ryn. The idea of both of them being rented out to one man at the same time will make them think that you are some sort of pervert who may hurt them."

Bob smiled and said, "No problem. I have been spending much of my adult life charming women and making them trust me."

Mary promptly said, "Excuse me while I upchuck my bologna sandwich. Bob is more in the mold of the Marquis de Sade than a lovable grandfather."

Bob shook his head and said, "So terribly untrue, Leta. Have you ever seen Mary come to breakfast with bruises or bite marks?"

Mary said, "Easy, big boy. I was just trying to throw out a historical character that only Leta and I would recognize to emphasize your abysmal lack of literary knowledge."

Bob shook his head and said, "Mary, you have a terrible habit of underestimating my genius and fund of general knowledge. The Marquis de Sade was an evil French nobleman who was known for his fondness of cruel sexual perversions."

Leta said, "And, as I recall, Marquis de Sade was born in 1740 in Paris and died in 1814."

Mary said, "Leta, you must have a photographic memory."

Leta replied modestly, "Yes, I think I do."

Bob finished his bottle of Dr Pepper and said, "Nectar for the gods. Good to the very last drop. This was a really great meal. My congratulations to Chef Leta Mitchell." Leta stood and took a small curtsy.

Bob then said, "I need to round up a few more things for our trip. Eagle Scouts like me always want to be prepared for any exigency. Let's all meet out back near the dune buggy at exactly nineteen hundred hours."

CHAPTER 48

CASH ON THE BARRELHEAD

At 7 PM the dune buggy left the compound and headed east. It was still daylight with an easy read of the path across the desert. Bob again detoured to enter Barlow from the east with a quiet engine. The sun had just set, and the entrance lights of the hotel were on. There were very few cars in front, which Leta said was typical for Sunday night.

"Men don't lust less on Sundays," she offered. "They just feel more guilty cheating on their wives that day. Looks like there is not much bedroom or gambling activity. Linda Kay and Ryn should be available."

Bob eased the dune buggy down the alley and circled around to the employee parking lot. All three of them were shocked to see a fancy black Cadillac Coup de Ville in the parking spot next to Randy Williams' Lincoln Continental. Leta angrily said, "That's Mike's car. He's the bastard who found me in Pecos and delivered me to Sadie with promises of safety and a good job in the hotel. He owns this operation, but is not here all the time. I hope that we can take that son of a bitch out while we are here."

Mary said, "Leta, control your anger. People who are upset often make very bad decisions. Our only goal is to free your friends—not to avenge all the wrongs in the world."

Bob said, "That Cadillac complicates things. It has a huge V8 engine that can keep up with the dune buggy on the open road. And it's a lot more stable at high speeds. I'm going to slip out and slash two of the Cadillac tires. And while I'm there, I'll just go ahead and pick the lock of the Continental for Leta."

Bob was quickly back in the dune buggy. "Almost the bewitching hour. I need to be in the hotel in three minutes. Leta, if you stay near here, are you sure that you can see the window to the room where I will be with your friends? Once I flash the lights twice, you need to deliver the grenade inmediatamente."

"Got it," Leta answered. "You can count on me."

Bob started walking toward the front of the hotel and entered the front door almost exactly at 8 PM. There was an overly made-up woman at the front desk whose face suggested a hard life. She had a beehive of blond hair stacked up on her head.

Bob approached the desk and said pleasantly, "I'm looking for some fun tonight."

The woman gave Bob a wary eye and said, "There are some older folks here who plan to meet in the lobby soon and play Monopoly. Maybe you can join them."

Bob smiled and said, "I'm looking for some fun with young women." He pulled a crisp $100 bill out of his pocket and gave it to the woman. "And there's a lot more where that came from. I'm here to spend a lot of money and have a really good time—if you know what I mean."

The woman seemed undecided and hesitated. Then she said, "I need to get the hotel manager." She left the desk and punched in a code on the lock of a door at the back of the room and disappeared down a hallway. After a few minutes, a middle-aged woman with generous breasts peeking out of the top of her dress came to the desk. She looked carefully at Bob, then said, "I'm Sadie, and I am the hotel manager. Are you looking for a room for the night?"

Bob shook his head and replied, "I told your assistant that I am looking for a good time and am willing to pay for it." He pulled out several hundred-dollar bills and asked, "How about $700 for an hour with two young women?"

Sadie looked at the money and replied, "Our women are simply companions for drinking together and talking. I think that you have the wrong idea about this place."

Bob smiled again and said, "I have a friend who has been here with Sheree one night, then Amber the next night. He said that they are spectacular in bed. I want to have both of them for one hour."

Sadie shook her head and replied, "We don't cater to kinky sex and perverts. I can let you choose one of the girls for an hour for $700."

Bob said, "I am a gentle soul and will treat the girls with extreme kindness." He pulled more money out of his pocket and added it to the $700 on the desk. "This adds up to $1400. You can take it or leave it. And for that kind of money, I don't want to waste any of my hour getting watered down drinks and making small talk with the girls. I want to be escorted to a room with a nice, clean bed with both of them waiting for me."

Sophie kept looking at the stack of bills and seemed to be wavering. After a minute she picked up the bills and stuffed them down the front of her dress.

"A deal," she said. "But I need to warn you that we have security guards a lot bigger than you who can really mess you up if you harm one of my girls. They are like daughters to me."

"Let me notify Sheree and Amber that they will be working tonight after all. I'll have one of the security guards escort you up to their room shortly. And, by the way, there is protection available in the bathroom if you prefer to use it."

A few minutes passed before a very large man with an impressive build came into the lobby. Sadie spoke to him and said, "Ricardo, please escort this gentleman to see Sheree and Amber." The man eyed Bob, then said harshly, "Come with me, buddy. I'll take you up to where the girls are. But, let me warn you. If you're rough with the girls, I'll kick your ass all the way out of Barlow. And, yes, I'm carrying, and I know how to take care of vermin and low life."

Bob smiled again and replied, "No problem, sir. If there's a Gideon Bible in the room, the girls and I may end up just reading scriptures."

The man stared intently at Bob and with no emotion. "I don't like wise-asses. So, watch your step. It doesn't take much to make me very mad."

CHAPTER 49

BROTHELBREAK

Bob followed the security guard up a flight of winding stairs that were carpeted in shag carpet with thin spots from the footsteps of many eager customers. They walked down the hall and stopped in front of a room with a tacky gold gilded sign that read 'Ecstasy Parlor.'

The guard gave Bob a cold stare, then said, "The girls are in there waiting. You can lock the door from the inside—but we can always get in if you cause any trouble. As Sadie told you, these sweet girls are like family members. So, treat them right—or else." The man made a fist and gestured at Bob. "You've got exactly one hour. And no free minutes. Finish your business on time, buster."

Bob entered the room and closed the door. Two young girls who were overly made up and wearing skimpy dresses stared at him from across the room with apprehension. Bob put his fingers to his lips. He looked up at the ceiling, then stood on a chair and used his pocket knife to cut the wire leading to a small microphone hidden near the gaudy chandelier.

He stepped down to the floor and smiled at the girls. "Relax. I'm not here for sex. Leta sent me to get you girls out of this hell hole. Listen very carefully since I am going to need your help. In a couple of minutes, I'm going to pull this black-out shade back slightly and flash the room lights twice. Almost immediately there is going to be a very loud explosion. Then all the lights will go out. I need you girls to lead us to the loading dock door. Leta and a friend of mine are waiting for us there."

Sheree stared at Bob and asked, "How can we trust you? We've been lied to ever since we were brought here."

Bob said, "Believe me—I am your only hope to escape from this terrible place. Leta said that if you questioned me, I was to call you Linda Kay and Ryn."

Both girls relaxed perceptively. As Bob reached for the shade, the door was suddenly crashed open, and the man Bob had crippled at the grocery store burst into the room. "Ah, we meet again, you son of a bitch. Ricardo told me that you were probably the one asking for the girls. This time you're the one who's going to get really messed up." The man pointed a snub-nosed revolver at Bob. With a snarl he asked, "Do you want me to shoot your balls off before or after I blow your head up?"

Sheree who was standing by the window leaned slightly into the shade causing it to gap at one side. Amber quickly flashed the lights twice. Almost immediately there was a deafening explosion, then total darkness. Bob had launched himself at the big man just after the explosion and knocked him to the ground. He bounced the man's head on and off the floor, then hit him in the head with the butt of his own pistol.

He stood up and ordered, "Time to run, girls. I have a flashlight. Take us to the loading dock."

There were women running down the hall screaming and bumping into each other in the darkness. Sheree grabbed Bob's flashlight and led Bob and Amber in the opposite direction to a back stairwell. Once on the ground floor, they ran through the kitchen to the landing dock door. Bob shoved the inside handle, but the door would not open. He stepped back, then kicked the handle as hard as he could. The door swung partially open.

As soon as Mary saw the light from the flashlight, she shouted, "Here, Woody! Here!" Bob, Linda Kay, and Ryn jumped into the dune buggy. Mary gunned the engine and popped the clutch. The vehicle leaped forward and swerved around the corner of the building. Mary left the headlights off, but there was enough light from the burning Lincoln Continental to show people running out of the employee door. Suddenly there were two quick gunshots, and a bullet crashed through the back window, showering people with shards of glass. Mary floorboarded the gas pedal. The tires screeched as the vehicle rapidly accelerated and raced through town.

Once Mary had the dune buggy safely on the road to the main highway, she eased off on the gas. Leta and her friends were hugging in the back seat. There were tears in the eyes of all three girls. Bob kept looking backwards, but there was no evidence that they were being followed.

At a steady sixty miles an hour, the engine noise was tolerable. Bob leaned toward the back seat and asked, "Leta told us that the black Cadillac belongs to the owner of the hotel. Does he stay at the hotel often?"

Ryn shook her head and replied, "One of the older women said that Randy, who is the boss of the two security guards Ricardo and Tony, was trying to buy the business from Mike. But Mike would not agree to sell. Two days ago, Mike was found dead in his bed. Smitty, who is the police chief and also a nasty old man, is the designated coroner. He declared that the owner died from a heart attack. But there was whispering that Mike had bruise marks on his neck like he had been strangled."

Linda Kay chimed in, "That same lady said that Randy had discussed building a funeral home in town. Makes no sense with so few people here. Randy supposedly said that if there was a cremation oven and low prices, the funeral home could attract business from as far away as Pecos."

Bob looked at Mary and said, "A new location for Bodies to Go. That must be a very lucrative business. Guess the Chicago crime boys are intent on franchising it."

Leta spoke up and asked, "Mary, why did you call Bob 'Woody' when you yelled at him at the loading dock?"

Mary kept her eyes intently on the road and answered, "That's a very long story. Now is not the time to go into it. We need to get your friends into safe hands."

Bob said, "Our timing is near perfect. We should reach the highway just before 9 PM. And, so far, no one is following us. But the trip back may be a very different story."

CHAPTER 50

NO PENIS–AFTER ALL

As the dune buggy got closer to Highway 18, Ryn asked with concern, "What's really going to happen to us? Neither one of us will ever agree to go back to our terrible home situations with fathers who starting molesting us even before we had our first period."

Mary replied, "You both are going to go to a safe place for a time to recover from your awful experiences. Deciding where you ultimately end up will not be a rushed decision. The people meeting you are government officials who will protect you from other predators like Mike and Sadie."

Linda Kay asked, "Will Leta be going with us?"

Leta quickly answered, "I've found a safe home with Bob and Mary—at least for now."

Mary came to a stop at the intersection of the Barlow cut off and Highway 18. Bob said, "Look across the highway. In our headlights you can see a black Suburban. It's bound to be the girls' ride. I wonder who Reagor sent."

Mary crossed the highway and pulled in behind the Suburban. Bob got out and walked around to the driver's side. The door opened, and a tall woman got out.

Bob gasped and said in shock, "Officer Reagor? I never, ever would have expected to see you here."

The woman said, "I took time off to come get your girls. Last year my sister's fourteen-year-old daughter was sexually assaulted by her husband's older brother. The court put the slimeball away for a long time in prison. But my poor niece is still in therapy and not doing well. So, I have a personal interest in helping young women. You can be certain that I will take good care of the two victims in your car. And, by the way, I'm off duty. Please call me Becky."

By this time, Mary, Leta, and her two friends had walked up to the side of the Suburban. Bob said, "Becky, I know that you remember Mary. Leta is the girl closest to you. She has been living with Mary and me out in the desert. Linda Kay is the blonde next to her, and Ryn is the third girl."

Becky stepped over to the girls and gave each of them a hug. "Linda Kay and Ryn, I promise that you women will be loved and safe from this point on." She then turned to Leta and asked, "Don't you think that it would be best for you to come with me along with your friends? I don't want to frighten you, but things may soon become very dangerous at the compound."

Leta shook her head firmly. "I'm not leaving Mary and Bob. They need my help."

Becky looked at Bob and Mary. "Don't you think that Leta should come with me?"

Bob spoke and said, "We will be responsible for Leta. She's a rather amazing young woman."

Becky said, "I don't think that is the best choice, but I will honor your wishes. Girls, if you will excuse us, I need to take Bob and Mary over near the tree to talk privately with them."

Once the three of them had walked several paces away, Becky said, "I want to give you an update. Your former case manager Officer Robertson has been relieved of duty and likely will be charged with treason for spying for the Russians. This has been tough on the director since Robertson is his son-in-law. Once again, you two have played a large role in finding traitors in the ranks of the CIA. The director is very grateful. Two other agents have been found to be complicit with Robertson and also are soon to be charged. The CIA should be clean now."

"Wow!" exclaimed Bob. "That's a real shocker about Robertson. You have to feel sorry for his wife and kids."

Becky continued, "We have learned that the KGB basically hired the Chicago crime group of which Randy Williams is a small player and offered them a million dollars to find and deliver Mary and you to them for torture and interrogation. So, the main people searching for you now are professional criminals."

Mary said, "We just heard from Leta's friends that the owner of the hotel in Barlow was likely murdered by Randy and his two thugs so that the crime syndicate could take over the whorehouse and gambling enterprise. Apparently, Randy mentioned a plan to build a funeral home in Barlow to offer cheap cremations."

"Déjà vu," said Bob. "Sounds like the business of making people disappear by cremating them continues to flourish."

Becky resumed, "The FBI and CIA are prepared to raid the Barlow hotel at any time, but that would just be catching minnows in the crime syndicate and letting the big fish escape. We likely would gain little helpful information regarding the KGB's partnership with the Chicago mafia group, which has tentacles all over the country. There is increasing evidence that the crime bosses are working with the Russians on a number of projects. But if the current leads and surveillance don't show promise very soon, you can count on all hell descending on Barlow."

Bob said, "Mary and I feel pretty secure at my Uncle Wilbur's compound. We have enough weapons to hold off a small army waiting for the cavalry to rescue us. And now that we know about the ham radio, we don't feel so isolated."

Becky paused, then said, "I need to tell you that the CIA director thinks that the KGB may grow tired of waiting for the crime people to deliver you two and may come out of hiding and become actively involved themselves again. This may give the CIA an opportunity to snag some of the big boys. But this keeps you two, or should I say three, at great risk. The director asked me to be certain that you know that he remains willing to relocate you out of the United States for your safety."

Bob smiled and answered, "Mary has fallen in love with cacti, squat toilets, and the desert life. I think that we will just stay put and roll the dice."

Mary asked, "What's next for Linda Kay and Ryn?"

Becky answered, "I'm going to drive them back to Odessa with me. We can hop an Air Force plane there and fly back to Virginia.

They can stay with me for a while since I have decided to take a several month sabbatical."

Bob said, "We cannot thank you enough for helping us escape from Langley and reach my uncle's compound. You probably won't admit it, but thank you also for the food and return of our guns in the VW camper."

Then Becky said, "One last little parting gift from the director. You can look behind us and see the plumber's panel truck that we used to spirit you out of Langley. It now has Texas plates and a sign that says 'Pecos Electric.' But in the back are several other tradesman signs that can be substituted. There is also an assortment of license plates from various states. I will pick up the driver as we head back to Odessa."

Bob said, "What should we do with the panel truck?"

Becky replied, "Drive it back to the compound. It is a very special truck that has been further modified since you rode in it. Your trip back to Barlow and across the desert to the compound may not be as safe as you hope. My suggestion would be for Mary to drive the panel truck and stay a mile or so behind you in case you run into trouble. I would also advise that Leta ride with Mary for the girl's safety."

Mary gave Becky a hug which was returned. Becky extended her hand to Bob, then changed her mind and gave him a hug also. She walked back to the girls, then ushered Linda Kay and Ryn into the Suburban. Becky made a U-turn and stopped briefly to let the driver of the panel truck get into the Suburban.

As the tail lights of the vehicle disappeared in the distance, Mary turned to Bob and said, "Now don't you feel bad for thinking at one time that Reagor probably had a penis?"

Leta asked, "What am I missing here?"

Mary smiled and said, "Sorry, Leta. It's an in joke. Time for us to hit the road and hope that nothing bad is waiting for us along the way. Come with me and we'll see just how hot that panel truck really is."

CHAPTER 51

PURSUIT

Bob pulled the dune buggy across the highway and started back along the road to Barlow. Mary and Leta waited in the panel truck, then began to follow a mile or so back. After a few minutes Mary pushed the gas pedal all the way down. The engine roared, and the panel truck surged forward, shoving Mary and Leta back against their seats. "My gosh!" Mary said. "I think I pulled three Gs on that one. I may need to see a chiropractor for my whiplash."

Mary kept the panel truck behind Bob as Becky had suggested, but began to close the gap as they got closer to Barlow. It was very dark, but the headlights illuminated the narrow road well. All of a sudden, new headlights swerved onto the road behind the dune buggy and rapidly accelerated. Then Mary and Leta heard gunshots. The dune buggy accelerated quickly, but the pursuit vehicle began gaining rapidly.

"Hang on and watch your neck!" Mary shouted as she punched the accelerator.

The van shot forward and began to eat up the distance. "I'm at one hundred miles an hour, and the engine is still loafing! Leta, take my Makarov and hang your head out of the window and let those people know that they have company."

Leta got off two rapid shots. There were a series of return muzzle flashes ahead of them as the shooters began firing at the panel truck. Bob suddenly veered off of the road into the loose desert sand. The dune buggy spun sideways, then corrected itself. The pursuing car tried to follow, but its wheels began to spin. The panel truck flashed by it as Mary headed straight into Barlow.

Leta shouted above the engine noise, "That's Sheriff Smitty's Crown Galaxie."

Mary answered, "That car won't be worth crap in the desert sand. Bob should be safe now. I plan to blast through town and head for the compound. This truck has been refitted with big tires, which should work well for sand."

Forty minutes later Mary reached the front of the compound just ahead of Bob in the dune buggy. They pulled both vehicles into the large barn. As Leta stepped out of the panel truck, she said, "My gosh, this barn looks like a used car lot. There is Wilbur's old Dodge truck, the dune buggy, the new acquisition panel truck, the Jeep you guys purchased, and the deuce and a half."

Bob replied, "As Benjamin Franklin once said, 'You can't ever have too much money or too many vehicles.'"

Leta smiled and said, "If that little adage was in *Poor Richard's Almanac*, I must have missed it."

Mary chimed in to say, "None of us ate much for supper. Let's thaw some of the ground meat in the freezer and make some cheeseburgers. Suddenly, I'm famished."

"Great idea," Leta answered. "I'll get it going."

Later, as the three of them were eating at the kitchen table, Mary said, "OK, Bob. Tell us what happened inside the bordello."

Bob finished chewing and replied, "It took money to buy my way into the back area and even more money to convince Sadie to let me have an hour with the two girls. Some security guard brute named Tony with a very nasty disposition escorted me upstairs to the girls' room. He warned me that if I wasn't nice to the girls, he would kick my ass all the way out of Barlow. The first thing I did was to eliminate a listening device in the ceiling. Then I assured Linda Kay and Ryn that I was there to rescue them and not for a threesome. I quickly told them about the plan to crack the blackout shade and flash the room light with the loud explosion to follow.

"Just as I started to move toward the window, the door crashed open and Ricardo, the man who hassled me about buying tampons at the store, rushed in with a pistol in his hand. He was super pissed and planned to kill me on the spot. The girls really saved me. Linda Kay leaned into the shade, and Ryn flashed the room light. Just as the explosion came, I dived at Ricardo and disabled him. The girls led us to the loading dock among all of the chaos, and the rest is history."

"Quite a story," Mary agreed. "Thank goodness for the girls. I'm not quite ready to lose you until I find a better upgrade."

Leta looked at Bob. "Well, that leads to one unanswered question. Why in the world did you want one of my tampons?"

Bob looked uncomfortable, then answered weakly, "I'd rather not say."

Mary said, "Fess up, big boy. If you are embarrassed, what you did with it must be awful."

Bob reluctantly responded, "When Ricardo messed with me when I was buying tampons for Leta, he said some pretty bad things that I won't repeat. After he swung at me, I had to hurt him. So, what I did tonight just before the girls and I rushed to the loading dock was tit for tat."

"I'm not sure that we want to know," Mary said. "But come on, let's have it so we can sleep tonight."

Bob hesitated, then admitted, "I crammed that little sucker way up one of Ricardo's nostrils."

"Gross," exclaimed Leta. "And Mary thinks that I lack refinement. Getting that tampon out may be a real challenge after it swells up."

"I'm not as bad a guy as you think. I left the string hanging out."

Mary shook her head. "Bob really never got out of the seventh grade intellectually. He probably still laughs hysterically at fart jokes. But we all need some sleep. It's still two hours until sunrise. I plan to crash."

Leta was suddenly very serious. "Mary and Bob, I can never express enough thanks to you two for rescuing Linda Kay and Ryn. You have literally saved their lives." She teared up and said with a catch in her voice, "And you have saved my life, too."

CHAPTER 52

RODENT HEAVEN

Despite the late night, Bob and Mary were up by 7:30 AM to exercise. Leta soon followed and joined them in laps around the compound. Bob insisted that it was his time to prepare breakfast. He conjured up some pancakes that had All-Bran cereal mixed in the batter.

Bob served the pancakes and said, "Pour a little syrup on these babies, and you will think that you have gone to Food Heaven."

Mary wrinkled up her nose and said, "They don't smell too good. What are these weird little dark things all throughout the pancake?"

"Sorry, I can't reveal that. This recipe is a Smith family secret. One of my ancestors brought it over on the Mayflower. Come on and dig in."

Mary and Leta both took a bite. Mary said, "Ugh!" as she spit into her napkin. "This is absolutely the nastiest thing that I have ever put into my mouth!"

Leta frowned and agreed, "It does taste awful."

Mary said, "Well, that settles one thing. We can never, ever let Bob cook again. He would kill us all. Leta, what say that you and I make some French toast?"

After breakfast as the three were drinking coffee, Mary asked, "What is likely to happen next?"

Bob replied, "I think that it's a sure bet that sooner or later Randy will round up some other heavies and make a trip out to visit us. The contract he has with the KGB to deliver Mary and me is worth a small fortune. But if what Becky said is true, the government may move in on Barlow sooner rather than later."

Mary said, "Well, so much for our disappearing into the desert for safety. NBC may just as well broadcast our location on the evening news."

Bob concurred, "With all of the leaks in the CIA, I think our search for geographic anonymity was doomed from the start."

Mary asked, "Thinking practically, let's assume that a group of unfriendlies attack the compound and more of them get inside the wall than we can take out. What would be our options?"

Bob replied, "I think that the best choice will be to retreat to the tower above the barn and try to pick people off."

Mary said, "But if people get into the barn, we would be trapped. They might even try to burn us out."

Bob thought a minute, then suggested, "We may not have an ace in the hole, but we do have a deuce in the hole."

Leta joined in, "Pretty clever, Bob. You obviously mean the deuce and a half."

"Yep. We could blast through a brick wall, and that baby would keep right on running."

Mary continued, "One big problem. If we are up in the tower and decide that we have to make a quick exit, there may be bad guys already in the barn that won't take kindly to our trying to escape."

"Good point," responded Bob. "But I suspect that Leta knows how to avoid that problem."

Leta thought a minute, then said, "Got it! We can take the pole from the radio room down to the barn's ground level and try to find a way to enter the barn from the wall near where the truck will be hidden behind bales of hay."

Mary interjected, "What about just continuing on down to the bunker and waiting it out there?"

Bob answered, "Randy and his buddies aren't stupid. At some point they would almost certainly find a way into the bunker. If things really get hot, I would rather try to blast our way out of the compound, guns a-blazing, and take our chances in the desert waiting for a federal rescue."

Mary paused, then said quietly, "If Bob and I were to get captured, at least we have a pharmaceutical escape. Leta, thank goodness you are not a high-value target. I don't think the crime boys will spend much time looking for you if they get Bob and me. Hiding out in the bunker and waiting to be rescued would likely be your best option."

Leta shook her head and stated resolutely, "Come what may, I'm not leaving you guys."

Bob said, "Leta, Mary and I will need to think that over very carefully. The last thing we would want is for you to get hurt. But, first things first. Let's head out to the barn and see if we can find a way into the barn in the area where we'll conceal the deuce and a half. Leta, why don't you go down the pole again and listen for us tapping on the wall to let you know where the deuce and a half will be hidden?"

Leta offered, "Remember, at the base of the pole there is a narrow passageway that leads in the direction of a likely second drop pole into the bunker. I did not get to explore the passageway all of the way, but to get near the bales of hay in the barn, I'll need to walk down the passageway. When I hear your tapping, we can all start looking for a possible hidden door."

Bob replied, "If we can't find a connecting door, we could always make an opening into the passageway from the barn and conceal it with hay bales."

Mary responded, "I'm ready to head to the barn. But, first, I need to wash my mouth out really well. That nasty taste of the famous Smith family poisonous pancake is still nauseating me."

Bob said with an assumed somber look, "Sweet Grandma Matilda is bound to be spinning in her grave."

Mary made a face and responded, "Matilda probably died after eating one of her own pancakes. I think those awful things might do better sending rats to rodent heaven than feeding humans."

CHAPTER 53

A NEW PASSAGEWAY

Mary, Bob, and Leta walked out to the barn. Leta climbed up into the loft and lowered the concealed trap door in the ceiling that led to the octagonal watch tower and pulled herself up into the radio room. Once there, she went into the closet and slowly descended the pole, shining a flashlight ahead of her. She reached the floor uneventfully and began moving down the small tunnel. After about twenty feet, she heard a faint tapping.

Leta moved to that location and shouted that she was there. But the wall was so thick that the voices she heard back were too muffled to understand. Leta shined the flashlight on the wall, looking for anything to suggest a hidden door. There was absolutely nothing that looked suspicious. Bob and Mary were inspecting the inside wall carefully, but they too discovered nothing to suggest a potential opening.

Leta crawled back to the pole and climbed up hand over hand. She quickly joined Mary and Bob. "No luck on my side. The wall looks solid. Maybe Wilbur never thought that he would need to get into the ground floor of the barn in an emergency since he would be hurrying from the tower to the bunker to fire up the dune buggy and escape."

"Probably true," Bob responded. "I think that we need to make our own opening. Wilbur has more tools than Sears and Roebuck in this barn. I saw a reciprocating saw the other day that is run by a compressor. There's electricity in the barn, so the saw should have plenty of power. I can use a large drill bit and make a tunnel through the wall large enough to accommodate the long saw blade."

It took over an hour to make an opening large enough for a person to crawl through. The wall was over a foot thick and was stuffed with sound-deadening insulation. After the passage was completed, they worked to conceal it by stacking bales of hay in front of it.

Bob said, "Heck of a job for us. Now, let's fire up the deuce and a half and take turns driving it around the compound to make sure that any one of us could be the driver if things get dicey." Each person took a turn starting the deuce and a half and working through the gears.

Mary asked, "Since this beast has a hard top, what if we needed to fire from the back or sides of the truck?"

Bob replied, "If you crawl into the back, you will find that clever Wilbur has constructed several flaps in the sides that can be opened for visibility and firing."

Leta said, "It's getting close to noon. This growing girl needs some food."

Bob said with a small grin, "The Smith family batter is still in the fridge, and it won't take me any time to whip out some steaming pancakes. After the batter sets a while, the wonderful flavor really comes out." Mary and Leta each put an index finger into their mouth and pretended to gag.

Mary said, "Such a kind offer, but Leta and I are planning on cheese sandwiches and a cold Dr Pepper. Lucky you. You can have all of the pancakes to yourself."

After lunch Bob moved the deuce and a half to the back of the barn. Mary and Leta joined him to hide the truck behind bales of hay. "Wait," Mary interrupted. "We need to put some weapons in the back of the truck before we cover it up." After several trips back and forth from the arms room, the truck had an impressive array of fire power and explosives.

"Now," Bob said, "let's cover the front of the deuce and a half with these bales of hay. We won't have to worry about moving them in an emergency since the deuce and a half will plow right through them."

After the truck was concealed, Mary turned to Leta and said, "I'm going to place some tin cans around the compound. Then you and I are going up to the top of the barn tower and see how good you are at hitting them."

Bob said, "With all those bullets flying around the compound, I'm going to join you ladies up in the tower for my own protection. Leta, do your best not to shoot our watch dog."

Leta shook her head and replied, "Fret not. I think I am a natural with guns. Those cans will be dancing."

Leta proved true to her words. Her shots were always close to the target, and some cans did indeed go skittering across the ground.

"Good job," Mary said. "If you can hit small cans, you can sure hit bad guys. When we get back to the house, I want to talk with you about lipstick while Bob does his push-ups and sit-ups."

Leta frowned and replied, "I've worn enough caked-on, cheap whore makeup to last a lifetime. I may never wear lipstick again."

Mary smiled and replied enigmatically, "I plan to show you how lipstick could be lifesaving."

CHAPTER 54

GETTING THE HELL OUT OF DODGE

A week went by and there were no unwelcome visitors to the compound. At breakfast one morning Bob mused, "It's been so quiet around here that it makes me wonder if Randy and his men have started attending church with Sadie."

"Ha!" Leta said. "The only reason those thugs would go to church would be to steal money out of the collection plate."

Mary added, "I'm betting that Randy is martialing forces to prepare for storming Fort Wilbur. There's way too much money for him to lick his wounds and hightail it out of the area. We really ought to move a couple of Thompson machine guns up into the tower to go along with the AK-47s already there."

Bob said, "Good idea. But the feds won't wait too long to move in on Barlow. You have sex trafficking of young girls, prostitution, illegal gambling, as well as a wanted person like Randy with a number of felonies. Unless someone really high up in the crime syndicate comes to help Randy or the KGB gets tired of waiting to dismember Mary and me, the potential gain by waiting is going to disappear."

Mary said, "The way I look at it is that Bob and I are high-priced bait."

That next morning at 5 AM, Avenger the Rottweiler started barking ferociously at the inside of the front gate. Bob and Mary were immediately up and on full alert. Leta joined them in the kitchen. Everyone grabbed a weapon. Bob left from the back door and walked carefully around the house. Mary followed him, but stayed behind a large support pole on the front porch as Bob walked closer to the gate.

A loud voice called out, "Woody Stressel, this is your old friend Randy Williams. I've come to settle a score and deliver you and your bitch girlfriend to some people who are really eager to see you both. We can do this smooth and easy, or we can make it hard. You are surrounded with no hope to get out of here alive if you don't play smart. What's it going to be?"

Bob slipped back to the porch and pointed to the tower in the barn. He and Mary dashed for the barn with Leta fast behind them. Once they were up in the highest part of the tower, there was enough daylight to make out a Suburban and four pickup trucks at the front gate as well as several people. There was a loud crash as one of the trucks plowed into the gate and forced it partially open. Three men with rifles rushed in through the gate and fanned out seeking cover. One of them shot Avenger when the dog leaped at him.

Leta called out, "I see two people coming over the wall at the back of the compound!"

Bob went to the window and looked. One of the men rushed straight toward the barn. Bob grabbed a rifle and started firing. There was a crash as a bullet from the second man sent splinters of glass all over the surveillance room. When a second bullet from the front of the barn ricocheted off of one of the steel window frames of the tower, Bob shouted, "No hope to defend this place now. We are outmanned. We need to bust out of here!"

Bob and the two women rushed down the small stairs into the radio room. Mary shouted, "Give me a minute to get the shortwave radio on. I'll send out a Mayday call and leave the radio on so the signal can be tracked. You two head for the deuce and a half, and I'll join you."

Leta opened the closet door and slid down the pole with Bob right behind her.

They crawled down the narrow passageway to the opening Bob had made with the reciprocal saw and pushed the small hay bales out of the way. Bob jumped up into the cab of the deuce and a half and started the engine. Leta crawled into the back and grabbed a rifle.

Mary crawled through the opening from the passageway and climbed up into the passenger's seat. One of her arms was bleeding. Bob took a look and asked, "Did you get hit?"

"There was a shot into the radio room that shattered the front of the ham radio just after I sent the Mayday signal out. Several shards of glass got my arm. But I'm all right."

Leta called out from the back of the truck, "I smell smoke!" Suddenly several of the bales of hay in front of the truck began blazing.

"Time to get the hell out of Dodge!" Bob shouted. "Randy is being paid to deliver Mary and me alive, so I think his men have been instructed to shoot out the tires rather than kill us."

The deuce and a half roared into action. The truck lurched forward, shoving flaming bales of hay ahead of it. Bob gunned the engine and knocked the large barn door off of its hinges as the truck picked up speed. Once outside the barn, Bob headed straight for the gate. A man stepped out from one side of the house and fired at the tires with a rifle. Leta instantaneously returned fire and miraculously hit the man in the leg. He screamed and dropped his rifle.

The pickup truck that had been used as a battering ram on the gate still partially blocked the exit. The deuce and a half flattened one side of the truck as it passed by it. Just outside the gate there were two pickup trucks forming a barrier.

Bob hit them, but the deuce and a half was slowed to a crawl as the diesel engine labored to move the vehicles.

Suddenly a man from behind the deuce and a half fired a tear gas canister into the back of the truck. The aerosolized particles filled the vehicle, and all three occupants immediately begin coughing with tears pouring out of their burning eyes. Bob jammed the accelerator to the floor just as there were two loud sounds of tires exploding. The truck stalled and the engine died.

Rough arms grabbed Bob and Mary and Leta and shoved them into the middle seats of a Suburban, which immediately made a U-turn and headed away from the compound. Randy's voice from the front seat said gloatingly, "Well, well, Superman and Superwoman have at last been found and captured. Such fun times are ahead for you two! You can't see yet, but please be advised that your old buddies Carlos and Ricardo are in the back with guns trained on your heads. So, please don't try anything stupid."

Bob began coughing. "Too many cigarettes, little buddy?" asked Ricardo mockingly. "Cramming that tampon up my nose was not too smart on your part. It really offended me. But payback time is coming soon. I think I'll suggest that the first thing your friendly questioners do is cut your balls off with a dull knife."

Randy spoke again, "And, as a cherry on top of this delicious sundae, we have the little whore Candy back again. Sadie will be so happy to see her. Some of her favorite customers will be thrilled that she is available again for their perverted pleasures."

CHAPTER 55

LIPSTICK WITH A BANG

Randy gave a mean chuckle as he drove and said, "I know that you three are all atwitter waiting to begin the next exciting phases of your life. But I have to drive carefully since you people are very valuable cargo. The good news is that this delay will give you more time to anticipate what wonderful experiences are in store for you with the waiting KGB interrogators. It is such a shame that the medical school dean is not available for postmortem entertainment with what remains of the lovely Ava after she spills her guts."

As the trip continued, Mary, Bob, and Leta could slowly begin to open their burning eyes and get a murky view of their surroundings. Ricardo spoke and said, "You turds, just so we understand each other, any funny business and each of the women gets a slug in the back of their heads. So, Stressel, don't try to be a hero."

Leta suddenly spoke up urgently, "You guys need to know that I was being held against my will at that compound. Crazy Wilbur kidnapped me and took me out there to be a love slave. He had a heart attack and died during forced sex. These two people showed up a day or two later. Bob claimed to be Wilbur's nephew. Once these people got inside the compound, they began making me do terrible things with both of them. They said if I tried to escape, they would kill me. I will be much better off back with Sadie."

Randy said, "Candy, you may not be as dumb a bitch as I first thought. Perhaps you learned some new sex tricks from these degenerate people that Sadie can charge more for."

Leta said, "I look so terrible with my messed-up hair and no makeup. Sadie may not want to take me back. Is it OK if I at least put some lipstick on?" Without waiting for an answer, Leta grabbed her lipstick out of her pants pocket and jammed it into the back of Randy's head. There was an explosion as the lipstick gun fired into the base of the driver's neck. Randy screamed and jerked the wheel violently. Bob and Mary had ducked as soon as the lipstick came out.

Ricardo and Tony had both fired just as the Suburban lurched to the side. One of the bullets grazed Leta's arm, the other one exited through the windshield. Bob and Mary immediately whirled around. Mary drove a finger into Ricardo's eye, causing it to rupture with a jet of blood and vitreous. Simultaneously, Bob grabbed Tony's long hair and smashed his face into the door. Leta crawled into the front seat and opened the door and shoved the paralyzed Randy out of the Suburban. She then grabbed the wheel, pushed the accelerator to the floor, and began rocking the vehicle violently back and forth.

Bob had wrestled the pistol away from Tony and hit him on the head with the butt of the gun. Ricardo had reached over the seat back and was choking Mary, who was gasping and struggling to breathe. Bob turned and shot Ricardo in the face. He gave a guttural scream and blood started pouring out of his mouth.

Several gun shots rang out as two tires exploded. The Suburban began to labor and slow down. There was a sudden jolt as a pickup truck rammed the vehicle and spun it sideways in the loose sand. Another pickup pulled in front of the Suburban. Several men leaped out and trained their rifles on Leta, Bob, and Mary.

One of the men shouted, "Those fucking Chicago idiots almost let these people get killed! I told that asshole Randy that we should take charge of the captives ourselves immediately!"

Mary had regained her breath. She whispered to Bob, "Russian accent. KGB."

The Russian pointed his rifle at Bob and screamed, "Drop that pistol, now!"

Bob let the gun fall to the floor. The speaker switched to Russian and ordered, "Drag them out of the Suburban and put them on the ground."

Mary and Bob were quickly lying face down in the sand. One of the men shoved Leta into the side of the Suburban and put a pistol to her head. He said in accented English, "Move if you want to die, whore."

Two men tied Bob's ankles together, then tied his hands behind his back. Mary was next, followed by Leta.

The leader then ordered in Russian, "Throw them into the back of my pickup truck. Mikhail, you and Andrei sit in the back and keep a gun on them at all times. No more screw ups. One last thing—that idiot Tony is starting to move. Shoot him."

Some of the men pulled Bob, Mary, and Leta up to their feet and made them hop to the pickup truck. As the three were being roughly deposited into the bed of the truck, the Russian leader said sarcastically, "I'm Pavel, and if there is anything I can do to make your trip more pleasant, please let me know. Not to give away any secrets, but we are heading back to the hotel in Barlow. There's actually a wonderful basement there with soundproof walls. Stressel and the traitor Ava will soon get to learn a lot about that room."

Mary said in Russian, "Let the girl go. She is no threat to you."

Pavel gave a deep laugh and said, "Dead women tell no tales."

Mary, who was lying next to Leta, felt her tense up.

As Pavel was getting into the truck he said ominously, "The countdown clock has begun."

CHAPTER 56

RUNNING OUT OF TIME

The pickup truck that Pavel was driving pulled up behind the hotel by the loading dock after a bumpy ride. Pavel got out and ordered in Russian, "Mikhail, you and Andrei unload our guests and cover their eyes with duct tape. Then, Yuri, cut their ankle ropes off so we can walk them up the loading dock steps and into the hotel. Stay ten paces ahead of them with your pistol ready, while Mikhail, Andrei, and I will bring up the rear with our weapons trained on them."

The three captives were herded with rifle butts up the stairs and into a back hall that led to a locked door. Yuri pulled a key from his pocket and turned the deadbolt and opened the door. Pavel said sweetly in English, "Careful, little sweeties, on the steep stairs. We wouldn't want any one of you to fall and hurt yourself. Omar doesn't like working on damaged goods." The other three men burst into laughter.

Leta was in front and tripped on the threshold and fell partway down the stairs.

"Get up, you clumsy bitch!" Pavel screamed. Bob was standing with his hands tied behind him near the open door. During a moment of temporary confusion, he used one of his hands to touch the box of the lock. The three blindfolded captives descended the stairs, carefully feeling ahead of themselves with their feet.

Once they were in the basement, Pavel said, "Just a few ground rules, my little friends. This room is totally soundproof. But I have sensitive ears. Please do not scream unless you want things to get worse for you. Yuri will handcuff you loosely one at a time to metal chairs that are bolted to the floor. He will then cut your wrist ropes and tighten the handcuffs. We don't like kickers, so your feet will be tied to the chair. Please don't think that this will give you a great opportunity to misbehave since you will have weapons pointed at your heads at all times."

Each person was quickly fixed to a chair. The handcuffs bit into their wrists, but no one made a sound. "Now, for the most exciting moment of all. Yuri, please take the tape off of their eyes."

Yuri jerked the tape off each person. He spoke to Ava and said in Russian, "Humble apologies, my princess. I seemed to have pulled some of your beautiful eyelashes off. Such a pity."

Bob, Mary, and Leta looked warily about the room. There was a gurney with restraining straps with a surgical tray beside it. There were bright spotlights on the ceiling. Leta was terrified and let out a short gasp, then composed herself.

Mary looked at Pavel and said quietly in Russian, "We know that we have no way out of here alive. But Leta is a young woman with a whole life ahead of her. You have no quarrel with her. Please let her go. She can return to work for Sadie and be watched closely."

Leta blurted out, "If Mary suggested letting me go back to work in the whorehouse, I had rather die."

Pavel looked at Leta and said, coldly, "Your wish will be granted." There was a pause, then Pavel continued in English, "And now for the most exciting moment of all, it's time to meet the star of the show, Omar."

A large, muscular man with a bushy beard and a pitted face stepped out of an alcove. He had a black eye patch. Omar looked eagerly at the three captives.

"Excellent, excellent," he said with a sinister smile. "I just love working on beautiful women."

Pavel said, "Omar is a very sensitive person. He rescues kittens and puppies. He wouldn't hurt a flea—but, then, I guess, you people aren't fleas, are you?" he asked with a chuckle.

Omar walked up to the chair Mary was in and said with a leer, "Oh, yes. I want to work on this beautiful lady first. I am so excited!"

Mikhail opened Mary's handcuffs while Andrei kept a pistol trained on her. He recuffed her wrists and lifted them above her face. Mikhail then attached a chain to them. The chain was connected to a pulley on the ceiling. Mikhail untied Mary's feet from the chair and forced her toward the center of the room. Omar pushed a button on the wall that slowly tightened the chain until Mary was barely able to touch the floor with her tiptoes.

Omar turned to leer at Leta and ordered, "Mikhail, go ahead and get the young sweetie ready with her hands cuffed in front. I love cutting up young women most of all." Leta looked defiantly at Omar, but her lower lip trembled slightly.

Yuri then faced Mary and spat out angrily, "Ava Volkov, you are a traitor to Mother Russia! You whored yourself out to this CIA man and turned on our country! Unlike you, your brother Viktar was a hero for his country. Now you are going to tell us everything, and I mean everything, that you have learned about the CIA. If you refuse to talk, Omar will encourage your memory by removing small body parts. If you tell us something useful, Omar will hold off."

Mary looked at Yuri. "I'm going to die anyway. Why should I tell you anything, you piece of human shit?"

Pavel shook his head. "Offending me is so stupid. Such a beautiful woman. But soon you won't be recognizable. Omar, let's start first with some fingers. Get out the heavy-duty snips. Now, Ava, do you have anything interesting to tell us before Omar removes one of your thumbs?"

Mary said, "I do have something important to say." She turned toward Woody and said softly, "I have loved you ever since the first day I saw you across the cadaver table in med school." Woody gave an audible groan.

"And one other thing… I just crushed a strychnine capsule in my mouth. You animals will need to work fast to kill me. And I will tell you nothing."

Bob screamed, "No! No!"

CHAPTER 57

AN EYE FOR AN EYE

Pavel rushed up to Ava and snarled, "Spit it out, you bitch!" Ava spat right into his face. Some of the spit went into one of his eyes. Pavel recoiled and started wiping his eye furiously.

Ava gave a short laugh and said, "Too late, you bastard. The strychnine is already in your system. We will die together, Comrade, for the glory of Mother Russia."

Pavel rushed over to a sink on the wall and began furiously washing out his eyes.

Omar shrieked, "The lady cannot die! I have such plans for her!" He pushed the button on the wall, lowering Ava who collapsed on the floor and began to have seizure movements. At that moment Leta shrieked, "I just bit into my capsule!" She slumped over and began to vomit.

Omar began to scream, "No! No! I need at least one woman!"

Pavel raised his head from the sink and shouted in Russian, "Let both of the bitches die! We still have Stressel who will squeal like a weasel when we start removing body parts. I rinsed my face off in time. I'm OK."

"Change in game plans, Stressel, with the women on the way out. We can carve their bodies up later and get some good pictures. Tell me something top secret about the CIA or Andrei will cut one of your fingers off to jog your memory."

Woody looked directly at Pavel and said calmly, "You are a piece of human garbage. I will tell you absolutely nothing."

Pavel walked over to Woody and slapped his face. "Tough guy. We'll see how long you stay tough when we slice your balls off. Andrei, let's start with the right thumb."

Andrei grabbed Woody's right hand that was cuffed to the chair and isolated his thumb and hesitated with the shears open. He gave a snicker and said, "It's going to be hard to play with yourself with no fingers. But I guess when you're dead it won't make any difference. Last chance to spit out some secrets for us."

Suddenly there was a loud crash as the door was kicked open. Everyone whirled around to see Smitty Edwards and a woman with gray hair rush in. Smitty had a sawed-off shotgun, and the woman had a rifle. Only Mikhail still had a pistol in his hand. He whirled to fire, but the woman was quicker and shot him in the chest. Mikhail yelled and collapsed to the floor as his pistol slipped from his grip.

Smitty said, "I am perfectly willing to blast each of you to hell. My wife Ellie was a sniper in the Army and handles weapons better than I do."

Pavel said, "You are making a big mistake, Smitty. The KGB will hound you and your wife to the ends of the earth. We can make it worth your time to back out of that door and mind your own business."

Smitty looked directly at Pavel and said, "I was willing to play along with the people who run the whorehouse and gambling. Selling pussy and running illegal card games was something I could tolerate. But when you commies showed up, it was a different game. We just got a telegram last week that our only son who was Army Special Forces in Nam was blown up by commies like you. When Randy told me yesterday that you Russians were coming in to help with a raid on crazy Wilbur's place, this was more than Ellie and I could stand."

Pavel looked furtively about the room. "Smitty, I'm talking big money if you and your wife walk out of here. You and your wife could move to Europe and live like a king and queen."

Smitty shook his head and replied, "Ellie and I got down on our knees last night and got right with the Lord. We ain't afraid to die. The Bible says 'an eye for an eye, a tooth for a tooth, a life for a life.' You commies killed my son. Ellie and I are going to speed up your trips to hell."

All four of the Russians suddenly dived for the floor while grabbing for their pistols. There were the loud staccato sounds of multiple weapons firing as well as two shotgun blasts. Smitty slumped over and fell to the floor with a wound to his chest. Omar lay on the floor with blood oozing from his abdomen. Yuri was leaning against the wall bleeding, with his face missing from a shotgun blast.

Pavel and Andrei were unscathed and had darted behind a large supporting pillar in the basement. Ellie was still armed and had taken cover behind a heavy metal cabinet. There was a growing blood stain on her blouse near one shoulder.

Pavel began firing rapidly at the cabinet as Andrei dashed toward Ellie, also firing. Woody had managed to free one foot from the chair and tripped Andrei as he ran by. His gun skittered to the floor and slid close to Leta, who grabbed it with one hand and shot Andrei in the back as he tried to stand. Pavel jumped from behind the pillar and fired at Ellie, spewing concrete particles from the wall behind her into the air. Ellie did not miss Pavel with a rifle blast. Her aim was perfect and shattered his arm with the gun.

Ellie came out from behind the cabinet with her rifle pointing at Pavel's chest and looked at him with utter hatred. "You are a lucky bastard that I chose not to kill you. Smitty told me that the CIA wants you. I decided to save you for them."

The sound of sirens could be heard through the open door of the basement.

Woody said, "Thank God! The cavalry has arrived." Then he had a sudden body jerk and turned toward Ava who was still lying on the floor and shouted, "Ava! Ava!"

CHAPTER 58

A LITTLE SECRET

Bob, Mary, Leta, and Reagor were sitting at the kitchen table at the compound a week after the raid on the hotel by the CIA and FBI. Mary said, "Becky, I cannot tell you how shocked we were when you drove up to the gate of the compound unannounced."

Becky answered, "As I recall, just before you two left Langley, Woody invited me to drop in. A lot has happened since the raid, and I wanted to give all of you an update now that I have seen the confidential report."

Woody said, "We have really appreciated the temporary security detail that the inspector ordered for the compound. The nights have been wonderful not having to sleep with one eye and one ear open."

Leta suddenly spoke. "I don't want to be rude and interrupt, but I have been dying to ask how Linda Kay and Ryn are doing. Are they somewhere safe?"

Becky smiled and replied, "They are at my home near Langley. My housekeeper and husband are taking care of them while I am gone. Your friends are still rather shell shocked and withdrawn. It is going to take some time for them to be able to resume any sort of normal life. My husband has a PhD in theoretical physics. He and I plan to do some home schooling for a few weeks until we can decide what is best for your friends."

Leta said quietly, "I would have killed myself if I had been kept at the whorehouse much longer. Wilbur gave me a reason to think living was better than suicide. Then Bob and Mary convinced me that despite my past, there can be a future for me. I hope that Linda Kay and Ryn will be as fortunate as I have been."

Bob asked, "Becky, what prompted the raid on the hotel? Mary sent a Mayday call out on the shortwave radio as we were fleeing the compound, but a bullet shattered the radio screen just after the message was sent. We figured that it likely never got out."

Becky answered, "The CIA never received a distress signal. However, we were monitoring KGB activity and learned that some important people were heading to Texas. The director immediately asked the FBI for help in staging a raid on the hotel in Barlow. Capturing Pavel was a real find. He's tough, but without going into any detail, our experts have been able to extract very important information from him. Andrei survived the gunshot wound to his back after emergency surgery. Once he is better, he will have his chance to sing. Yuri died from the shotgun blast to his face. Mikhail did not survive his chest wound, and Omar bled out from a bullet that exploded his liver."

Mary asked, "What about Smitty and his wife Ellie?"

"Smitty had a bullet through his heart and died quickly. His wife was hit in the upper chest and shoulder. She lost a lot of blood and had a collapsed lung. Ellie is still in the hospital in Odessa, but is going to survive. That woman could really shoot."

Bob said, "We are all alive thanks to Smitty and his wife. Their arrival was just in the nick of time."

Mary asked, "How in the world were they able to get into the basement with a heavy locked door?"

Bob made the sign of the cross on his chest. "Talk about a guardian angel. When Leta tripped on the stairs going down into the basement, there was brief confusion. I was able to use one of my handcuffed hands to fish a piece of Kleenex out of my back pocket and stuff it into the box of the door lock. The KGB people were able to lock the door, but the paper kept the bolt from being completely engaged in the box. So, Smitty was able to kick the door open."

Mary asked, "What about Randy Williams? Leta showed incredible bravery and shot him in the back of the neck with a lipstick pistol, then pushed him out of the truck."

"As Mary knows, it was the Russians who invented the lipstick pistol as something that their agents could easily conceal. It has such a small bullet and powder charge that it is only effective at very close range. Randy has temporary paralysis from the shot. He was found in the desert and also flown to the hospital in Odessa. The doctors tell us that he will survive with limited use of his lower extremities. He is well guarded in the hospital. The FBI is eager to talk with him about the Chicago crime syndicate."

Leta asked, "What happened to that witch Sadie who managed the whorehouse?"

Becky answered, "Sadie and several other people at the hotel were arrested and will be charged with compelling prostitution. Since Leta, Linda Kay, and Ryn are all underage, this will be a first-degree felony in Texas with beaucoup prison time."

There was a lull in the conversation, then Woody looked at Ava and said in a choked voice, "I thought that you really had crushed your strychnine tablet in your mouth. When you started having seizure movements, I was convinced that you were surely dying. You will never know what a relief it was when you sat up and began talking when the shooting was over."

Mary smiled and said, "I was not eager to have Omar the oaf start removing my body parts. The poison ruse was just a way to stall for time. And, just look. I still have all of my fingers."

Bob turned to Leta and asked, "What inspired you to pretend to join Mary in a suicide pact? You never even had a strychnine capsule."

"I was just trying to add more confusion and delay. Ever since I was a kid, I have been able to vomit any time I want to. I thought a little upchuck would add authenticity to my suicide."

Becky finished her coffee and stood up. "Time for me to head back to Virginia. Woody and Ava, you will be protected here for several weeks until the director decides what is the safest next step. He and the entire organization are very indebted to you two for smoking out the CIA traitors. And, Leta, at some point you will need to think about getting back in school. But for now, staying with Ava and Woody seems to be in your best interest."

Woody, Ava, and Leta walked out to the front of the house with Becky. She hesitated before getting into the government Suburban she had driven out in. With a smile she turned to Woody and Ava and said,

"Despite all of your training, neither of you seemed to learn that even the walls have ears at Langley. Woody, it may be a bitter disappointment for you to learn that I really do not have a penis."

Woody actually blushed and said, "Humble apologies, Becky. But in my defense, when you coached Ava and me at Langley, you were so tough and all business that I thought that the estrogen fairy must have been MIA at your conception."

Becky laughed and said with a smile, "Just remember, if in the future we ever meet at Langley, I plan to be hard-ass Officer Reagor once again."

Mary walked over to Becky and gave her a hug, then whispered something into her ear.

Becky looked surprised, then asked, "Have you told him yet?"

Mary shook her head no.

Woody looked puzzled and asked, "Can I share in this little secret?"

Mary smiled and answered, "Just one more thing for me to know and you to find out."

Becky gave Woody a hug, then got into the Suburban quickly and drove out of the gate without ever looking back.

Dwain Gordon Fuller is a retired Dallas retinal surgeon who finally has found time to try his hand at writing. A demanding premedical curriculum in college has a way of damping down literary interests. However, Dr. Fuller found time to write stories and poems for the college creative writing journal. The mantra in medical school was survive—not write fiction. But during residency, Dr. Fuller was able to rekindle his interest in writing and pen and publish several nonscientific articles. Once in practice, Dr. Fuller coauthored a medical book about evaluating eyes with opaque media and also published a number of articles in scientific journals. Being retired has given Dr. Fuller the time to unleash whatever creative spark remains.